A Mortal Antipathy

Oliver Wendell Holmes

Contents

A MORTAL ANTIPATHY

BY

Oliver Wendell Holmes

A MORTAL ANTIPATHY.
FIRST OPENING OF THE NEW PORTFOLIO.

INTRODUCTION.

"AND why *the* New Portfolio, I would ask?"

Pray, do you remember, when there was an accession to the nursery in which you have a special interest, whether the new-comer was commonly spoken of as *a* baby? Was it not, on the contrary, invariably, under all conditions, in all companies, by the whole household, spoken of as *the* baby? And was the small receptacle provided for it commonly spoken of as *a* cradle; or was it not always called *the* cradle, as if there were no other in existence?

Now this New Portfolio is the cradle in which I am to rock my new-born thoughts, and from which I am to lift them carefully and show them to callers, namely, to the whole family of readers belonging to my list of intimates, and such other friends as may drop in by accident. And so it shall have the definite article, and not be lost in the mob of its fellows as *a* portfolio.

There are a few personal and incidental matters of which I wish to say something before reaching the contents of the Portfolio, whatever these may be. I have had other portfolios before this,—two, more especially, and the first thing I beg leave to introduce relates to these.

Do not throw this volume down, or turn to another page, when I tell you that the earliest of them, that of which I now am about to speak, was opened more than fifty years ago. This is a very dangerous confession. For fifty years make everything hopelessly old-fashioned, without giving it the charm of real antiquity. If I could say a hundred years, now, my readers would accept all I had to tell them with a curious interest; but fifty years ago,—there are too many talkative old people who know all about that time, and at best half a century is a half-baked bit of ware. A coin-fancier would say that your fifty-year-old facts have just enough of antiquity to spot them with rust, and not enough to give them the delicate and durable *patina* which is time's exquisite enamel.

When the first Portfolio was opened the coin of the realm bore for its legend,— or might have borne if the more devout hero-worshippers could have had their way,—Andreas Jackson, Populi Gratia, Imp. Cœsar. Aug. Div. Max., etc., etc. I never happened to see any gold or silver with that legend, but the truth is I was not very familiarly acquainted with the precious metals at that period of my career, and there might have been a good deal of such coin in circulation without my handling it, or knowing much about it.

Permit me to indulge in a few reminiscences of that far-off time.

In those days the Athenæum Picture Gallery was a principal centre of attraction to young Boston people and their visitors. Many of us got our first ideas of art, to say nothing of our first lessons in the comparatively innocent flirtations of our city's primitive period, in that agreeable resort of amateurs and artists.

How the pictures on those walls in Pearl Street do keep their places in the mind's gallery! Trumbull's Sortie of Gibraltar, with red enough in it for one of our sunset after-glows; and Neagle's full-length portrait of the blacksmith in his shirt-sleeves; and Copley's long-waistcoated gentlemen and satin-clad ladies,—they looked like gentlemen and ladies, too; and Stuart's florid merchants and high-waisted matrons; and Allston's lovely Italian scenery and dreamy, unimpassioned women, not forgetting Florimel in full flight on her interminable rocking-horse,—you may still see her at the Art Museum; and the rival landscapes of Doughty and Fisher, much talked of and largely praised in those days; and the Murillo,—not from Marshal Soult's collection; and the portrait of Annibale Caracci by himself, which cost the Athenæum a hundred dollars; and Cole's allegorical pictures, and his immense and dreary canvas, in which the prostrate shepherds and the angel in Joseph's coat of many colors look as if they must have been thrown in for nothing; and West's brawny Lear tearing his clothes to pieces. But why go on with the catalogue, when most of these pictures can be seen either at the Athenæum building in Beacon Street or at the Art Gallery, and admired or criticised perhaps more justly, certainly not more generously, than in those earlier years when we looked at them through the japanned fish-horns?

If one happened to pass through Atkinson Street on his way to the Athenæum, he would notice a large, square, painted, brick house, in which lived a leading representative of old-fashioned coleopterous Calvinism, and from which emerged one of the liveliest of literary butterflies. The father was editor of the "Boston Recorder," a very respectable, but very far from amusing paper, most largely patronised by that class of the community which spoke habitually of the first day of the week as "the Sahbuth." The son was the editor of several different periodicals in succession, none of them over severe or serious, and of many pleasant books, filled with lively descriptions of society, which he studied on the outside with a quick eye for form and color, and with a certain amount of sentiment, not very deep, but real, though somewhat frothed over by his worldly experiences.

Nathaniel Parker Willis was in full bloom when I opened my first Portfolio. He had made himself known by his religious poetry, published in his father's paper, I think, and signed "Roy." He had started the "American Magazine," afterwards merged in the "New York Mirror." He had then left off writing scripture pieces, and taken to lighter forms of verse. He had just written

"I'm twenty-two, I'm twenty-two,— They idly give me joy, As if I should be glad to know That I was less a boy."

He was young, therefore, and already famous. He came very near being very handsome. He was tall; his hair, of light brown color, waved in luxuriant abundance; his cheek was as rosy as if it had been painted to show behind the footlights; he dressed with artistic elegance. He was something between a remembrance of Count D'Orsay and an anticipation of Oscar Wilde. There used to be in the gallery of the Luxembourg a picture of Hippolytus and Phædra, in which the beautiful young man, who had kindled a passion in the heart of his wicked step-mother, always reminded me of Willis, in spite of the shortcomings of the living face as compared with the ideal. The painted youth is still blooming on the canvas, but the fresh-cheeked, jaunty young author of the year 1830 has long faded out of human sight I took the leaves which lie before me at this moment, as I write, from his coffin, as it lay just outside the door of Saint Paul's Church, on a sad, overclouded

winter's day, in the year 1867. At that earlier time, Willis was by far the most prom-
inent young American author. Cooper, Irving, Bryant, Dana, Halleck, Drake, had
all done their best work. Longfellow was not yet conspicuous. Lowell was a school-
boy. Emerson was unheard of. Whittier was beginning to make his way against the
writers with better educational advantages whom he was destined to outdo and to
outlive. Not one of the great histories, which have done honour to our literature,
had appeared. Our school-books depended, so far as American authors were concerned, on extracts from the orations and speeches of Webster and Everett; on Bryant's Thanatopsis, his lines To a Waterfowl, and the Death of the Flowers, Halleck's
Marco Bozzaris, Red-Jacket, and Burns; on Drake's American Flag, and Percival's
Coral Grove, and his Genius Sleeping and Genius Waking,—and not getting very
wide awake, either. These could be depended upon. A few other copies of verses
might be found, but Dwight's "Columbia, Columbia," and Pierpont's Airs of Pales-
tine, were already effaced, as many of the favorites of our own day and generation
must soon be, by the great wave which the near future will pour over the sands in
which they still are legible.

About this time, in the year 1832, came out a small volume entitled "Truth, a
Gift for Scribblers," which made some talk for a while, and is now chiefly valuable
as a kind of literary tombstone on which may be read the names of many whose
renown has been buried with their bones. The "London Athenæum" spoke of it as
having been described as a "tomahawk sort of satire." As the author had been a trap-
per in Missouri, he was familiarly acquainted with that weapon and the warfare of
its owners. Born in Boston, in 1804, the son of an army officer, educated at West
Point, he came back to his native city about the year 1830. He wrote an article on
Bryant's Poems for the "North American Review," and another on the famous Indian Chief, Black Hawk. In this last-mentioned article he tells this story as the great
warrior told it himself. It was an incident of a fight with the Osages.

"Standing by my father's side, I saw him kill his antagonist, and tear the scalp
from his head. Fired with valor and ambition, I rushed furiously upon another,
smote him to the earth with my tomahawk, ran my lance through his body, took
off his scalp, and returned in triumph to my father. He said nothing, but looked
pleased."

This little red story describes very well Snelling's style of literary warfare. His handling of his most conspicuous victim, Willis, was very much like Black Hawk's way of dealing with the Osage. He tomahawked him in heroics, ran him through in prose, and scalped him in barbarous epigrams. Bryant and Halleck were abundantly praised; hardly any one else escaped.

If the reader wishes to see the bubbles of reputation that were floating, some of them gay with prismatic colors, half a century ago, he will find in the pages of "Truth" a long catalogue of celebrities he never heard of. I recognize only three names, of all which are mentioned in the little book, as belonging to persons still living; but as I have not read the obituaries of all the others, some of them may be still flourishing in spite of Mr. Snelling's exterminating onslaught. Time dealt as hardly with poor Snelling, who was not without talent and instruction, as he had dealt with our authors. I think he found shelter at last under a roof which held numerous inmates, some of whom had seen better and many of whom had known worse days than those which they were passing within its friendly and not exclusive precincts. Such, at least, was the story I heard after he disappeared from general observation.

That was the day of Souvenirs, Tokens, Forget-me-nots, Bijous, and all that class of showy annuals. Short stories, slender poems, steel engravings, on a level with the common fashion-plates of advertising establishments, gilt edges, resplendent binding,—to manifestations of this sort our lighter literature had very largely run for some years. The "Scarlet Letter" was an unhinted possibility. The "Voices of the Night" had not stirred the brooding silence; the Concord seer was still in the lonely desert; most of the contributors to those yearly volumes, which took up such pretentious positions on the centre table, have shrunk into entire oblivion, or, at best, hold their place in literature by a scrap or two in some omnivorous collection.

What dreadful work Snelling made among those slight reputations, floating in swollen tenuity on the surface of the stream, and mirroring each other in reciprocal reflections! Violent, abusive as he was, unjust to any against whom he happened to have a prejudice, his castigation of the small littérateurs of that day was not harmful, but rather of use. His attack on Willis very probably did him good; he needed a little discipline, and though he got it too unsparingly, some cautions came with it which were worth the stripes he had to smart under. One noble writer Snelling treated with rudeness, probably from some accidental pique, or equally insignificant reason. I myself, one of the three survivors before referred to, escaped with a love-pat, as the youngest son of the Muse. Longfellow gets a brief nod of acknowledgment. Bailey, an American writer, "who made long since a happy snatch at fame," which must have been snatched away from him by envious time, for I cannot identify him; Thatcher, who died early, leaving one poem, The Last Request, not wholly unremembered; Miss Hannah F. Gould, a very bright and agreeable writer of light verse,—all these are commended to the keeping of that venerable public carrier, who finds his scythe and hour-glass such a load that he generally drops the burdens committed to his charge, after making a show of paying every possible attention to them so long as he is kept in sight.

It was a good time to open a portfolio. But my old one had boyhood written on every page. A single passionate outcry when the old war-ship I had read about in the broadsides that were a part of our kitchen literature, and in the "Naval Monument," was threatened with demolition; a few verses suggested by the sight of old Major Melville in his cocked hat and breeches, were the best scraps that came out of that first Portfolio, which was soon closed that it should not interfere with the duties of a profession authorized to claim all the time and thought which would have been otherwise expended in filling it.

During a quarter of a century the first Portfolio remained closed for the greater part of the time. Only now and then it would be taken up and opened, and something drawn from it for a special occasion, more particularly for the annual reunions of a certain class of which I was a member.

In the year 1857, towards its close, the "Atlantic Monthly," which I had the honour of naming, was started by the enterprising firm of Phillips & Sampson, under the editorship of Mr. James Russell Lowell. He thought that I might bring something out of my old Portfolio which would be not unacceptable in the new magazine. I looked at the poor old receptacle, which, partly from use and partly from neglect, had lost its freshness, and seemed hardly presentable to the new company expected to welcome the new-comer in the literary world of Boston, the least provincial of American centres of learning and letters. The gilded covering where the emblems of hope and aspiration had looked so bright had faded; not wholly, perhaps, but how was the gold become dim!—how was the most fine gold changed!

Long devotion to other pursuits had left little time for literature, and the waifs and strays gathered from the old Portfolio had done little more than keep alive the memory that such a source of supply was still in existence. I looked at the old Portfolio, and said to myself, "Too late! too late. This tarnished gold will never brighten, these battered covers will stand no more wear and tear; close them, and leave them to the spider and the bookworm."

In the meantime the nebula of the first quarter of the century had condensed into the constellation of the middle of the same period. When, a little while after the establishment of the new magazine, the "Saturday Club," gathered about the long table at "Parker's," such a representation of all that was best in American literature had never been collected within so small a compass. Most of the Americans whom educated foreigners cared to see—leaving out of consideration official dignitaries, whose temporary importance makes them objects of curiosity—were seated at that board. But the club did not yet exist, and the "Atlantic Monthly" was an experiment. There had already been several monthly periodicals, more or less successful and permanent, among which "Putnam's Magazine" was conspicuous, owing its success largely to the contributions of that very accomplished and delightful writer, Mr. George William Curtis. That magazine, after a somewhat prolonged and very honorable existence, had gone where all periodicals go when they die, into the archives of the deaf, dumb, and blind recording angel whose name is Oblivion. It had so well deserved to live that its death was a surprise and a source of regret. Could another monthly take its place and keep it when that, with all its attractions and excellences, had died out, and left a blank in our periodical literature which it would be very hard to fill as well as that had filled it?

This was the experiment which the enterprising publishers ventured upon, and I, who felt myself outside of the charmed circle drawn around the scholars and poets of Cambridge and Concord, having given myself to other studies and duties, wondered somewhat when Mr. Lowell insisted upon my becoming a contributor. And so, yielding to a pressure which I could not understand, and yet found myself unable to resist, I promised to take a part in the new venture, as an occasional writer in the columns of the new magazine.

That was the way in which the second Portfolio found its way to my table, and was there opened in the autumn of the year 1857. I was already at least

Net mezzo del cammin di mia *vita,*

when I risked myself, with many misgivings, in little-tried paths of what looked at first like a wilderness, a *selva oscura,* where, if I did not meet the lion or the wolf, I should be sure to find the critic, the most dangerous of the carnivora, waiting to welcome me after his own fashion.

The second Portfolio is closed and laid away. Perhaps it was hardly worth while to provide and open a new one; but here it lies before me, and I hope I may find something between its covers which will justify me in coming once more before my old friends. But before I open it I want to claim a little further indulgence.

There is a subject of profound interest to almost every writer, I might say to almost every human being. No matter what his culture or ignorance, no matter what his pursuit, no matter what his character, the subject I refer to is one of which he rarely ceases to think, and, if opportunity is offered, to talk. On this he is eloquent, if on nothing else. The slow of speech becomes fluent; the torpid listener becomes electric with vivacity, and alive all over with interest.

The sagacious reader knows well what is coming after this prelude. He is accustomed to the phrases with which the plausible visitor, who has a subscription book in his pocket, prepares his victim for the depressing disclosure of his real errand. He is not unacquainted with the conversational amenities of the cordial and interesting stranger, who, having had the misfortune of leaving his carpet-bag in the cars, or of having his pocket picked at the station, finds himself without the means of reaching that distant home where affluence waits for him with its luxurious welcome, but to whom for the moment the loan of some five and twenty dollars would be a convenience and a favor for which his heart would ache with gratitude during the brief interval between the loan and its repayment.

I wish to say a few words in my own person relating to some passages in my own history, and more especially to some of the recent experiences through which I have been passing.

What can justify one in addressing himself to the general public as if it were his private correspondent? There are at least three sufficient reasons: first, if he has a story to tell that everybody wants to hear,—if he has been shipwrecked, or has been in a battle, or has witnessed any interesting event, and can tell anything new about it; secondly, if he can put in fitting words any common experiences not already well told, so that readers will say, "Why, yes! I have had that sensation, thought, emotion, a hundred times, but I never heard it spoken of before, and I never saw any mention of it in print;" and thirdly, anything one likes, provided he can so tell it as to make it interesting.

I have no story to tell in this Introduction which can of itself claim any general attention. My first pages relate the effect of a certain literary experience upon myself,—a series of partial metempsychoses of which I have been the subject. Next follows a brief tribute to the memory of a very dear and renowned friend from whom I have recently been parted. The rest of the Introduction will be consecrated to the memory of my birthplace.

I have just finished a Memoir, which will appear soon after this page is written, and will have been the subject of criticism long before it is in the reader's hands. The experience of thinking another man's thoughts continuously for a long time; of living one's self into another man's life for a month, or a year, or more, is a very curious one. No matter how much superior to the biographer his subject may be, the man who writes the life feels himself, in a certain sense, on the level of the person whose life he is writing. One cannot fight over the battles of Marengo or Austerlitz with Napoleon without feeling as if he himself had a fractional claim to the victory, so real seems the transfer of his personality into that of the conqueror while he reads. Still more must this identification of "subject" and "object" take place when one is writing of a person whose studies or occupations are not unlike his own.

Here are some of my metempsychoses:—

Ten years ago I wrote what I called A Memorial Outline of a remarkable student of nature. He was a born observer, and such are far from common. He was also a man of great enthusiasm and unwearying industry. His quick eye detected what others passed by without notice: the Indian relic, where another would see only pebbles and fragments; the rare mollusk, or reptile, which his companion would poke with his cane, never suspecting that there was a prize at the end of it. Getting his single facts together with marvellous sagacity and long-breathed patience, he arranged them, classified them, described them, studied them in their relations, and before those around him were aware of it the collector was an accomplished naturalist. When he died his collections remained, and they still remain, as his record in the hieratic language of science. In writing this memoir the spirit of his quiet pursuits, the even temper they bred in him, gained possession of my own mind, so that I seemed to look at nature through his gold-bowed spectacles, and to move about his beautifully ordered museum as if I had myself prepared and arranged its specimens. I felt wise with his wisdom, fair-minded with his calm impartiality; it seemed as if for the time his placid, observant, inquiring, keen-sighted nature "slid into my soul," and if I had looked at myself in the glass I should almost have expected to see the image of the Hersey professor whose life and character I was sketching.

A few years later I lived over the life of another friend in writing a Memoir of which he was the subject. I saw him, the beautiful, bright-eyed boy, with dark, waving hair; the youthful scholar, first at Harvard, then at Göttingen and Berlin, the friend and companion of Bismarck; the young author, making a dash for renown as a novelist, and showing the elements which made his failures the promise of success in a larger field of literary labor; the delving historian, burying his fresh young manhood in the dusty alcoves of silent libraries, to come forth in the face of Europe and America as one of the leading historians of the time; the diplomatist, accomplished, of captivating presence and manners, an ardent American, and in the time of trial an impassioned and eloquent advocate of the cause of freedom; reaching at last the summit of his ambition as minister at the Court of Saint James. All this I seemed to share with him as I tracked his career from his birthplace in Dorchester, and the house in Walnut Street where he passed boyhood, to the palaces of Vienna and London. And then the cruel blow which struck him from the place he adorned; the great sorrow that darkened his later years; the invasion of illness, a threat that warned of danger, and after a period of invalidism, during a part of which I shared his most intimate daily life, the sudden, hardly unwelcome, final summons. Did not my own consciousness migrate, or seem, at least, to transfer itself into this brilliant life history, as I traced its glowing record? I, too, seemed to feel the delight of carrying with me, as if they were my own, the charms of a presence which made its own welcome everywhere. I shared his heroic toils, I partook of his literary and social triumphs, I was honored by the marks of distinction which gathered about him, I was wronged by the indignity from which he suffered, mourned with him in his sorrow, and thus, after I had been living for months with his memory, I felt as if I should carry a part of his being with me so long as my self-consciousness might remain imprisoned in the ponderable elements.

The years passed away, and the influences derived from the companionships I have spoken of had blended intimately with my own current of being. Then there came to me a new experience in my relations with an eminent member of the medical profession, whom I met habitually for a long period, and to whose memory I consecrated a few pages as a prelude to a work of his own, written under very peculiar circumstances. He was the subject of a slow, torturing, malignant, and almost necessarily fatal disease. Knowing well that the mind would feed upon itself if it were not supplied with food from without, he determined to write a treatise on a subject which had greatly interested him, and which would oblige him to bestow much of his time and thought upon it, if indeed he could hold out to finish the work. During the period while he was engaged in writing it, his wife, who had seemed in perfect health, died suddenly of pneumonia. Physical suffering, mental distress, the prospect of death at a near, if uncertain, time always before him, it was hard to conceive a more terrible strain than that which he had to endure. When, in the hour of his greatest need, his faithful companion, the wife of many years of happy union, whose hand had smoothed his pillow, whose voice had consoled and cheered him, was torn from him after a few days of illness, I felt that my friend's trial was such that the cry of the man of many afflictions and temptations might well have escaped from his lips: " I was at ease, but he hath broken me asunder; he hath also taken me by my neck and shaken me to pieces, and set me up for his mark. His archers compass me round about, he cleaveth my reins asunder, and doth not spare; he poureth out my gall upon the ground."

I had dreaded meeting him for the first time after this crushing blow. What a lesson he gave me of patience under sufferings which the fearful description of the Eastern poet does not picture too vividly! We have been taught to admire the calm philosophy of Haller, watching his faltering pulse as he lay dying; we have heard the words of pious resignation said to have been uttered with his last breath by Addison: but here was a trial, not of hours, or days, or weeks, but of months, even years, of cruel pain, and in the midst of its thick darkness the light of love, which had burned steadily at his bedside, was suddenly extinguished.

There were times in which the thought would force itself upon my consciousness, How long is the universe to look upon this dreadful experiment of a malarious planet, with its unmeasurable freight of suffering, its poisonous atmosphere, so sweet to breathe, so sure to kill in a few scores of years at farthest, and its heart-breaking woes which make even that brief space of time an eternity? There can be but one answer that will meet this terrible question, which must arise in every thinking nature that would fain "justify the ways of God to men." So must it be until that

"one far-off divine event To which the whole creation moves"

has become a reality, and the anthem in which there is no discordant note shall be joined by a voice from every life made " perfect through sufferings."

Such was the lesson into which I lived in those sad yet placid years of companionship with my suffering and sorrowing friend, in retracing which I seemed to find another existence mingled with my own.

And now for many months I have been living in daily relations of intimacy with one who seems nearer to me since he has left us than while he was here in living form and feature. I did not know how difficult a task I had undertaken in venturing upon a memoir of a man whom all, or almost all, agree upon as one of the great lights of the New World, and whom very many regard as an unpredicted Messiah. Never before was I so forcibly reminded of Carlyle's description of the work of a newspaper editor,—that threshing of straw already thrice beaten by the flails of other laborers in the same field. What could be said that had not been said of "transcendentalism" and of him who was regarded as its prophet; of the poet whom some admired without understanding, a few understood, or thought they did, without admiring, and many both understood and admired,—among these there being not a small number who went far beyond admiration, and lost themselves in devout worship? While one exalted him as "the greatest man that ever lived," another, a friend, famous in the world of letters, wrote expressly to caution me against the danger of overrating a writer whom he is content to recognize as an American Montaigne, and nothing more.

After finishing this Memoir, which has but just left my hands, I would gladly have let my brain rest for a while. The wide range of thought which belonged to the subject of the Memoir, the occasional mysticism and the frequent tendency toward it, the sweep of imagination and the sparkle of wit which kept his reader's mind on the stretch, the union of prevailing good sense with exceptional extravagances, the modest audacity of a nature that showed itself in its naked truthfulness and was not ashamed, the feeling that I was in the company of a sibylline intelligence which was discounting the promises of the remote future long before they were due,—all this made the task a grave one. But when I found myself amidst the vortices of uncounted, various, bewildering judgments, Catholic and Protestant, orthodox and liberal, scholarly from under the tree of knowledge and instinctive from over the potato-hill; the passionate enthusiasm of young adorers and the cool, if not cynical, estimate of hardened critics, all intersecting each other as they whirled each around its own centre, I felt that it was indeed very difficult to keep the faculties clear and the judgment unbiassed.

It is a great privilege to have lived so long in the society of such a man. "He nothing common," said, "or mean." He was always the same pure and high-souled companion. After being with him virtue seemed as natural to man as its opposite did according to the old theologies. But how to let one's self down from the high level of such a character to one's own poor standard? I trust that the influence of this long intellectual and spiritual companionship never absolutely leaves one who has lived in it. It may come to him in the form of self-reproach that he falls so far short of the superior being who has been so long the object of his contemplation. But it also carries him at times into the other's personality, so that he finds himself thinking thoughts that are not his own, using phrases which he has unconsciously borrowed, writing, it may be, as nearly like his long-studied original as Julio Romano's painting was like Raphael's; and all this with the unquestioning conviction that he is talking from his own consciousness in his own natural way. So far as tones and expressions and habits which belonged to the idiosyncrasy of the original are borrowed by the student of his life, it is a misfortune for the borrower. But to share the inmost consciousness of a noble thinker, to scan one's self in the white light of a pure and radiant soul,—this is indeed the highest form of teaching and discipline.

I have written these few memoirs, and I am grateful for all that they have taught me. But let me write no more. There are but two biographers who can tell the story of a man's or a woman's life. One is the person himself or herself; the other is the Recording Angel. The autobiographer cannot be trusted to tell the whole truth, though he may tell nothing but the truth, and the Recording Angel never lets his book go out of his own hands. As for myself, I would say to my friends, in the Oriental phrase, "Live forever!" Yes, live forever, and I, at least, shall not have to wrong your memories by my imperfect record and unsatisfying commentary.

In connection with these biographies, or memoirs, more properly, in which I have written of my departed friends, I hope my readers will indulge me in another personal reminiscence. I have just lost my dear and honored contemporary of the last century. A hundred years ago this day, December 13, 1784, died the admirable and ever to be remembered Dr. Samuel Johnson. The year 1709 was made ponderous and illustrious in English biography by his birth. My own humble advent to the world of protoplasm was in the year 1809 of the present century. Summer was just ending when those four letters, "son b." were written under the date of my birth, August 29th. Autumn had just begun when my great pre-contemporary entered this un-Christian universe and was made a member of the Christian church on the same day, for he was born and baptized on the 18th of September.

Thus there was established a close bond of relationship between the great English scholar and writer and myself Year by year, and almost month by month, my life has kept pace in this century with his life in the last century. I had only to open my Boswell at any time, and I knew just what Johnson at my age, twenty or fifty or seventy, was thinking and doing; what were his feelings about life; what changes the years had wrought in his body, his mind, his feelings, his companionships, his reputation. It was for me a kind of unison between two instruments, both playing that old familiar air, "Life,"—one a bassoon, if you will, and the other an oaten pipe, if you care to find an image for it, but still keeping pace with each other until the players both grew old and gray. At last the thinner thread of sound is heard by itself, and its deep accompaniment rolls out its thunder no more.

I feel lonely now that my great companion and friend of so many years has left me. I felt more intimately acquainted with him than I do with many of my living friends. I can hardly remember when I did not know him. I can see him in his bushy wig, exactly like that of the Reverend Dr. Samuel Cooper (who died in December, 1783) as Copley painted him,—he hangs there on my wall, over the revolving bookcase. His ample coat, too, I see, with its broad flaps and many buttons and generous cuffs, and beneath it the long, still more copiously buttoned waistcoat, arching in front of the fine, crescentic, almost semi-lunar Falstaffian prominence, involving no less than a dozen of the above-mentioned buttons, and the strong legs with their sturdy calves, fitting columns of support to the massive body and solid capacious brain enthroned over it. I can hear him with his heavy tread as he comes into the Club, and a gap is widened to make room for his portly figure. "A fine day," says Sir Joshua. "Sir," he answers, "it seems propitious, but the atmosphere is humid and the skies are nebulous," at which the great painter smiles, shifts his trumpet, and takes a pinch of snuff.

Dear old massive, deep-voiced dogmatist and hypochondriac of the eighteenth century, how one would like to sit at some ghostly Club, between you and the bony, "mighty-mouthed," harsh-toned termagant and dyspeptic of the nineteenth! The growl of the English mastiff and the snarl of the Scotch terrier would make a duet which would enliven the shores of Lethe. I wish I could find our "spiritualist's" paper in the Portfolio, in which the two are brought together, but I hardly know what I shall find when it is opened.

Yes, my life is a little less precious to me since I have lost that dear old friend; and when the funeral train moves to Westminster Abbey next Saturday,—for I feel as if this were 1784, and not 1884,—I seem to find myself following the hearse, one of the silent mourners.

Among the events which have rendered the past year memorable to me has been the demolition of that venerable and interesting old dwelling-house, precious for its intimate association with the earliest stages of the war of the Revolution, and sacred to me as my birthplace and the home of my boyhood.

The "Old Gambrel-roofed House" exists no longer. I remember saying something, in one of a series of papers published long ago, about the experience of dying out of a house,—of leaving it forever, as the soul dies out of the body. We may die out of many houses, but the house itself can die but once; and so real is the life of a house to one who has dwelt in it, more especially the life of the house which held him in dreamy infancy, in restless boyhood, in passionate youth,—so real, I say, is its life, that it seems as if something like a soul of it must outlast its perishing frame.

The slaughter of the Old Gambrel-roofed House was, I am ready to admit, a case of justifiable domicide. Not the less was it to be deplored by all who love the memories of the past. With its destruction are obliterated some of the footprints of the heroes and martyrs who took the first steps in the long and bloody march which led us through the wilderness to the promised land of independent nationality. Personally, I have a right to mourn for it as a part of my life gone from me. My private grief for its loss would be a matter for my solitary digestion, were it not that the experience through which I have just passed is one so familiar to my fellow-countrymen that, in telling my own reflections and feelings, I am repeating those of great numbers of men and women who have had the misfortune to outlive their birthplace.

It is a great blessing to be born surrounded by a natural horizon. The Old Gambrel-roofed House could not boast an unbroken ring of natural objects encircling it. Northerly it looked upon its own outbuildings and some unpretending two-story houses which had been its neighbors for a century and more. To the south of it the square brick dormitories and the belfried hall of the university helped to shut out the distant view. But the west windows gave a broad outlook across the common, beyond which the historical "Washington elm" and two companions in line with it, spread their leaves in summer and their networks in winter. And far away rose the hills that bounded the view, with the glimmer here and there of the white walls or the illuminated casements of some embowered, half-hidden villa. Eastwardly also, the prospect was, in my earlier remembrance, widely open, and I have frequently seen the sunlit sails gliding along as if through the level fields, for no water was visible. So there were broad expanses on two sides at least, for my imagination to wander over.

I cannot help thinking that we carry our childhood's horizon with us all our days. Among these western wooded hills my day-dreams built their fairy palaces, and even now, as I look at them from my library window, across the estuary of the Charles, I find myself in the familiar home of my early visions. The "clouds of glory" which we trail with us in after life need not be traced to a pre-natal state. There is enough to account for them in that unconsciously remembered period of existence before we have learned the hard limitations of real life. Those earliest months in which we lived in sensations without words, and ideas not fettered sentences, have all the freshness of proofs of an engraving "before the letter." I am very thankful that the first part of my life was not passed shut in between high walls and treading the unimpressible and unsympathetic pavement.

Our university town was very much like the real country, in those days of which I am thinking. There were plenty of huckleberries and blueberries within half a mile of the house. Blackberries ripened in the fields, acorns and shagbarks dropped from the trees, squirrels ran among the branches, and not rarely the hen-hawk might be seen circling over the barnyard. Still another rural element was not wanting, in the form of that far-diffused, infragrant effluvium, which, diluted by a good half mile of pure atmosphere, is no longer odious, nay is positively agreeable, to many who have long known it, though its source and centre has an unenviable reputation. I need not name the animal whose Parthian warfare terrifies and puts to flight the mightiest hunter that ever roused the tiger from his jungle or faced the lion of the desert. Strange as it may seem, an aerial hint of his personality in the far distance always awakens in my mind pleasant remembrances and tender reflections. A whole neighborhood rises up before me; the barn, with its hay-mow, where the hens laid their eggs to hatch, and we boys hid our apples to ripen, both occasionally illustrating the *sic vos non vobis;* the shed, where the annual Tragedy of the Pig was acted with a realism that made Salvini's Othello seem but a pale counterfeit; the ricketty old outhouse, with the "corn-chamber" which the mice knew so well; the paved yard, with its open gutter,—these and how much else come up at the hint of my far-off friend, who is my very near enemy. Nothing is more familiar than the power of smell in reviving old memories. There was that quite different fragrance of the wood-house, the smell of fresh sawdust. It comes back to me now, and with it the hiss of the saw; the tumble of the divorced logs which God put together and man has just put asunder; the coming down of the axe and the hah! that helped it,— the straight-grained stick opening at the first appeal of the implement as if it were a pleasure, and the stick with a knot in the middle of it that mocked the blows and the hahs! until the beetle and wedge made it listen to reason,—there are just such straight-grained and just such knotty men and women. All this passes through my mind while Biddy, whose parlor-name is Angela, contents herself with exclaiming "egh! * **** * *****!"

How different distances were in those young days of which I am thinking! From the old house to the old yellow meeting-house, where the head of the family preached and the limbs of the family listened, was not much more than two or three times the width of Commonwealth Avenue. But of a hot summer's afternoon, after having already heard one sermon, which could not in the nature of things have the charm of novelty of presentation to the members of the home circle, and the theology of which was not too clear to tender apprehensions; with three hymns more or less lugubrious, rendered by a village-choir, got into voice by many preliminary snuffles and other expiratory efforts, and accompanied by the snort of a huge bass-viol which wallowed through the tune like a hippopotamus, with other exercises of the customary character,—after all this in the forenoon, the afternoon walk to the meeting-house in the hot sun counted for as much, in my childish dead-reckoning, as from old Israel Porter's in Cambridge to the Exchange Coffee-house in Boston did in after years. It takes a good while to measure the radius of the circle that is about us, for the moon seems at first as near as the watch-face. Who knows but that, after a certain number of ages, the planet we live on may seem to us no bigger than our neighbor Venus appeared when she passed before the sun a few months ago, looking as if we could take her between our thumb and finger, like a bullet or a marble? And time, too; how long was it from the serious sunrise to the joyous "sundown" of an old-fashioned, puritanical, judaical first day of the week, which a pious fraud christened "the Sabbath"? Was it a fortnight, as we now reckon duration, or only a week? [Curious entities, or non-entities, space and time? When you see a metaphysician trying to wash his hands of them and get rid of these accidents, so as to lay his dry, clean palm on ***the absolute,*** does it not remind you of the hopeless task of changing the color of the blackamoor by a similar proceeding? For space is the fluid in which he is washing, and time is the soap which he is using up in the process, and he cannot get free from them until he can wash himself in a mental vacuum.]

In my reference to the old house in a former paper, published years ago, I said,—

"By and by the stony foot of the great University will plant itself on this whole territory, and the private recollections which clung so tenaciously to the place and its habitations will have died with those who cherished them."

What strides the great University has taken since those words were written! During all my early years our old Harvard Alma Mater sat still and lifeless as the colossi in the Egyptian desert. Then all at once, like the statue in Don Giovanni, she moved from her pedestal. The fall of that "stony foot" has effected a miracle like the harp that Orpheus played, like the teeth which Cadmus sowed. The plain where the moose and the bear were wandering while Shakespeare was writing Hamlet, where a few plain dormitories and other needed buildings were scattered about in my school-boy days, groans under the weight of the massive edifices which have sprung up all around them, crowned by the tower of that noble structure which stands in full view before me as I lift my eyes from the portfolio on the back of which I am now writing.

For I must be permitted to remind you that I have not yet opened it. I have told you that I have just finished a long memoir, and that it has cost me no little labor to overcome some of its difficulties,—if I have overcome them, which others must decide. And I feel exactly as honest Dobbin feels when his harness is slipped off after a long journey with a good deal of uphill work. He wants to rest a little, then to feed a little; then, if you will turn him loose in the pasture, he wants to *roll*. I have left my starry and ethereal companionship,—not for a long time, I hope, for it has lifted me above my common self, but for a while. And now I want, so as to speak, to roll in the grass and among the dandelions with the other pachyderms. So I have kept to the outside of the portfolio as yet, and am disporting myself in reminiscences, and fancies, and vagaries, and parentheses.

How well I understand the feeling which led the Pisans to load their vessels with earth from the Holy Land, and fill the area of the Campo Santo with that sacred soil! The old house stood upon about as perverse a little patch of the planet as ever harbored a half-starved earth-worm. It was as sandy as Sahara and as thirsty as Tantalus. The rustic aid-de-camps of the household used to aver that all fertilizing matters "leached" through it. I tried to disprove their assertion by gorging it with the best of terrestrial nourishment, until I became convinced that I was feeding the tea-plants of China, and then I gave over the attempt. And yet I did love, and do love, that arid patch of ground. I wonder if a single flower could not be made to grow in a pot of earth from that Campo Santo of my childhood! One noble product of nature did not refuse to flourish there,—the tall, stately, beautiful, soft-haired, many-jointed, generous maize or Indian corn, which thrives on sand and defies the blaze of our shrivelling summer. What child but loves to wander in its forest-like depths, amidst the rustling leaves and with the lofty tassels tossing their heads high above him! There are two aspects of the cornfield which always impress my imagination: the first when it has reached its full growth, and its ordered ranks look like an army on the march with its plumed and bannered battalions; the second when, after the battle of the harvest, the girdled stacks stand on the field of slaughter like so many ragged Niobes,—say rather like the crazy widows and daughters of the dead soldiery.

Once more let us come back to the old house. It was far along in its second century when the edict went forth that it must stand no longer.

The natural death of a house is very much like that of one of its human tenants. The roof is the first part to show the distinct signs of age. Slates and tiles loosen and at last slide off, and leave bald the boards that supported them; shingles darken and decay, and soon the garret or the attic lets in the rain and the snow; by and by the beams sag, the floors warp, the walls crack, the paper peels away, the ceilings scale off and fall, the windows are crusted with clinging dust, the doors drop from their rusted hinges, the winds come in without knocking and howl their cruel death-songs through the empty rooms and passages, and at last there comes a crash, a great cloud of dust rises, and the home that had been the shelter of generation after generation finds its grave in its own cellar. Only the chimney remains as its monument. Slowly, little by little, the patient solvents that find nothing too hard for their chemistry pick out the mortar from between the bricks; at last a mighty wind roars around it and rushes against it, and the monumental relic crashes down among the wrecks it has long survived. So dies a human habitation left to natural decay, all that was seen above the surface of the soil sinking gradually below it,

Till naught remains the saddening tale to tell Save home's last wrecks, the cellar and the well.

But if this sight is saddening, what is it to see a human dwelling fall by the hand of violence! The ripping off of the shelter that has kept out a thousand storms, the tearing off of the once ornamental wood-work, the wrench of the inexorable crow-bar, the murderous blows of the axe, the progressive ruin, which ends by rending all the joints asunder and flinging the tenoned and mortised timbers into heaps that will be sawed and split to warm some new habitation as firewood,—what a brutal act of destruction it seems!

Why should I go over the old house again, having already described it more than ten years ago? Alas! how many remember anything they read but once, and so long ago as that? How many would find it out if one should say over in the same words that which he said in the last decade? But there is really no need of telling the story a second time, for it can be found by those who are curious enough to look it up in a volume of which it occupies the opening chapter.

In order, however, to save any inquisitive reader that trouble, let me remind him that the old house was General Ward's headquarters at the breaking out of the Revolution; that the plan for fortifying Bunker's Hill was laid, as commonly believed, in the southeast lower room, the floor of which was covered with dents, made, it was alleged, by the butts of the soldiers' muskets. In that house, too, General Warren probably passed the night before the Bunker Hill battle, and over its threshold must the stately figure of Washington have often cast its shadow.

But the house in which one drew his first breath, and where he one day came into the consciousness that he was a personality, an *ego,* a little universe with a sky over him all his own, with a persistent identity, with the terrible responsibility of a separate, independent, inalienable existence,—that house does not ask for any historical associations to make it the centre of the earth for him.

If there is any person in the world to be envied, it is the one who is born to an ancient estate, with a long line of family traditions and the means in his hands of shaping his mansion and his domain to his own taste, without losing sight of all the characteristic features which surrounded his earliest years. The American is, for the most part, a nomad, who pulls down his house as the Tartar pulls up his tent-poles. If I had an ideal life to plan for him it would be something like this:—

His grandfather should be a wise, scholarly, large-brained, large-hearted country minister, from whom he should inherit the temperament that predisposes to cheerfulness and enjoyment, with the finer instincts which direct life to noble aims and make it rich with the gratification of pure and elevated tastes and the carrying out of plans for the good of his neighbors and his fellow-creatures. He should, if possible, have been born, at any rate have passed some of his early years, or a large part of them, under the roof of the good old minister. His father should be, we will say, a business man in one of our great cities,—a generous manipulator of millions, some of which have adhered to his private fortunes, in spite of his liberal use of his means. His heir, our ideally placed American, shall take possession of the old house, the home of his earliest memories, and preserve it sacredly, not exactly like the Santa Casa, but, as nearly as may be, just as he remembers it. He can add as many acres as he will to the narrow house-lot. He can build a grand mansion for himself, if he chooses, in the not distant neighborhood. But the old house, and all immediately round it, shall be as he recollects it when he had to stretch his little arm up to reach the door-handles. Then, having well provided for his own household, himself included, let him become the providence of the village or the town where he finds himself during at least a portion of every year. Its schools, its library, its poor,—and perhaps the new clergyman who has succeeded his grandfather's successor may be one of them,—all its interests, he shall make his own. And from this centre his beneficence shall radiate so far that all who hear of his wealth shall also hear of him as a friend to his race.

Is not this a pleasing programme? Wealth is a steep hill, which the father climbs slowly and the son often tumbles down precipitately; but there is a table-land on a level with it, which may be found by those who do not lose their head in looking down from its sharply cloven summit. Our dangerously rich men can make themselves hated, held as enemies of the race, or beloved and recognized as its benefactors. The clouds of discontent are threatening, but if the gold-pointed lightning-rods are rightly distributed the destructive element may be drawn off silently and harmlessly. For it cannot be repeated too often that the safety of great wealth with us lies in obedience to the new version of the Old World axiom, RICHESSE *oblige*.

THE NEW PORTFOLIO: FIRST OPENING.

A MORTAL ANTIPATHY

I.
GETTING READY.

IT is impossible to begin a story which must of necessity tax the powers of belief of readers unacquainted with the class of facts to which its central, point of interest belongs without some words in the natural of the preparation. Readers of Charles Lamb remember that Sarah Battle insisted on a clean-swept hearth before sitting down to her favorite game of whist.

The narrator wishes to sweep the hearth, as it were, in these opening pages, before sitting down to tell his story. He does not intend to frighten the reader away by prolix explanation, but he does mean to warn him against hasty judgments when facts are related which are not within the range of every-day experience. Did he ever see the Siamese twins, or any pair like them? Probably not, yet he feels sure that Chang and Eng really existed; and if he has taken the trouble to inquire, he has satisfied himself that similar cases have been recorded by credible witnesses, though at long intervals and in countries far apart from each other.

This is the first sweep of the brush, to clear the hearth of the skepticism and incredulity which must be got out of the way before we can begin to tell and to listen in peace with ourselves and each other.

One more stroke of the brush is needed before the stage will be ready for the chief characters and the leading circumstances to which the reader's attention is invited. If the principal personages made their entrance at once, the reader would have to create for himself the whole scenery of their surrounding conditions. In point of fact, no matter how a story is begun, many of its readers have already shaped its chief actors out of any hint the author may have dropped, and provided from their own resources locality and a set of outward conditions to environ these imagined personalities. These are all to be brushed away, and the actual surroundings of the subject of the narrative represented as they were, at the risk of detaining the reader a little while from the events most likely to interest him. The choicest egg that ever was laid was not so big as the nest that held it. If a story were so interesting that a maiden would rather heat it than listen to the praise of her own beauty, or a poet would rather read it than recite his own verses, still it would have to be wrapped in some tissue of circumstance, or it would lose half its effectiveness.

It may not be easy to find the exact locality referred to in this narrative by looking into the first gazetteer that is at hand. Recent experiences have shown that it is unsafe to be too exact in designating places and the people who live in them. There are, it may be added, so many advertisements disguised under the form of stories and other literary productions that one naturally desires to avoid the suspicion of being employed by the enterprising proprietors of this or that celebrated resort to use his gifts for their especial benefit. There are no doubt many persons who remember the old sign and the old tavern and its four chief personages presently to be mentioned. It is to be hoped that they will not furnish the public with a key to this narrative, and perhaps bring trouble to the writer of it, as has happened to other authors. If the real names are a little altered, it need not interfere with the important facts relating to those who bear them. It might not be safe to tell a damaging story about John or James Smythe; but if the slight change is made of spelling the name Smith, the Smythes would never think of bringing an action, as if the allusion related to any of them. The same gulf of family, distinction separates the Thompsons with a *p* from the Thomsons without that letter.

There are few pleasanter places in the Northern States for a summer residence than that known from the first period of its settlement by the name of Arrowhead Village. The Indians had found it out, as the relics they left behind them abundantly testified. The commonest of these were those chipped stones which the medals of barbarism, and from which the place took its name,—the heads of arrows, of various sizes, material, and patterns; some small enough for killing fish and little birds, some large enough for such game as the moose and the bear, to say nothing of the hostile Indian and the white settler; some of flint, now and then one of white quartz, and others of variously colored jasper. The Indians must have lived here for many generations, and it must have been a kind of factory village of the stone age,—which lasted up to near the present time, if we may judge from the fact that many of these relics are met with close to the surface of the ground.

No wonder they found this a pleasant residence, for it is to-day one of the most attractive of all summer resorts; so inviting, indeed, that those who know it do not like to say too much about it, lest the swarms of tourists should make it unendurable to those who love it for itself, and not as a centre of fashionable display and extra-mural cockneyism.

There is the lake, in the first place,—Cedar Lake,—about five miles long, and from half a mile to a mile and a half wide, stretching from north to south. Near the northern extremity are the buildings of Stoughton University, a flourishing young college with an ambitious name but well equipped and promising, the grounds of which reach the water. At the southern end of the lake are the edifices of the Corinna Institute, a favorite school for young ladies, where large numbers of the daughters of America are fitted, so far as education can do it, for all stations in life, from camping out with a husband at the mines in Nevada to acting the part of chief lady of the land in the White House at Washington.

Midway between the two extremities, on the eastern shore of the lake is a valley between two hills, which come down to the very edge of the lake, leaving only room enough for a road between their base and the water. This valley, half a mile in width, has been long settled, and here for a century or more has stood the old Anchor Tavern. A famous place it was so long as its sign swung at the side of the road: famous for its landlord, portly, paternal, whose welcome to a guest that looked worthy of the attention was like that of a parent to a returning prodigal, and whose parting words were almost as good as a marriage benediction; famous for its landlady, ample in person, motherly, seeing to the whole household with her own eyes, mistress of all culinary secrets that Northern kitchens are most proud of; famous also for its ancient servant, as city people would call her,—help, as she was called in the tavern and would have called herself,—the unchanging, seemingly immortal Miranda, who cared for the guests as if she were their nursing mother, and pressed the specially favorite delicacies on their attention as a connoisseur calls the wandering eyes of an amateur to the beauties of a picture. Who that has ever been at the old Anchor Tavern forgets Miranda's

"A little of this fricassee?—it is vér-y nice;"

or

"Some of these cakes? You will find them vér-y good."

Nor would it be just to memory to forget that other notable and noted member of the household,—the- unsleeping, unresting, omnipresent Pushee, ready for everybody and everything, everywhere within the limits of the establishment at all hours of the day and night. He fed, nobody could say accurately when or where. There were rumors of a "bunk," in which he lay down with his clothes on, but he seemed to be always wide awake, and at the service of as many guests at once as if there had been a half a dozen of him.

So much for old reminiscences.

The landlord of the Anchor Tavern had taken down his sign. He had had the house thoroughly renovated and furnished it anew, and kept it open in summer for a few boarders. It happened more than once that the summer boarders were so much pleased with the place that they stayed on through the autumn, and some of them through the winter. The attractions of the village were really remarkable. Boating in summer, and skating in winter; ice-boats, too, which the wild ducks could hardly keep up with; fishing, for which the lake was renowned; varied and beautiful walks through the valley and up the hill-sides; houses sheltered from the north and northeasterly winds, and refreshed in the hot summer days by the breeze which came over the water,—all this made the frame for a pleasing picture of rest and happiness. But there was a great deal more than this. There was a fine library in the little village, presented and richly endowed by a wealthy native of the place. There was a small permanent population of a superior character to that of an every-day country town; there was a pretty little Episcopal church, with a good-hearted rector, broad enough for the Bishop of the diocese to be a little afraid of, and hospitable to all outsiders, of whom, in the summer season, there were always some who wanted a place of worship to keep their religion from dying out during the heathen months, while the shepherds of the flocks to which they belonged were away from their empty folds.

What most helped to keep the place alive all through the year was the frequent coming together of the members of a certain literary association. Some time before the tavern took down its sign the landlord had built a hall, where many a ball had been held, to which the young folks of all the country round had resorted. It was still sometimes, used for similar occasions, but it was especially notable as being the place of meeting of the famous PANSOPHLAN SOCIETY.

This association, the name of which might be invidiously interpreted as signifying that its members knew everything, had no such pretensions, but, as its Constitution said very plainly and modestly, held itself open to accept knowledge on any and all subjects from such as had knowledge to impart. Its President was the rector of the little chapel, a man who, in spite of the Thirty-Nine Articles, could stand fire from the widest-mouthed heretical blunderbuss without flinching or losing his temper. The hall of the old Anchor Tavern was a convenient place of meeting for the students and instructors of the University and the Institute. Sometimes in boat-loads, sometimes in carriage-loads, sometimes in processions of skaters, they came to the meetings in Pansophian Hall, as it was now commonly called.

These meetings had grown to be occasions of great interest. It was customary to have papers written by members of the Society, for the most part, but now and then by friends of the members, sometimes by the students of the College or the Institute, and in rarer instances by anonymous personages, whose papers, having been looked over and discussed by the Committee appointed for that purpose, were thought worth listening to. The variety of topics considered was very great. The young ladies of the village and the Institute had their favorite subjects, the young gentlemen a different set of topics, and the occasional outside contributors their own; so that one who happened to be admitted to a meeting never knew whether he was going to hear an account of recent arctic discoveries, or an essay on the freedom of the will, or a psychological experience, or a story, or even a poem.

Of late there had been a tendency to discuss the questions relating to the true status and the legitimate social functions of woman. The most conflicting views were held on the subject. Many of the young ladies and some of the University students were strong in defence of all the "woman's rights" doctrines. Some of these young people were extreme in their views. They had read about Semiramis and Boadicea and Queen Elizabeth, until they were ready, if they could get the chance, to vote for a woman as President of the United States or as General of the United States Army. They were even disposed to assert the physical equality of woman to man, on the strength of the rather questionable history of the Amazons, and especially of the story, believed to be authentic, of the female body-guard of the King of Dahomey,—females frightful enough to need no other weapon than their looks to scare off an army of Cossacks.

Miss Lurida Vincent, gold medallist of her year at the Corinna Institute, was the leader of these advocates of virile womanhood. It was rather singular that she should have elected to be the apostle of this extreme doctrine, for she was herself far better equipped with brain than muscles. In fact, she was a large-headed, large-eyed, long-eyelashed, slender-necked, slightly developed young woman; looking almost like a child at an age when many of the girls had reached their full stature and proportions. In her studies she was so far in advance of her different classes that there was always a wide gap between her and the second scholar. So fatal to all rivalry had she proved herself that she passed under the school name of *The Terror.* She learned so easily that she under-valued her own extraordinary gifts, and felt the deepest admiration for those of her friends endowed with faculties of an entirely different and almost opposite nature. After sitting at her desk until her head was hot and her feet were like ice, she would go and look at the blooming young girls exercising in the gymnasium of the school, and feel as if she would give all her knowledge, all her mathematics and strange tongues and history, all those accomplishments that made her the encyclopædia of every class she belonged to, if she could go through the series of difficult and graceful exercises in which she saw her schoolmates delighting.

One among them, especially, was the object of her admiration, as she was of all who knew her exceptional powers in the line for which nature had specially organized her. All the physical perfections which Miss Lurida had missed had been united in Miss Euthymia Tower, whose school name was *The Wonder.* Though of full womanly stature, there were several taller girls of her age. While all her contours and all her movements betrayed a fine muscular development, there was no lack of proportion, and her finely shaped hands and feet showed that her organization was one of those carefully finished masterpieces of nature which sculptors are always in search of, and find it hard to detect among the imperfect products of the living laboratory.

This girl of eighteen was more famous than she cared to be for her performances in the gymnasium. She commonly contented herself with the same exercises that her companions were accustomed to. Only her dumbbells, with which she exercised easily and gracefully, were too heavy for most of the girls to do more with than lift them from the floor. She was fond of daring feats on the trapeze, and had to be checked in her indulgence in them. The Professor of gymnastics at the University came over to the Institute now and then, and it was a source of great excitement to watch some of the athletic exercises in which the young lady showed her remarkable muscular strength and skill in managing herself in the accomplishment of feats which looked impossible at first sight. How often The Terror had thought to her-self that she would gladly give up all her knowledge of Greek and the differential and integral calculus if she could only perform the least of those feats which were mere play to The Wonder! Miss Euthymia was not behind the rest in her attainments in classical or mathematical knowledge, and she was one of the very best students in the out-door branches,—botany, mineralogy, sketching from nature,—to be found among the scholars of the Institute.

There was an eight-oared boat rowed by a crew of the young ladies, of which Miss Euthymia was the captain and pulled the bow oar. Poor little Lurida could not pull an oar, but on great occasions, when there were many boats out, she was wanted as coxswain, being a mere feather-weight, and quick-witted enough to serve well in the important office where brains are more needed than muscle.

There was also an eight-oared boat belonging to the University, and rowed by a picked crew of stalwart young fellows. The bow oar and captain of the University crew was a powerful young man, who, like the captain of the girls' boat, was a noted gymnast. He had had one or two quiet trials with Miss Euthymia, in which, according to the ultras of the woman's rights party, he had not vindicated the superiority of his sex in the way which might have been expected. Indeed, it was claimed that he let a cannon-ball drop when he ought to have caught it, and it was not disputed that he had been ingloriously knocked over by a sand-bag projected by the strong arms of the young maiden. This was of course a story that was widely told and laughingly listened to, and the captain of the University crew had become a little sensitive on the subject. When there was a talk, therefore, about a race between the champion boats of the two institutions there was immense excitement in both of them, as well as among the members of the Pansophian Society and all the good people of the village.

There were many objections to be overcome. Some thought it unladylike for the young maidens to take part in a competition which must attract many lookers-on, and which it seemed to them very hoidenish to venture upon. Some said it was a shame to let a crew of girls try their strength against an equal number of powerful young men. These objections were offset by the advocates of the race by the following arguments. They maintained that it was no more hoidenish to row a boat than it was to take a part in the calisthenic exercises, and that the girls had nothing to do with the young men's boat, except to keep as much ahead of it as possible. As to strength, the woman's righters believed that, weight for weight, their crew was as strong as the other, and of course due allowance would be made for the difference of weight and all other accidental hindrances. It was time to test the boasted superiority of masculine muscle. Here was a chance. If the girls beat, the whole country would know it, and after that female suffrage would be only a question of time. Such was the conclusion, from rather iusufficient premises, it must be confessed; but if nature does nothing **per saltum,**—by jumps,—as the old adage has it, youth is very apt to take long leaps from a fact to a possible sequel or consequence. So it had come about that a contest between the two boat-crews was looked forward to with an interest almost equal to that with which the combat between the Horatii and Curiatii was regarded.

The terms had been at last arranged between the two crews, after cautious protocols and many diplomatic discussions. It was so novel in its character that it naturally took a good deal of time to adjust it in such a way as to be fair to both parties. The course must not be too long for the lighter and weaker crew, for the staying power of the young persons who made it up could not be safely reckoned upon. A certain advantage must be allowed them at the start, and this was a delicate matter to settle. The weather was another important consideration. June would be early enough, in all probability, and if the lake should be tolerably smooth the grand affair might come off some time in that month. Any roughness of the water would be unfavorable to the weaker crew. The rowing-course was on the eastern side of the lake, the starting-point being opposite the Anchor Tavern; from that three quarters of a mile to the south, where the turning-stake was fixed, so that the whole course of one mile and a half would bring the boats back to their starting-point.

The race was to be between the Algonquin, eight-oared boat with outriggers, rowed by young men, students of Stoughton University, and the Atalanta, also eight-oared and outrigger boat, by young ladies from the Corinna Institute. Their boat was three inches wider than the other, for various sufficient reasons, one of which was to make it a little less likely to go over and throw its crew into the water, which was a sound precaution, though all the girls could swim, and one at least, the bow oar, was a famous swimmer, who had pulled a drowning man out of the water after a hard struggle to keep him from carrying her down with him.

Though the coming trial had not been advertised in the papers, so as to draw together a rabble of betting men and ill-conditioned lookers-on, there was a considerable gathering, made up chiefly of the villagers and the students of the two institutions. Among them were a few who were disposed to add to their interest in the trial by small wagers. The bets were rather in favor of the "Quins," as the University boat was commonly called, except where the natural sympathy of the young ladies or the gallantry of some of the young men led them to risk their gloves or cigars, or whatever it might be, on the Atalantas. The elements of judgment were these: average weight of the Algonquins one hundred and sixty-five pounds; average weight of the Atalantas, one hundred and forty-eight pounds; skill in practice about equal; advantage of the narrow boat equal to three lengths; whole distance allowed the Atalantas eight lengths,—a long stretch to be made up in a mile and a half.

And so both crews began practising for the grand trial.

II.
THE BOAT-RACE.

THE tenth of June was a delicious summer day,—rather warm, but still and bright. The water was smooth, and the crews were in the best possible condition. All was expectation, and for some time nothing but expectation. No boat-race or regatta ever began at the time appointed for the start. Somebody breaks an oar, or somebody fails to appear in season, or something is the matter with a seat or an out-rigger; or if there is no such excuse, the crew of one or both or all the boats to take part in the race must paddle about to get themselves ready for work, to the infinite weariness of all the spectators, who naturally ask why all this getting ready is not attended to beforehand. The Algonquins wore plain gray flannel suits and white caps. The young ladies were all in dark blue dresses, touched up with a red ribbon here and there, and wore light straw hats. The little coxswain of the Atalanta was the last to step on board. As she took her place she carefully deposited at her feet a white handkerchief wrapped about something or other,—perhaps a sponge, in case the boat should take in water.

At last the Algonquin shot out from the little nook where she lay,—long, nar-row, shining, swift as a pickerel when he darts from the reedy shore. It was a beau-tiful sight to see the eight young fellows in their close-fitting suits, their brown muscular arms bare, bending their backs for the stroke and recovering, as if they were parts of a single machine.

"The gals can't stan' it agin them fellers," said the old blacksmith from the vil-lage.

"You wait till the gals get agoin'," said the carpenter, who had often worked in the gymnasium of the Corinna Institute, and knew something of their muscular accomplishments. "Y' ought to see 'em climb ropes, and swing dumb-bells, and pull in them rowin'-machines. Ask Jake there whether they can't row a mild in double-quick time,—he knows all about it."

Jake was by profession a fisherman, and a fresh-water fisherman in a country village is inspector-general of all that goes on out-of-doors, being a lazy, wander-ing sort of fellow, whose study of the habits and habitats of fishes gives him a kind of shrewdness of observation, just as dealing in horses is an education of certain faculties, and breeds a race of men peculiarly cunning, suspicious, wary, and wide awake, with a rhetoric of appreciation and depreciation all its own.

Jake made his usual preliminary signal, and delivered himself to the following effect:—

"Wahl, I don' know jest what to say. I've seed 'em both often enough when they was practisin', an' I tell ye the' wa'n't no slouch abaout neither on 'em. But them boats is allfired long, 'n' eight on 'em stretched in a straight line eendways makes a consid'able piece aout 'f a mile 'n' a haaf. I'd bate on them gals if it wa'n't that them fellers is naterally longer winded, as the gals 'll find aout by the time they git raound the stake 'n' over agin the big ellum. I'll go ye a quarter on the pahnts agin the petticoats."

The fresh-water fisherman had expressed the prevailing belief that the young ladies were overmatched. Still there were not wanting those who thought the advantage allowed the "Lantas," as they called the Corinna boat-crew, was too great, and that it would be impossible for the "Quins," to make it up and go by them.

The Algonquins rowed up and down a few times before the spectators. They appeared in perfect training, neither too fat nor too fine, mettlesome as colts, steady as draught-horses, deep-breathed as oxen, disciplined to work together as symmetrically as a single sculler pulls his pair of oars. The fisherman offered to make his quarter fifty cents. No takers.

Five minutes passed, and all eyes were strained to the south, looking for the Atalanta. A clump of trees hid the edge of the lake along which the Corinna's boat was stealing towards the starting-point. Presently the long shell swept into view, with its blooming rowers, who, with their ample dresses, seemed to fill it almost as full as Raphael fills his skiff on the edge of the Lake of Galilee. But how steadily the Atalanta came on!—no rocking, no splashing, no apparent strain; the bow oar turning to look ahead every now and then, and watching her course, which seemed to be straight as an arrow, the beat of the strokes as true and regular as the pulse of the healthiest rower among them all. And if the sight of the other boat and its crew was beautiful, how lovely was the look of! Eight young girls,—young ladies, for those who prefer that more dignified and less attractive expression,—all in the flush of youth, all in vigorous health; every muscle taught its duty; each rower alert, not to be a tenth of a second out of time, or let her oar dally with the water so as to lose an ounce of its propelling virtue; every eye kindling with the hope of victory. Each of the boats was cheered as it came in sight, but the cheers for the Atalanta were naturally the loudest, as the gallantry of one sex and the clear, high voices of the other gave it life and vigor.

"Take your places!" shouted the umpire, five minutes before the half hour. The two boats felt their way slowly and cautiously to their positions, which had been determined by careful measurement. After a little backing and filling they got into line, at the proper distance from each other, and sat motionless, their bodies bent forward, their arms outstretched, their oars in the water, waiting for the word.

"Go!" shouted the umpire.

Away sprang the Atalanta, and far behind her leaped the Algonquin, her oars bending like so many long Indian bows as their blades flashed through the water.

"A stern chase is a long chase," especially when one craft is a great distance behind the other. It looked as if it would be impossible for the rear boat to overcome the odds against it. Of course the Algonquin kept gaining, but could it possibly gain enough? That was the question. As the boats got farther and farther away, it became more and more difficult to determine what change there was in the interval between them. But when they came to rounding the stake it was easier to guess at the amount of space which had been gained. It was clear that something like half the distance, four lengths, as nearly as could be estimated, had been made up in rowing the first three quarters of a mile. Could the Algonquins do a little better than this in the second half of the race-course, they would be sure of winning.

The boats had turned the stake, and were coming in rapidly. Every minute the University boat was getting nearer the other.

"Go it, Quins!" shouted the students.

"Pull away, Lantas!" screamed the girls, who were crowding down to the edge of the water.

Nearer,—nearer,—the rear boat is pressing the other more and more closely,—a few more strokes, and they will be even, for there is but one length between them, and thirty rods will carry them to the line. It looks desperate for the Atalantas. The bow oar of the Algonquin turns his head. He sees the little coxswain leaning forward at every stroke, as if her trivial weight were of such mighty consequence,— but a few ounces might turn the scale of victory. As he turned he got a glimpse of the stroke oar of the Atalanta. What a flash of loveliness it was! Her face was like the reddest of June roses, with the heat and the strain and the passion of expected triumph. The upper button of her close-fitting flannel suit had strangled her as her bosom heaved with exertion, and it had given way before the fierce clutch she made at it. The bow oar was a staunch and steady rower, but he was human. The blade of his oar lingered in the water; a little more and he would have caught a crab, and perhaps lost the race by his momentary bewilderment.

The boat, which seemed as if it had all the life and nervousness of a Derby three-year-old, felt the slight check, and all her men bent more vigorously to their oars. The Atalantas saw the movement, and made a spurt to keep their lead and gain upon it if they could. It was of no use. The strong arms of the young men were too much for the young maidens; only a few lengths remained to be rowed, and they would certainly pass the Atalanta before she could reach the line.

The little coxswain saw that it was all up with the girls' crew if she could not save them by some strategic device.

"Dolus an virtus quis in hoste requirat?"

she whispered to herself,—for The Terror remembered her Virgil as she did everything else she ever studied. As she stooped, she lifted the handkerchief at her feet, and took from it a flaming bouquet. "Look!" she cried, and flung it just forward of the track of the Algonquin. The captain of the University boat turned his head, and there was the lovely vision which had a moment before bewitched him. The owner of all that loveliness must, he thought, have flung the bouquet. It was a challenge: how could he be such a coward as to decline accepting it! He was sure he could win the race now, and he would sweep past the line in triumph with the great bunch of flowers at the stem of his boat, proud as Van Tromp in the British channel with the broom at his mast-head.

He turned the boat's head a little by backing water. He came up with the floating flowers, and near enough to reach them. He stooped and snatched them up, with the loss perhaps of a second in all,—no more. He felt sure of his victory.

How can one tell the story of the finish in cold-blooded preterites? Are we not there ourselves? Are not our muscles straining with those of these sixteen young creatures, full of hot, fresh blood, their nerves all tingling like so many tight-strained harp-strings, all their life concentrating itself in this passionate moment of supreme effort? No! We are seeing, not telling about what somebody else once saw!

—The bow of the Algonquin passes the stern of the Atalanta!

—The bow of the Algonquin is on a level with the middle of the Atalanta!

—Three more lengths' rowing and the college crew will pass the girls!

—"Hurrah for the Quins!" The Algonquin ranges up alongside of the Atalanta!

"Through with her!" shouts the captain of the Algonquin.

"Now, girls!" shrieks the captain of the Atalanta.

They near the line, every rower straining desperately, almost madly.

—Crack goes the oar of the Atalanta's captain, and up flash its splintered fragments, as the stem of her boat springs past the line, eighteen inches at least ahead of the Algonquin.

Hooraw for the Lantas! Hooraw for the girls! Hooraw for the Institoot! shout a hundred voices.

"Hurrah for woman's rights and female suffrage!" pipes the small voice of The Terror, and there is loud laughing and cheering all round.

She had not studied her classical dictionary and her mythology for nothing. "I have paid off one old score," she said. "Set down my damask roses against the golden apples of Hippomenes!"

It was that one second lost in snatching up the bouquet which gave the race to the Atalantas.

III.
THE WHITE CANOE.

WHILE the two boats were racing, other boats with lookers-on in them were rowing or sailing in the neighborhood of the race-course. The scene on the water was a gay one, for the young people in the boats were, many of them, acquainted with each other. There was a good deal of lively talk until the race became too exciting. Then many fell silent, until, as the boats neared the line, and still more as they crossed it, the shouts burst forth which showed how a cramp of attention finds its natural relief in a fit of convulsive exclamation.

But far away, on the other side of the lake, a birch-bark canoe was to be seen, in which sat a young man, who paddled it skilfully and swiftly. It was evident enough that he was watching the race intently, but the spectators could see little more than that. One of them, however, who sat upon the stand, had a powerful spyglass, and could distinguish his motions very minutely and exactly. It was seen by this curious observer that the young man had an opera-glass with him, which he used a good deal at intervals. The spectator thought he kept it directed to the girls' boat, chiefly, if not exclusively. He thought also that the opera-glass was more particularly pointed towards the bow of the boat, and came to the natural conclusion that the bow oar, Miss Euthymia Tower, captain of the Atalantas, "The Wonder" of the Corinna Institute, was the attraction which determined the direction of the instrument.

"Who is that in the canoe over there?" asked the owner of the spy-glass.

"That's just what we should like to know," answered the old landlord's wife. "He and his man boarded with us when they first came, but we could never find out anything about him only just his name and his ways of living. His name is Kirkwood,—Maurice Kirkwood, Esq., it used to come on his letters. As for his ways of living, he was the solitariest human being that I ever came across. His man carried his meals up to him. He used to stay in his room pretty much all day, but at night he would be off, walking, or riding on horseback, or paddling about in the lake, sometimes till nigh morning. There's something very strange about that Mr. Kirkwood. But there don't seem to be any harm in him. Only nobody can guess what his business is. They got up a story about him at one time. What do you think? They said he was a counterfeiter! And so they went one night to his room, when he was out, and that man of his was away too, and they carried keys, and opened pretty much everything; and they found—well, they found just nothing at all except writings and letters,—letters from places in America and in England, and some with Italian postmarks: that was all. Since that time the sheriff and his folks have let him alone and minded their own business. He was a gentleman,—anybody ought to have known that; and anybody that knew about his nice ways of living and behaving, and knew the kind of wear he had for his underclothing, might have known it. I could have told those officers that they had better not bother him. I know the ways of real gentlemen and real ladies, and I know those fellows in store clothes that look a little too fine,—outside. Wait till washing-day comes !"

The good lady had her own standards for testing humanity, and they were not wholly unworthy of consideration; they were quite as much to be relied on as the judgments of the travelling phrenologist, who sent his accomplice on before him to study out the principal personages in the village, and in the light of these revelations interpreted the bumps, with very little regard to Gall and Spurzheim, or any other authorities.

Even with the small amount of information obtained by the search among his papers and effects, the gossips of the village had constructed several distinct histories for the mysterious stranger. He was an agent of a great publishing house; a leading contributor to several important periodicals; the author of that anonymously published novel which had made so much talk; the poet of a large clothing establishment; a spy of the Italian, some said the Russian, some said the British, Government; a proscribed refugee from some country where he had been plotting; a school-master without a school, a minister without a pulpit, an actor without an engagement; in short, there was no end to the perfectly senseless stories that were told about him, from that which made him out an escaped convict to the whispered suggestion that he was the eccentric heir to a great English title and estate.

The one unquestionable fact was that of his extraordinary seclusion. Nobody in the village, no student in the University, knew his history. No young lady in the Corinna Institute had ever had a word from him. Sometimes, as the boats of the University or the Institute were returning at dusk, their rowers would see the canoe stealing into the shadows as they drew near it. Sometimes on a moonlight night, when a party of the young ladies were out upon the lake, they would see the white canoe gliding ghost-like in the distance. And it had happened more than once that when a boat's crew had been out with singers among them, while they were in the midst of a song, the white canoe would suddenly appear and rest upon the water,— not very near them, but within hearing distance,—and so remain until the singing was over, when it would steal away and be lost sight of in some inlet or behind some jutting rock.

Naturally enough, there was intense curiosity about this young man. The landlady had told her story, which explained nothing. There was nobody to be questioned about him except his servant, an Italian, whose name was Paolo, but who to the village was known as Mr. Paul.

Mr. Paul would have seemed the easiest person in the world to worm a secret out of. He was good-natured, child-like as a Heathen Chinee, talked freely with everybody in such English as he had at command, knew all the little people of the village, and was followed round by them, partly from his personal attraction for them, and partly because he was apt to have a stick of candy or a handful of peanuts or other desirable luxury in his pocket for any of his little friends he met with. He had that wholesome, happy look, so uncommon in our arid countrymen,—a look hardly to be found except where figs and oranges ripen in the open air. A kindly climate to grow up in, a religion which takes your money and gives you a stamped ticket good at Saint Peter's box office, a roomy chest and a good pair of lungs in it, an honest digestive apparatus, a lively temperament, a cheerful acceptance of the place in life assigned to one by nature and circumstance,—these are conditions under which life may be quite comfortable to endure, and certainly is very pleasant to contemplate. All these conditions were united in Paolo. He was the easiest, pleasantest creature to talk with that one could ask for a companion. His southern vivacity, his amusing English, his simplicity and openness, made him friends everywhere.

It seemed as if it would be a very simple matter to get the history of his master out of this guileless and unsophisticated being. He had been tried by all the village experts. The rector had put a number of well-studied careless questions, which failed of their purpose. The old librarian of the town library had taken note of all the books he carried to his master, and asked about his studies and pursuits. Paolo found it hard to understand his English, apparently, and answered in the most irrelevant way. The leading gossip of the village tried her skill in pumping him for information. It was all in vain.

His master's way of life was peculiar,—in fact, eccentric He had hired rooms in an old-fashioned three-story house. He had two rooms in the second and third stories of this old wooden building: his study in the second, his sleeping room in the one above it. Paolo lived in the basement, where he had all the conveniences for cooking, and played the part of *chef* for his master and himself. This was only a part of his duty, for he was a man-of-all-work, purveyor, steward, chambermaid,—as universal in his services for one man as Pushee at the Anchor Tavern used to be for everybody.

It so happened that Paolo took a severe cold one winter's day, and had such threatening symptoms that he asked the baker, when he called, to send the village physician to see him. In the course of his visit the doctor naturally inquired about the health of Paolo's master.

"Signor Kirkwood well,—*motto bene*," said Paolo.

"Why does he keep out of sight as he does?" asked the doctor.

"He always so," replied Paolo. *"Una antipatia."*

Whether Paolo was off his guard with the doctor, whether he revealed it to him as to a father confessor, or whether he thought it time that the reason of his master's seclusion should be known, the doctor did not feel sure. At any rate, Paolo was not disposed to make any further revelations. *Una antipatia,*—an antipathy,—that was all the doctor learned. He thought the matter over, and the more he reflected the more he was puzzled. What could an antipathy be that made a young man a recluse! Was it a dread of blue sky and open air, of the smell of flowers, or some electrical impression to which he was unnaturally sensitive?

Dr. Butts carried these questions home with him. His wife was a sensible, discreet woman, whom he could trust with many professional secrets. He told her of Paolo's revelation, and talked it over with her in the light of his experience and her own; for she had known some curious cases of constitutional likes and aversions.

Mrs. Butts buried the information in the grave of her memory, where it lay for nearly a week. At the end of that time it emerged in a confidential whisper to her favorite sister-in-law, a perfectly safe person. Twenty-four hours later the story was all over the village that Maurice Kirkwood was the subject of a strange, mysterious, unheard- of antipathy to something,—nobody knew what; and the whole neighborhood naturally resolved itself into an unorganized committee of investigation.

IV.
THE YOUNG SOLITARY.

WHAT is a country village without its mysterious personage? Few are now living who can remember the advent of the handsome young man who was the mystery of our great university town "sixty years since,"—long enough ago for a romance to grow out of a narrative, as Waverley may remind us. The writer of this narrative remembers him well, and is not sure that he has not told the strange story in some form or other to the last generation, or to the one before the last. No matter: if he has told it they have forgotten it,—that is, if they have ever read it; and whether they have or have not, the story is singular enough to justify running the risk of repetition.

This young man, with a curious name of Scandinavian origin, appeared unheralded in the town, as it was then, of Cantabridge. He wanted employment, and soon found it in the shape of manual labor, which he undertook and performed cheerfully. But his whole appearance showed plainly enough that he was bred to occupations of a very different nature, if, indeed, he had been accustomed to any kind of toil for his living. His aspect was that of one of gentle birth. His hands were not those of a laborer, and his features were delicate and refined, as well as of remarkable beauty. Who he was, where he came from, why he had come to Cantabridge, was never clearly explained. He was alone, without friends, except among the acquaintances he had made in his new residence. If he had any correspondents, they were not known to the neighborhood where he was living. But if he had neither friends nor correspondents, there was some reason for believing that he had enemies. Strange circumstances occurred which connected themselves with him in an ominous and unaccountable way. A threatening letter was slipped under the door of a house where he was visiting. He had a sudden attack of illness, which was thought to look very much like the effect of poison. At one time he disappeared, and was found wandering, bewildered, in a town many miles from that where he was residing. When questioned how he came there, he told a coherent story that he had been got, under some pretext, or in some not incredible way, into a boat, from which, at a certain landing-place, he had escaped and fled for his life, which he believed was in danger from his kidnappers.

Whoever his enemies may have been,—if they really existed,—he did not fall a victim to their plots, so far as known to or remembered by this witness.

Various interpretations were put upon his story. Conjectures were as abundant as they were in the case of Kaspar Hauser. That he was of good family seemed probable; that he was of distinguished birth, not impossible; that he was the dangerous rival of a candidate for a greatly coveted position in one of the northern states of Europe was a favorite speculation of some of the more romantic young persons. There was no dramatic ending to this story,—at least none is remembered by the present writer.

"He left a name," like the royal Swede, of whose lineage he may have been for aught that the village people knew, but not a name at which anybody "grew pale;" for he had swindled no one, and broken no woman's heart with false vows. Possibly some withered cheeks may flush faintly as they recall the handsome young man who came before the Cantabridge maidens fully equipped for a hero of romance when the century was in its first quarter.

The writer has been reminded of the handsome Swede by the incidents attending the advent of the unknown and interesting stranger who had made his appearance at Arrowhead Village.

It was a very insufficient and unsatisfactory reason to assign for the young man's solitary habits that he was the subject of an antipathy. For what do we understand by that word? When a young lady screams at the sight of a spider, we accept her explanation that she has a natural antipathy to the creature. When a person expresses a repugnance to some wholesome article of food, agreeable to most people, we are satisfied if he gives the same reason. And so of various odors, which are pleasing to some persons and repulsive to others. We do not pretend to go behind the fact. It is an individual, and it may be a family, peculiarity. Even between different personalities there is an instinctive elective dislike as well as an elective affinity. We are not bound to give a reason why Dr. Fell is odious to us any more than the prisoner who peremptorily challenges a juryman is bound to say why he does it; it is enough that he "does not like his looks."

There was nothing strange, then, that Maurice Kirk-wood should have his special antipathy; a great many other people have odd likes and dislikes. But it was a very curious thing that this antipathy should be alleged as the reason for his singular mode of life. All sorts of explanations were suggested, not one of them in the least satisfactory, but serving to keep the curiosity of inquirers active until they were superseded by a new theory. One story was that Maurice had a great fear of dogs. It grew at last to a connected narrative, in which a fright in childhood from a rabid mongrel was said to have given him such a sensitiveness to the near presence of dogs that he was liable to convulsions if one came close to him.

This hypothesis had some plausibility. No other creature would be so likely to trouble a person who had an antipathy to it. Dogs are very apt to make the acquaintance of strangers, in a free and easy way. They are met with everywhere,—in one's daily walk, at the thresholds of the doors one enters, in the gentleman's library, on the rug of my lady's sitting-room and on the cushion of her carriage. It is true that there are few persons who have an instinctive repugnance to this "friend of man." But what if this so-called antipathy were only a fear, a terror, which borrowed the

so saying, he gave it a fling to the box marked P, as if it burned his fingers. Why a grown-up young woman allowed herself to be cheapened in the way so many of them do by the use of names which become them as well as the frock of a ten-year-old schoolgirl would become a graduate of the Corinna Institute, the old postmaster could not guess. He was a queer old man.

The letter thus scornfully treated runs over with a young girl's written loquacity:—

"Oh, Lulu, there is *such* a sensation as you never saw or heard of 'in all your born days,' as mamma used to say. He has been at the village for some time, but Lately we have had—oh, the *weirdest stories* about him! 'The Mysterious Stranger is the name some give him, but we girls call him the *Sachem,* because he paddles about in an Indian canoe. If I should tell you *all* the things that are said about him I should use up all my paper *ten times over.* He has never made a visit to the Institute, and none of the girls have ever spoken to him, but the people at the village say he is *very, very* handsome. We are *dying* to get a look at him, of course—though there is a horrid story about him—that he has *the evil eye*—did you ever hear about *the evil eye?* If a person who is born with it *looks* at you, you die, or something happens—*awful*—isn't it?

"The rector says he *never goes to church,* but then you know a good many of the people that pass the summer at the village never do—they think their *religion must have vacations*?that's what I've heard them say—vacations, just like other *hard work*—it ought not to be hard work, I'm sure, but I suppose they feel so about it. Should you feel afraid to have him look at you? Some of the girls say they wouldn't have him *for the whole world,* but *I* shouldn't mind it—especially if I had on my eye-glasses. Do you suppose if there *is* anything in the evil eye it would go through glass? I don't believe it. Do you think *blue* eye-glasses would be better than common ones? Don't *laugh* at me—they tell such weird stories! *The Terror*—Lurida Vincent, you know—makes fun of all they say about it, but then she 'knows everything and doesn't believe anything,' the girls say—Well, I should be *awfully scared,* I know, if anybody that had the evil eye should look at me—but—oh, I don't know—but if it was a young man—and if he was very—*very* good-looking—I think—perhaps I would run the risk—but don't tell anybody I said any such *horrid* thing—and ***burn this letter right up***—there's a dear good girl."

It is to be hoped that no reader will doubt the genuineness of this letter. There are not quite so many "awfuls" and "awfullys" as one expects to find in young ladies' letters, but there are two "weirds," which may be considered a fair allowance. How it happened that "jolly" did not show itself can hardly be accounted for; no doubt it turns up two or three times at least in the postscript.

Here is an extract from another letter. This was from one of the students of Stoughton University to a friend whose name as it was written on the envelope was Mr. Frank Mayfield. The old postmaster who found fault with Miss "Lulu's" designation would probably have quarrelled with this address, if it had come under his eye. "Frank" is a very pretty, pleasant-sounding name, and it is not strange that many persons use it in common conversation all their days when speaking of a friend. Were they really christened by that name, any of these numerous Franks? Perhaps they were, and if so there is nothing to be said. But if not, was the baptismal name Francis or Franklin? The mind is apt to fasten in a very perverse and unpleasant way upon this question, which too often there is no possible way of settling. One might hope, if he outlived the bearer of the appellation, to get at the fact; but since even gravestones have learned to use the names belonging to childhood and infancy in their solemn record, the generation which docks its Christian names in such an un-Christian way will bequeath whole churchyards full of riddles to posterity. How it will puzzle and distress the historians and antiquarians of a coming generation to settle what was the real name of Dan and Bert and "Billy," which last is legible on a white marble slab, raised in memory of a grown person, in a certain burial-ground in a town in Essex County, Massachusetts!

But in the mean time we are forgetting the letter directed to Mr. Frank Mayfield.

"DEAR FRANK,—Hooray! Hurrah! Rah!

"I have made the acquaintance of 'The Mysterious Stranger!' It happened by a queer sort of accident, which came pretty near relieving you of the duty of replying to this letter. I was out in my little boat, which carries a sail too big for her, as I know and ought to have remembered. One of those fitful flaws of wind to which the lake is so liable struck the sail suddenly, and over went my boat. My feet got tangled in the sheet somehow, and I could not get free. I had hard work to keep my head above water, and I struggled desperately to escape from my toils; for if the boat were to go down I should be dragged down with her. I thought of a good many things in the course of some four or five minutes, I can tell you, and I got a lesson about time better than anything Kant and all the rest of them have to say of it. After I had been there about an ordinary lifetime, I saw a white canoe making toward me, and I knew that our shy young gentleman was coming to help me, and that we should become acquainted without an introduction. So it was, sure enough. He saw what the trouble was, managed to disentangle my feet without drowning me in the process or upsetting his little flimsy craft, and, as I was somewhat tired with my struggle, took me in tow and carried me to the landing where he kept his canoe. I can't say that there is anything odd about his manners or his way of talk. I judge him to be a native of one of our Northern States,—perhaps a New Englander. He has lived abroad during some parts of his life. He is not an artist, as it was at one time thought he might be. He is a good-looking fellow, well developed, manly in appearance, with nothing to excite special remark unless it be a certain look of anxiety or apprehension which comes over him from time to time. You remember our old friend Squire B., whose companion was killed by lightning when he was standing close to him. You know the look he had whenever anything like a thundercloud came up in the sky. Well, I should say there was a look like that came over this Maurice Kirkwood's face every now and then. I noticed that he looked round once or twice as if to see whether some object or other was in sight. There was a little rustling in the grass as if of footsteps, and this look came over his features. A rabbit ran by us, and I watched to see if he showed any sign of that antipathy we have heard so much of, but he seemed to be pleased watching the creature.

"If you ask me what my opinion is about this Maurice Kirkwood, I think he is eccentric in his habit of life, but not what they call a 'crank' exactly. He talked well enough about such matters as we spoke of,—the lake, the scenery in general, the climate. I asked him to come over and take a look at the college. He didn't promise, but I should not be surprised if I should get him over there some day. I asked him why he didn't go to the Pansophian meetings. He didn't give any reason, but he shook his head in a very peculiar way, as much as to say that it was impossible.

"On the whole, I think it is nothing more than the same feeling of dread of human society, or dislike for it, which under the name of religion used to drive men into caves and deserts. What a pity that Protestantism does not make special provision for all the freaks of individual character! If we had a little more faith and a few more caverns, or convenient places for making them, we should have hermits in these holes as thick as wood-chucks or prairie dogs. I should like to know if you never had the feeling,

'Oh, that the desert were my dwelling-place!'

I know what your answer will be, of course. You will say, 'Certainly,

"With one fair spirit for my minister;" '

but I mean alone,—all alone. Don't you ever feel as if you should like to have been a pillar-saint in the days when faith was as strong as lye (spelt with a *y*), instead of being as weak as dish-water? (Jerry is looking over my shoulder, and says this pun is too bad to send, and a disgrace to the University—but never mind.) *I* often feel as if I should like to roost on a pillar a hundred feet high,—yes, and have it soaped from top to bottom. Wouldn't it be fun to look down at the bores and the duns? Let us get up a pillar-roosters' association. (Jerry—still looking over—says there is an absurd contradiction in the idea.)

"What a matter-of-fact idiot Jerry is!
"How do you like looking over, Mr. Inspector-general?"

The reader will not get much information out of this lively young fellow's letter but he may get a little. It is something to know that the mysterious resident of Arrowhead Village did not look nor talk like a crazy person; that he was of agreeable aspect and address, helpful when occasion offered, and had nothing about him, so far as yet appeared, to prevent his being an acceptable member of society.

Of course the people in the village could never be contented without learning everything there was to be learned about their visitor. All the city papers were examined for advertisements. If a cashier had absconded, if a broker had disappeared, if a railroad president was missing, some of the old stories would wake up and get a fresh currency, until some new circumstance gave rise to a new hypothesis. Unconscious of all these inquiries and fictions, Maurice Kirkwood lived on in his inoffensive and unexplained solitude, and seemed likely to remain an unsolved enigma. The "Sachem" of the boating girls became the "Sphinx" of the village ramblers, and it was agreed on all hands that Egypt did not hold any hieroglyphics harder to make out than the meaning of this young man's odd way of living.

V.
THE ENIGMA STUDIED.

IT was a curious, if it was not a suspicious, circumstance that a young man, seemingly in good health, of comely aspect, looking as if made for companionship, should keep himself apart from all the world around him in a place where there was a general feeling of good neighborhood and a pleasant social atmosphere. The Public Library was a central point which brought people together. The Pansophian Society did a great deal to make them acquainted with each other, for many of the meetings were open to outside visitors, and the subjects discussed in the meetings furnished the material for conversation in their intervals. A card of invitation had been sent by the Secretary to Maurice, in answer to which Paolo carried back a polite note of regret. The paper had a narrow rim of black, implying apparently some loss of relative or friend, but not any very recent and crushing bereavement. This refusal to come to the meetings of the society was only what was expected. It was proper to ask him, but his declining the invitation showed that he did not wish for attentions or courtesies. There was nothing further to be done to bring him out of his shell, and seemingly nothing more to be learned about him at present.

In this state of things it was natural that all which had been previously gathered by the few who had seen or known anything of him should be worked over again. When there is no new ore to be dug, the old refuse heaps are looked over for what may still be found in them. The landlord of the Anchor Tavern, now the head of the boarding-house, talked about Maurice, as everybody in the village did at one time or another. He had not much to say, but he added a fact or two.

The young gentleman was good pay,—so they all said. Sometimes he paid in gold; sometimes in fresh bills, just out of the bank. He trusted his man, Mr. Paul, with the money to pay his bills. He knew something about horses; he showed that by the way he handled that colt,—the one that threw the hostler and broke his collar-bone. "Mr. Paul come down to the stable. 'Let me see that colt you all 'fraid of,' says he. 'My master, he ride any hoss,' says Paul. 'You saddle him,' says he: and so they did, and Paul, he led that colt—the kickinest and ugliest young beast you ever see in your life—up to the place where his master, as he calls him, and he lives. What does that Kirkwood do but clap on a couple of long spurs and jump on to that colt's back, and off the beast goes, tail up, heels flying, standing up on end, trying all sorts of capers, and at last going it full run for a couple of miles, till he'd got about enough of it. That colt went off as ferce as a wild-cat, and come back as quiet as a cosset lamb. A man that pays his bills regular, in good money, and knows how to handle a hoss is three quarters of a gentleman, if he isn't a whole one,—and most likely he *is* a whole one."

So spake the patriarch of the Anchor Tavern. His wife had already given her favorable opinion of her former guest. She now added something to her description as a sequel to her husband's remarks.

"I call him," she said, "about as likely a young gentleman as ever I clapped my eyes on. He is rather slighter than I like to see a young man of his age; if he was my son, I should like to see him a little more fleshy. I don't believe he weighs more than a hundred and thirty or forty pounds. Did *y'* ever look at those eyes of his, M'randy? Just as blue as succory flowers. I do like those light-complected young fellows, with their fresh cheeks and their curly hair; somehow, curly hair doos set off anybody's face. He isn't any foreigner, for all that he talks Italian with that Mr. Paul that's his help. He looks just like our kind of folks,—the college kind, that's brought up among books, and is handling 'em, and reading of 'em, and making of 'em, as like as not, all their lives. All that you say about his riding the mad colt is just what I should think he was up to, for he's as spry as a squirrel; you ought to see him go over that fence, as I did once. I don't believe there's any harm in that young gentleman,—I don't care what people say. I suppose he likes this place just as other people like it, and cares more for walking in the woods and paddling about in the water than he doos for company; and if he doos, whose business is it, I should like to know?"

The third of the speakers was Miranda, who had her own way of judging people.

"I never see him but two or three times," Miranda said. "I should like to have waited on him, and got a chance to look stiddy at him when he was eatin' his vittles. That's the time to watch folks, when their jaws get a-goin' and their eyes are on what's afore 'em. Do you remember that chap the sheriff come and took away when we kep' tahvern? Eleven year ago it was, come nex' Thanksgivin' time. A mighty grand gentleman from the City he set up for. I watched him, and I watched him. Says I, I don't believe you're no gentleman, says I. He eat with his knife, and that ain't the way city folks eats. Every time I handed him anything I looked closeter and closeter. Them whiskers never growed on them cheeks, says I to myself. Them's paper collars, says I. That dimun in your shirt-front hain't got no life to it, says I. I don't believe it's nothin' more 'n a bit o' winderglass. So says I to Pushee, 'You jes' step out and get the sheriff to come in and take a look at that chap.' I knowed he was after a fellah. He come right in, an' he goes up to the chap. 'Why, Bill,' says he, 'I'm mighty glad to see yer. We've had the hole in the wall you got out of mended, and I want your company to come and look at the old place,' says he, and he pulls out a couple of handcuffs and has 'em on his wrists in less than no time, an' off they goes together! I know one thing about that young gentleman, anyhow,—there ain't no better judge of what's good eatin' than he is. I cooked him some maccaroni myself one day, and he sends word to me by that Mr. Paul, 'Tell Miss Miranda,' says he, 'that the Pope o' Rome don't have no better cooked maccaroni than what she sent up to me yesterday,' says he. I don' know much about the Pope o' Rome except that he's a Roman Catholic, and I don' know who cooks for him, whether it's a man or a woman; but when it comes to a dish o' maccaroni, I ain't afeard of their *shefs,* as they call 'em,—them he-cooks that can't serve up a cold potater without callin' it by some name nobody can say after 'em. But this gentleman knows good cookin', and that's as good a sign of a gentleman as I want to tell 'em by."

VI.
STILL AT FAULT.

THE house in which Maurice Kirkwood had taken up his abode was not a very inviting one. It was old, and had been left in a somewhat dilapidated and disorderly condition by the tenants who had lived in the part which Maurice now occupied. They had piled their packing-boxes in the cellar, with broken chairs, broken china, and other household wrecks. A cracked mirror lay on an old straw mattress, the contents of which were airing themselves through wide rips and rents. A lame clothes-horse was saddled with an old rug fringed with a ragged border, out of which all the colors had been completely trodden. No woman would have gone into a house in such a condition. But the young man did not trouble himself much about such matters, and was satisfied when the rooms which were to be occupied by himself and his servant were made decent and tolerably comfortable. During the fine season all this was not of much consequence, and if Maurice made up his mind to stay through the winter he would have his choice among many more eligible places.

The summer vacation of the Corinna Institute had now arrived, and the young ladies had scattered to their homes. Among the graduates of the year were Miss Euthymia Tower and Miss Lurida Vincent, who had now returned to their homes in Arrowhead Village. They were both glad to rest after the long final examinations and the exercises of the closing day, in which each of them had borne a conspicuous part. It was a pleasant life they led in the village, which was lively enough at this season. Walking, riding, driving, boating, visits to the Library, meetings of the Pansophian Society, hops, and picnics made the time pass very cheerfully, and soon showed their restoring influences. The Terror's large eyes did not wear the dull, glazed look by which they had too often betrayed the after effects of over-excitement of the strong and active brain behind them. The Wonder gained a fresher bloom, and looked full enough of life to radiate vitality into a statue of ice. They had a boat of their own, in which they passed many delightful hours on the lake, rowing, drifting, reading, telling of what had been, dreaming of what might be.

The Library was one of the chief centres of the fixed population, and visited often by strangers. The old Librarian was a peculiar character, as these officials are apt to be. They have a curious kind of knowledge, sometimes immense in its way. They know the backs of books, their title-pages, their popularity or want of it, the class of readers who call for particular works, the value of different editions, and a good deal besides. Their minds catch up hints from all manner of works on all kinds of subjects. They will give a visitor a fact and a reference which they are surprised to find they remember and which the visitor might have hunted for a year. Every good librarian, every private book-owner, who has grown into his library, finds he has a bunch of nerves going to every bookcase, a branch to every shelf, and a twig to every book. These nerves get very sensitive in old librarians, sometimes, and they do not like to have a volume meddled with any more than they would like to have their naked eyes handled. They come to feel at last that the books of a great collection are a part, not merely of their own property, though they are only the agents for their distribution, but that they are, as it were, outlying portions of their own organization. The old Librarian was getting a miserly feeling about *his* books, as he called them. Fortunately, he had a young lady for his assistant, who was never so happy as when she could find the work any visitor wanted and put it in his hands,—or her hands, for there were more readers among the wives and daughters, and especially among the aunts, than there were among their male relatives. The old Librarian knew the books, but the books seemed to know the young assistant; so it looked, at least, to the impatient young people who wanted their services.

Maurice had a good many volumes of his own,—a great many, according to Paolo's account; but Paolo's ideas were limited, and a few well-filled shelves seemed a very large collection to him. His master frequently sent him to the Public Library for books, which somewhat enlarged his notions; still, the Signor was a very learned man, he was certain, and some of his white books (bound in vellum and richly gilt) were more splendid, according to Paolo, than anything in the Library.

There was no little curiosity to know what were the books that Maurice was in the habit of taking out, and the Librarian's record was carefully searched by some of the more inquisitive investigators. The list proved to be a long and varied one. It would imply a considerable knowledge of modern languages and of the classics; a liking for mathematics and physics, especially all that related to electricity and magnetism; a fancy for the occult sciences, if there is any propriety in coupling these words; and a whim for odd and obsolete literature, like the Parthenologia of Fortunius Licetus, the quaint treatise "De Sternutatione," books about alchemy, and witchcraft, apparitions, and modern works relating to Spiritualism. With these were the titles of novels and now and then of books of poems; but it may be taken for granted that his own shelves held the works he was most frequently in the habit of reading or consulting. Not much was to be made out of this beyond the fact of wide scholarship,—more or less deep it might be, but at any rate implying no small mental activity; for he appeared to read very rapidly, at any rate exchanged the books he had taken out for new ones very frequently. To judge by his reading, he was a man of letters. But so wide-reading a man of letters must have an object, a literary purpose in all probability. Why should not he be writing a novel? Not a novel of society, assuredly, for a hermit is not the person to report the talk and manners of a world which he has nothing to do with. Novelists and lawyers understand the art of "cramming" better than any other persons in the world. Why should not this young man be working up the picturesque in this romantic region to serve as a background for some story with magic, perhaps, and mysticism, and hints borrowed from science, and all sorts of out-of-the-way knowledge which his odd and miscellaneous selection of books furnished him? That might be, or possibly he was only reading for amusement. Who could say?

The funds of the Public Library of Arrowhead Village allowed the managers to purchase many books out of the common range of reading. The two learned people of the village were the rector and the doctor. These two worthies kept up the old controversy between the professions, which grows out of the fact that one studies nature from below upwards, and the other from above downwards. The rector maintained that physicians contracted a squint which turns their eyes inwardly, while the muscles which roll their eyes upward become palsied. The doctor retorted that theological students developed a third eyelid,—the ***nictitating membrane,*** which is so well known in birds, and which serves to shut out, not all light, but all the light they do not want. Their little skirmishes did not prevent their being very good friends, who had a common interest in many things and many persons. Both were on the committee which had the care of the Library and attended to the purchase of books. Each was scholar enough to know die wants of scholars, and disposed to trust the judgment of the other as to what books should be purchased. Consequently, the clergyman secured the addition to the Library of a good many old theological works which the physician would have called brimstone divinity, and held to be just the thing to kindle fires with,—good books still for those who know how to use them, oftentimes as awful examples of the extreme of disorganization the whole moral system may undergo when a barbarous belief has strangled the natural human instincts. The physician, in the meantime, acquired for the collection some of those medical works where one may find recorded various rare and almost incredible cases, which may not have their like for a whole century, and then repeat themselves, so as to give a new lease of credibility to stories which had come to be looked upon as fables.

Both the clergyman and the physician took a very natural interest in the young man who had come to reside in their neighborhood for the present, perhaps for a long period. The rector would have been glad to see him at church. He would have liked more especially to have had him hear his sermon on the Duties of Young Men to Society. The doctor meanwhile, was meditating on the duties of society to young men, and wishing that he could gain the young man's confidence, so as to help him out of any false habit of mind or any delusion to which he might be subject, if he had the power of being useful to him.

Dr. Butts was the leading medical practitioner, not only of Arrowhead Village, but of all the surrounding region. He was an excellent specimen of the country doctor, self-reliant, self-sacrificing, working a great deal harder for his living than most of those who call themselves the laboring classes,—as if none but those whose hands were hardened by the use of farming or mechanical implements had any work to do. He had that sagacity without which learning is a mere incumbrance, and he had also a fair share of that learning without which sagacity is like a traveller with a good horse, but who cannot read the directions on the guideboards. He was not a man to be taken in by names. He well knew that oftentimes very innocent-sounding words mean very grave disorders; that all degrees of disease and disorder are frequently confounded under the same term; that "run down" may stand for a fatigue of mind or body from which a week or a month of rest will completely restore the overworked patient, or an advanced stage of a mortal illness; that "seedy" may signify the morning's state of feeling, after an evening's over-indulgence, which calls for a glass of soda-water and a cup of coffee, or a dangerous malady which will pack off the subject of it, at the shortest notice, to the south of France. He knew too well that what is spoken lightly of as a "nervous disturbance" may imply that the whole machinery of life is in a deranged condition, and that every individual organ would groan aloud if it had any other language than the terrible inarticulate one of pain by which to communicate with the consciousness.

When, therefore, Dr. Butts heard the word *antipatia* he did not smile, and say to himself that this was an idle whim, a foolish fancy, which the young man had got into his head. Neither was he satisfied to set down everything to the account of insanity, plausible as that supposition might seem. He was prepared to believe in some exceptional, perhaps anomalous, form of exaggerated sensibility, relating to what class of objects he could not at present conjecture, but which was as vital to the subject of it as the insulating arrangement to a piece of electrical machinery. With this feeling he began to look into the history of antipathies as recorded in all the books and journals on which he could lay his hands.

The holder of the Portfolio asks leave to close it for a brief interval. He wishes to say a few words to his readers, before offering them some verses which have no connection with the narrative now in progress.

If one could have before him a set of photographs taken annually, representing the same person as he or she appeared for thirty or forty or fifty years, it would be interesting to watch the gradual changes of aspect from the age of twenty, or even of thirty or forty, to that of threescore and ten. The face might be an uninteresting one; still, as sharing the inevitable changes wrought by time, it would be worth looking at as it passed through the curve of life,—the vital parabola, which betrays itself in the symbolic changes of the features. An inscription is the same thing, whether we read it on slate-stone, or granite, or marble. To watch the lights and shades, the reliefs and hollows, of a countenance through a lifetime, or a large part of it, by the aid of a continuous series of photographs would not only be curious; it would teach us much more about the laws of physiognomy than we could get from casual and unconnected observations.

The same kind of interest, without any assumption of merit to be found in them, I would claim for a series of annual poems, beginning in middle life and continued to what many of my correspondents are pleased to remind me—as if I required to have the fact brought to my knowledge—is no longer youth. Here is the latest of a series of annual poems read during the last thirty-four years. There seems to have been one interruption, but there may have been other poems not recorded or remembered. This, the latest poem of the series, was listened to by the scanty remnant of what was a large and brilliant circle of classmates and friends when the first of the long series was read before them, then in the flush of ardent manhood:—

THE OLD SONG.

The minstrel of the classic lay

Of love and wine who sings
Still found the fingers run astray
That touched the rebel strings.

Of Cadmus he would fain have sung,
Of Atreus and his line;
But all the jocund echoes rung
With songs of love and wine.

Ah, brothers! I would fain have caught
Some fresher fancy's gleam;
My truant accents find, unsought,
The old familiar theme.

Love, Love! but not the sportive child
With shaft and twanging bow,
Whose random arrows drove us wild
Some threescore years ago;

Not Eros, with his joyous laugh,
The urchin blind and bare,
But Love, with spectacles and staff,
And scanty, silvered hair.

Our heads with frosted locks are white,
Our roofs are thatched with snow,
But red, in chilling winter's spite,
Our hearts and hearthstones glow.

Our old acquaintance, Time, drops in,
And while the running sands

Their golden thread unheeded spin,
He warms his frozen hands.

Stay, winged hours, too swift, too sweet,
And waft this message o'er
To all we miss, from all we meet
On life's fast-crumbling shore:

Say that to old affection true
We hug the narrowing chain
That binds our hearts,—alas, how few
The links that yet remain!

The fatal touch awaits them all
That turns the rocks to dust;
From year to year they break and fall,—
They break, but never rust.

Say if one note of happier strain
This worn-out harp afford,—
One throb that trembles, not in vain,—
Their memory lent its chord.

Say that when Fancy closed her wings
And Passion quenched his fire,
Love, Love, still echoed from the strings
As from Anacreon's lyre!

January 8, 1885.

VII.
A RECORD OF ANTIPATHIES.

IN thinking the whole matter over, Dr. Butts felt convinced that, with care and patience and watching his opportunity, he should get at the secret, which so far had yielded nothing but a single word. It might be asked why he was so anxious to learn what, from all appearances, the young stranger was unwilling to explain. He may have been to some extent infected by the general curiosity of the persons around him, in which good Mrs. Butts shared, and which she had helped to intensify by revealing the word dropped by Paolo. But this was not really his chief motive. He could not look upon this young man, living a life of unwholesome solitude, without a natural desire to do all that his science and his knowledge of human nature could help him to do towards bringing him into healthy relations with the world about him. Still, he would not intrude upon him in any way. He would only make certain general investigations, which might prove serviceable in case circumstances should give him the right to counsel the young man as to his course of life. The first thing to be done was to study systematically the whole subject of antipathies. Then, if any further occasion offered itself, he would be ready to take advantage of it. The resources of the Public Library of the place and his own private collection were put in requisition to furnish him the singular and widely scattered facts of which he was in search.

It is not every reader who will care to follow Dr. Butts in his study of the natural history of antipathies. The stories told about them are, however, very curious; and if some of them may be questioned, there is no doubt that many of the strangest are true, and consequently take away from the improbability of others which we are disposed to doubt.

But in the first place, what do we mean by an antipathy? It is an aversion to some object, which may vary in degree from mere dislike to mortal horror. What the cause of this aversion is we cannot say. It acts sometimes through the senses, sometimes through the imagination, sometimes through an unknown channel. The relations which exist between the human being and all that surrounds him vary in consequence of some adjustment peculiar to each individual. The brute fact is expressed in the phrase "One man's meat is another man's poison."

In studying the history of antipathies the doctor began with those referable to the sense of taste, which are among the most common. In any collection of a hundred persons there will be found those who cannot make use of certain articles of food generally acceptable. This may be from the disgust they occasion or the effects they have been found to produce. Every one knows individuals who cannot venture on honey, or cheese, or veal, with impunity. Carlyle, for example, complains of having veal set before him,—a meat he could not endure. There is a whole family connection in New England, and that a very famous one, to many of whose members, in different generations, all the products of the dairy are the subjects of a congenital antipathy. Montaigne says there are persons who dread the smell of apples more than they would dread being exposed to a fire of musketry. The readers of the charming story "A Week in a French Country-House" will remember poor Monsieur Jacque's piteous cry in the night: "Ursula, art thou asleep? Oh, Ursula, thou sleepest, but I cannot close my eyes. Dearest Ursula, there is such a dreadful smell! Oh, Ursula, it is such a smell! I do so wish thou couldst smell it! Good-night, my angel!—Dearest! I have found them! . . . They are apples!" The smell of roses, of peonies, of lilies, has been known to cause faintness. The sight of various objects has had singular effects on some persons. A boar's head was a favorite dish at the table of great people in Marshal d'Albret's time; yet he used to faint at the sight of one. It is not uncommon to meet with persons who faint at the sight of blood. One of the most inveterately pugnacious of Dr. Butts's college-mates confessed that he had this infirmity. Stranger and far more awkward than this is the case mentioned in an ancient collection, where the subject of the antipathy fainted at the sight of any object of a red color. There are sounds, also, which have strange effects on some individuals. Among the obnoxious noises are the crumpling of silk stuffs, the sound of sweeping, the croaking of frogs. The effects in different cases have been spasms, a sense of strangling, profuse sweating,—all showing a profound disturbance of the nervous system.

All these effects were produced by impressions on the organs of sense, seemingly by direct agency on certain nerve centres. But there is another series of cases in which the imagination plays a larger part in the phenomena. Two notable examples are afforded in the lives of two very distinguished personages. Peter the Great was frightened, when an infant, by falling from a bridge into the water. Long afterward, when he had reached manhood, this hardy and resolute man was so affected by the sound of wheels rattling over a bridge that he had to discipline himself by listening to the sound, in spite of his dread of it, in order to overcome his antipathy. The story told by Abbé Boileau of Pascal is very similar to that related of Peter. As he was driving in his coach and four over the bridge at Neuilly, his horses took fright and ran away, and the leaders broke from their harness and sprang into the river, leaving the wheel-horses and the carriage on the bridge. Ever after this fright it is said that Pascal had the terrifying sense that he was just on the edge of an abyss, ready to fall over.

What strange early impression was it which led a certain lady always to shriek aloud if she ventured to enter a church, as it is recorded? The old and simple way of accounting for it would be the scriptural one, that it was an unclean spirit who dwelt in her, and who, when she entered the holy place and brought her spiritual tenant into the presence of the sacred symbols, "cried with a loud voice, and came out of her. A very singular case, the doctor himself had recorded, and which the reader may accept as authentic, is the following: At the head of the doctor's front stairs stood, and still stands, a tall clock, of early date and stately presence. A middle-aged visitor, noticing it as he entered the front door, remarked that he should feel a great unwillingness to pass that clock. He could not go near one of those tall timepieces without a profound agitation, which he dreaded to undergo. This very singular idiosyncrasy he attributed to a fright when he was an infant in the arms of his nurse. She was standing near one of those tall clocks, when the cord which supported one of its heavy leaden weights broke, and the weight came crashing down to the bottom of the case. Some effect must have been produced upon the pulpy nerve centres from which they never recovered. Why should not this happen, when we know that a sudden mental shock may be the cause of insanity? The doctor remembered the verse of "The Ancient Mariner:"—

"I moved my lips; the pilot shrieked And fell down in a fit; The holy hermit raised his eyes And prayed where he did sit. I took the oars; the pilot's boy, **Who now doth crazy go,** Laughed loud and long, and all the while His eyes went to and fro."

This is only poetry, it is true, but the poet borrowed the description from nature, and the records of our asylums could furnish many cases where insanity was caused by a sudden fright.

More than this, hardly a year passes that we do not read of some person, a child commonly, killed outright by terror,—***scared to death,*** literally. Sad cases they often are, in which, nothing but a surprise being intended, the shock has instantly arrested the movements on which life depends. If a mere instantaneous impression can produce effects like these, such an impression might of course be followed by consequences less fatal or formidable, but yet serious in their nature. If here and there a person is killed, as if by lightning, by a sudden startling sight or sound, there must be more numerous cases in which a terrible shock is produced by similar apparently insignificant causes,—a shock which falls short of overthrowing the reason and does not destroy life, yet leaves a lasting effect upon the subject of it.

This point, then, was settled in the mind of Dr. Butts, namely, that, as a violent emotion caused by a sudden shock can kill or craze a human being, there is no perversion of the faculties, no prejudice, no change of taste or temper, no eccentricity, no antipathy, which such a cause may not rationally account for. He would not be surprised, he said to himself, to find that some early alarm, like that which was experienced by Peter the Great or that which happened to Pascal, had broken some spring in this young man's nature, or so changed its mode of action as to account for the exceptional remoteness of his way of life. But how could any conceivable antipathy be so comprehensive as to keep a young man aloof from all the world, and make a hermit of him? He did not hate the human race; that was clear enough. He treated Paolo with great kindness, and the Italian was evidently much attached to him. He had talked naturally and pleasantly with the young man he had helped out of his dangerous situation when his boat was upset. Dr. Butts heard that he had once made a short visit to this young man, at his rooms in the University. It was not misanthropy, therefore, which kept him solitary. What could be broad enough to cover the facts of the case? Nothing that the doctor could think of, unless it were some color, the sight of which acted on him as it did on the individual before mentioned, who could not look at anything red without fainting. Suppose this were a case of the same antipathy. How very careful it would make the subject of it as to where he went and with whom he consorted! Time and patience would be pretty sure to bring out new developments, and physicians, of all men in the world, know how to wait as well as how to labor.

Such were some of the crude facts as Dr. Butts found them in books or gathered them from his own experience. He soon discovered that the story had got about the village that Maurice Kirkwood was the victim of an "antipathy," whatever that word might mean in the vocabulary of the people of the place. If he suspected the channel through which it had reached the little community, and, spreading from that centre, the country round, he did not see fit to make out of his suspicions a domestic *casus belli.* Paolo might have mentioned it to others as well as to himself. Maurice might have told some friend, who had divulged it. But to accuse Mrs. Butts, good Mrs. Butts, of petit treason in telling one of her husband's professional secrets was too serious a matter to be thought of. He would be a little more careful, he promised himself, the next time, at any rate; for he had to concede, in spite of every wish to be charitable in his judgment, that it was among the possibilities that the worthy lady had forgotten the rule that a doctor's patients must put their tongues out, and a doctor's wife must keep her tongue in.

VIII.
THE PANSOPHIAN SOCIETY.

THE Secretary of this Association was getting somewhat tired of the office, and the office was getting somewhat tired of him. It occurred to the members of the Society that a little fresh blood infused into it might stir up the general vitality of the organization. The woman suffragists saw no reason why the place of Secretary need as a master of course be filled by a person of the male sex. They agitated, they made domiciliary visits, they wrote notes to influential citizens, and finally announced as their candidate the young lady who had won and worn the school name of "The Terror," who was elected. She was just the person for the place: wide awake, with all her wits about her, full of every kind of knowledge, and, above all, strong on points of order and details of management, so that she could prompt the presiding officer, to do which is often the most essential duty of a Secretary. The President, the worthy rector, was good at plain sailing in the track of the common moralities and proprieties, but was liable to get muddled if anything came up requiring swift decision and off-hand speech. The Terror had schooled herself in the debating societies of the Institute, and would set up the President when he was floored by an awkward question, as easily as if he were a ninepin which had been bowled over.

It has been already mentioned that the Pansophian Society received communications from time to time from writers outside of its own organization. Of late these had been becoming more frequent. Many of them were sent in anonymously, and as there were numerous visitors to the village, and two institutions not far removed from it, both full of ambitious and intelligent young persons, it was often impossible to trace the papers to their authors. The new Secretary was alive with curiosity, and at sagacious a little body as one might find if in want of a detective. She could make a pretty shrewd guess whether a paper was written by a young or old person, by one of her own sex or the other, by an experienced hand or a novice.

Among the anonymous papers she received was one which exercised her curiosity to an extraordinary degree. She felt a strong suspicion that "the Sachem," as the boat-crews used to call him, "the Recluse," "the Night-Hawk," "the Sphinx," as others named him, must be the author of it. It appeared to her the production of a young person of a reflective, poetical turn of mind. It was not a woman's way of writing; at least, so thought the Secretary. The writer had travelled much; had resided in Italy, among other places. But so had many of the summer visitors and residents of Arrowhead Village. The handwriting was not decisive; it had some points of resemblance with the pencilled orders for books which Maurice sent to the Library, but there were certain differences, intentional or accidental, which weakened this evidence. There was an undertone in the essay which was in keeping with the mode of life of the solitary stranger. It might be disappointment, melancholy, or only the dreamy sadness of a young person who sees the future he has to climb, not as a smooth ascent, but as overhanging him like a cliff, ready to crush him, with all his hopes and prospects. This interpretation may have been too imaginative, but here is the paper, and the reader can form his own opinion:—

MY THREE COMPANIONS.

"I have been from my youth upwards a wanderer. I do not mean constantly flitting from one place to another, for my residence has often been fixed for considerable periods. From time to time I have put down in a notebook the impressions made upon me by the scenes through which I have passed. I have long hesitated whether to let any of my notes appear before the public My fear has been that they were too subjective, to use the metaphysician's term,—that I have seen myself reflected in Nature, and not the true aspects of Nature, as she was meant to be understood. One who should visit the Harz Mountains would see—might see, rather—his own colossal image shape itself on the morning mist. But if in every mist that rises from the meadows, in every cloud that hangs upon the mountain, he always finds his own reflection, we cannot accept him as an interpreter of the landscape.

"There must be many persons present at the meetings of the Society to which this paper is offered who have had experiences like that of its author. They have visited the same localities, they have had many of the same thoughts and feelings. Many, I have no doubt. Not all,—no, not all. Others have sought the companionship of Nature; I have been driven to it Much of my life has been passed in that communion. These pages record some of the intimacies I have formed with her under some of her various manifestations.

"I have lived on the shore of the great ocean, where its waves broke wildest and its voice rose loudest.

"I have passed whole seasons on the banks of mighty and famous rivers.

"I have dwelt on the margin of a tranquil lake, and floated through many a long, long summer day on its clear waters.

"I have learned the 'various language' of Nature, of which poetry has spoken,—at least, I have learned some words and phrases of it. I will translate some of these as I best may into common speech.

"The OCEAN says to the dweller on its shores:—

" 'You are neither welcome nor unwelcome. I do not trouble myself with the living tribes that come down to my waters. I have my own people, of an older race than yours, that grow to mightier dimensions than your mastodons and elephants; more numerous than all the swarms that fill the air or move over the thin crust of the earth. Who are you that build your gay palaces on my margin? I see your white faces as I saw the dark faces of the tribes that came before you, as I shall look upon the unknown family of mankind that will come after you. And what is your whole human family but a parenthesis in a single page of my history? The raindrops stereotyped themselves on my beaches before a living creature left his footprints there. This horseshoe-crab I fling at your feet is of older lineage than your Adam,—perhaps, indeed, you count your Adam as one of his descendants. What feeling have I for you? Not scorn,—not hatred,—not love,—not loathing. No!—indifference,—blank indifference to you and your affairs: that is my feeling, say rather absence of feeling, as regards you.—Oh yes, I will lap your feet, I will cool you in the hot summer days, I will bear you up in my strong arms, I will rock you on my rolling undulations, like a babe in his cradle. Am I not gentle? Am I not kind? Am I not harmless? But hark! The wind is rising, and the wind and I are rough playmates! What do you say to my voice now? Do you see my foaming lips? Do you feel the rocks tremble as my huge billows crash against them? Is not my anger terrible as I dash your argosy, your thunder-bearing frigate, into fragments, as you would crack an eggshell?—No, not anger; deaf, blind, unheeding indifference,—that is all. Out of me all things arose; sooner or later, into me all things subside. All changes around me; I change not. I look not at you, vain man, and your frail transitory concerns, save in momentary glimpses: I look on the white face of my dead mistress, whom I follow as the bridegroom follows the bier of her who has changed her nuptial raiment for the shroud.

   " 'Ye whose thoughts are of eternity, come dwell at my side. Continents and islands grow old, and waste and disappear. The hardest rock crumbles; vegetable and animal kingdoms come into being, wax great, decline, and perish, to give way to others, even as human dynasties and nations and races come and go. Look on me! "Time writes no wrinkle" on my forehead. Listen to me! All tongues are spoken on my shores, but I have only one language: the winds taught me their vowels, the crags and the sounds schooled me in my rough or smooth consonants. Few words are mine but I have whispered them and sung them and shouted them to men of all tribes from the time when the first wild wanderer strayed into my awful presence. Have you a grief that gnaws at your heart-strings? Come with it to my shore, as of old the priest of far-darting Apollo carried his rage and anguish to the margin of the loud-roaring sea. There, if anywhere, you will forget your private and short-lived woe, for my voice speaks to the infinite and the eternal in your consciousness.'

   "To him who loves the pages of human history, who listens to the voices of the world about him, who frequents the market and the thoroughfare, who lives in the study of time and its accidents rather than, in the deeper emotions in abstract speculation and spiritual contemplation, the RIVER addresses itself as his natural companion.

" 'Come live with me. I am active, cheerful, communicative, a natural talker and story-teller. I am not noisy, like the ocean, except occasionally when I am rudely interrupted, or when I stumble and get a fall. When I am silent you can still have pleasure in watching my changing features. My idlest babble, when I am toying with the trifles that fall in my way, if not very full of meaning, is at least musical. I am not a dangerous friend, like the ocean; no highway is absolutely safe, but my nature is harmless, and the storms that strew the beaches with wrecks cast no ruins upon my flowery borders. Abide with me, and you shall not die of thirst, like the forlorn wretches left to the mercies of the pitiless salt waves. Trust yourself to me, and I will carry you far on your journey, if we are travelling to the same point of the compass. If I sometimes run riot and overflow your meadows, I leave fertility behind me when I withdraw to my natural channel. Walk by my side toward the place of my destination. I will keep pace with you, and you shall feel my presence with you as that of a self-conscious being like yourself. You will find it hard to be miserable in my company; I drain you of ill-conditioned thoughts as I carry away the refuse of your dwelling-house and its grounds.'

"But to him whom the ocean chills and crushes with its sullen indifference, and the river disturbs with its never-pausing and never-ending story, the silent LAKE shall be a refuge and a place of rest for his soul

" 'Vex not yourself with thoughts too vast for your limited faculties,' it says; 'yield not yourself to the babble of the running stream. "Leave the ocean, which cares nothing for you or any living thing that walks the solid earth; leave the river too busy with its own errand, too talkative about its own affairs, and find peace with me, whose smile will cheer you, whose whisper will soothe you. Come to me when the morning sun blazes across my bosom like a golden baldric; come to me in the still midnight, when I hold the inverted firmament like a cup brimming with jewels, nor spill one star of all the constellations that float in my ebon goblet. Do you know the charm of melancholy? Where will you find a sympathy like mine in your hours of sadness? Does the ocean share your grief? Does the river listen to your sighs? The salt wave, that called to you from under last month's full moon, to-day is dashing on the rocks of Labrador; the stream, that ran by you pure and sparkling, has swallowed the poisonous refuse of a great city, and is creeping to its grave in the wide cemetery that buries all things in its tomb of liquid crystal. It is true that my waters exhale and are renewed from one season to another; but are your features the same, absolutely the same, from year to year? We both change, but we know each other through all changes. Am I not mirrored in those eyes of yours? And does not Nature plant me as an eye to behold her beauties while she is dressed in the glories of leaf and flower, and draw the icy lid over my shining surface when she stands naked and ashamed in the poverty of winter?'

"I have had strange experiences and sad thoughts in the course of a life not very long, but with a record which much longer lives could not match in incident. Oftentimes the temptation has come over me with dangerous urgency to try a change of existence, if such change is a part of human destiny,—to seek rest, if that is what we gain by laying down the burden of life. I have asked who would be the friend to whom I should appeal for the last service I should have need of. Ocean was there, all ready, asking no questions, answering none. What strange voyages, downward through its glaucous depths, upwards to its boiling and frothing surface, wafted by tides, driven by tempests, disparted by rude agencies; one remnant whitening on the sands of a northern beach, one perhaps built into the circle of a coral reef in the Pacific, one settling to the floor of the vast laboratory where continents are built, to emerge in far-off ages! What strange companions for my pallbearers! Unwieldy sea-monsters, the stories of which are counted fables by the spectacled collectors who think their catalogues have exhausted nature; naked-eyed creatures, staring, glaring, nightmare-like spectres of the ghastly-green abysses; pulpy islands, with life in gelatinous immensity,—what a company of hungry heirs at every ocean funeral! No! No! Ocean claims great multitudes, but does not invite the solitary who would fain be rid of himself.

"Shall I seek a deeper slumber at the bottom of the lake I love than I have ever found when drifting idly over its surface? No, again. I do not want the sweet, clear waters to know me in the disgrace of nature, when life, the faithful body-servant, has ceased caring for me. That must not be. The mirror which has pictured me so often shall never know me as an unwelcome object.

"If I must ask the all-subduing element to be my last friend, and lead me out of my prison, it shall be the busy, whispering, not unfriendly, pleasantly companionable river.

"But Ocean and River and Lake have certain relations to the periods of human life which they who are choosing their places of abode should consider. Let the child play upon the seashore. The wide horizon gives his imagination room to grow in, untrammelled. That background of mystery, without which life is a poor mechanical arrangement, is shaped and colored, so far as it can have outline, or any hue but shadow, on a vast canvas, the contemplation of which enlarges and enriches the sphere of consciousness. The mighty ocean is not too huge to symbolize the aspirations and ambitions of the yet untried soul of the adolescent.

"The time will come when his indefinite mental horizon has found a solid limit, which shuts his prospect in narrower bounds than he would have thought could content him in the few years of undefined possibilities. Then he will find the river a more natural intimate than the ocean. It is individual, which the ocean, with all its gulfs and inlets and multitudinous shores, hardly seems to be. It does not love you very dearly, and will not miss you much when you disappear from its margin; but it means well to you, bids you good-morning with its coming waves, and good-evening with those which are leaving. It will lead your thoughts pleasantly away, upwards to its source, downwards to the stream to which it is tributary, or the wide waters in which it is to lose itself. A river, by choice, to live by in middle age.

"In hours of melancholy reflection, in those last years of life which have little left but tender memories, the still companionship of the lake, embosomed in woods, sheltered, fed by sweet mountain brooks and hidden springs, commends itself to the wearied and saddened spirit I am not thinking of those great inland seas, which have many of the features and much of the danger that belong to the ocean, but of those 'ponds,' as our countrymen used to call them until they were rechristened by summer visitors; beautiful sheets of water from a hundred to a few thousand acres in extent, scattered like raindrops over the map of our Northern sovereignties. The loneliness of contemplative old age finds its natural home in the near neighborhood of one of these tranquil basins.

"Nature does not always plant her poets where they belong, but if we look carefully their affinities betray themselves. The youth will carry his Byron to the rock which overlooks the ocean the poet loved so well. The man of maturer years will remember that the sonorous couplets of Pope which ring in his ears were written on the banks of the Thames. The old man, as he nods over the solemn verse of Wordsworth, will recognize the affinity between the singer and the calm sheet that lay before him as he wrote,—the stainless and sleepy Windermere.

"The dwellers by Cedar Lake may find it an amusement to compare their own feelings with those of one who has lived by the Atlantic and the Mediterranean, by the Nile and the Tiber, by Lake Leman and by one of the fairest sheets of water that our own North America embosoms in its forests."

Miss Lurida Vincent, Secretary of the Pansophian Society, read this paper, and pondered long upon it She was thinking very seriously of studying medicine, and had been for some time in frequent communication with Dr. Butts, under whose direction she had begun reading certain treatises, which added to such knowledge of the laws of life in health and in disease as she had brought with her from the Corinna Institute. Naturally enough, she carried the anonymous paper to the doctor, to get his opinion about it, and compare it with her own. They both agreed that it was probably, they would not say certainly, the work of the solitary visitor. There was room for doubt, for there were visitors who might well have travelled to all the places mentioned, and resided long enough on the shores of the waters the writer spoke of to have had all the experiences mentioned in the paper. The Terror remembered a young lady, a former schoolmate, who belonged to one of those nomadic families common in this generation, the heads of which, especially the female heads, can never be easy where they are, but keep going between America and Europe, like so many pith-balls in the electrical experiment, alternately attracted and repelled, never in contented equilibrium. Every few years they pull their families up by the roots, and by the time they have begun to take hold a little with their radicles in the spots to which they have been successively transplanted up they come again, so that they never get a tap-root anywhere. The Terror suspected the daughter of one of these families of sending certain anonymous articles of not dissimilar character to the one she had just received. But she knew the style of composition common among the young girls, and she could hardly believe that it was one of them who had sent this paper. Could a brother of this young lady have written it? Possibly; she knew nothing more than that the young lady had a brother, then a student at the University. All the chances were that Mr. Maurice Kirkwood was the author. So thought Lurida, and so thought Dr. Butts.

Whatever faults there were in this essay, it interested them both. There was nothing which gave the least reason to suspect insanity on the part of the writer, whoever he or she might be. There were references to suicide, it is true, but they were of a purely speculative nature, and did not look to any practical purpose in that direction. Besides, if the stranger were the author of the paper, he certainly would not choose a sheet of water like Cedar Lake to perform the last offices for him, in case he seriously meditated taking unceremonious leave of life and its accidents. He could find a river easily enough, to say nothing of other methods of effecting his purpose; but he had committed himself as to the impropriety of selecting a lake, so they need not be anxious about the white canoe and its occupant, as they watched it skimming the surface of the deep waters.

The holder of the Portfolio would never have ventured to come before the public if he had not counted among his resources certain papers belonging to the records of the Pansophian Society, which he can make free use of, either for the illustration of the narrative, or for a diversion during those intervals in which the flow of events is languid, or even ceases for the time to manifest any progress. The reader can hardly have failed to notice that the old Anchor Tavern had become the focal point where a good deal of mental activity converged. There were the village people, including a number of cultivated families; there were the visitors, among them many accomplished and widely travelled persons; there was the University, with its learned teachers and aspiring young men; there was the Corinna Institute, with its eager, ambitious, hungry-souled young women, crowding on, class after class coming forward on the broad stream of liberal culture, and rounding the point which, once passed, the boundless possibilities of womanhood opened before them. All this furnished material enough and to spare for the records and the archives of the society.

The new Secretary infused fresh life into the meetings. It may be remembered that the girls had said of her, when she was The Terror, that "she knew everything and didn't believe anything." That was just the kind of person for a secretary of such an association. Properly interpreted, the saying meant that she knew a great deal, and wanted to know a great deal more, and was consequently always on the lookout for information; that she believed nothing without sufficient proof that it was true, and therefore was perpetually asking for evidence where others took assertions on trust.

It was astonishing to see what one little creature like The Terror could accomplish in the course of a single season. She found out what each member could do and wanted to do. She wrote to the outside visitors whom she suspected of capacity, and urged them to speak at the meetings, or send written papers to be read. As an official, with the printed title at the head of her notes, PANSOPHIAN SOCIETY, she was a privileged personage. She begged the young persons who had travelled to tell something of their experiences. She had contemplated getting up a discussion on the woman's rights question, but being a wary little body, and knowing that the debate would become a dispute and divide the members into two hostile camps, she deferred this project indefinitely. It would be time enough after she had her team well in hand, she said to herself,—had felt their mouths and tried their paces. This expression, as she used it in her thoughts, seems rather foreign to her habits, but there was room in her large brain for a wide range of illustrations and an ample vocabulary. She could not do much with her own muscles, but she had known the passionate delight of being whirled furiously over the road behind four scampering horses, in a rocking stage-coach, and thought of herself in the Secretary's chair as not unlike the driver on his box. A few weeks of rest had allowed her nervous energy to store itself up, and the same powers which had distanced competition in the classes of her school had of necessity to expend themselves in vigorous action in her new office.

Her appeals had their effect. A number of papers were very soon sent in; some with names, some anonymously. She looked these papers over, and marked those which she thought would be worth reading and listening to at the meetings. One of them has just been presented to the reader. As to the authorship of the following one there were many conjectures. A well-known writer, who had spent some weeks at Arrowhead Village, was generally suspected of being its author. Some, however, questioned whether it was not the work of a new hand, who wrote, not from experience, but from his or her ideas of the condition to which a story-teller, a novelist, must in all probability be sooner or later reduced. The reader must judge for himself whether this first paper is the work of an old hand or a novice.

SOME EXPERIENCES OF A NOVELIST.

"I have written a frightful number of stories,—forty or more, I think. Let me see. For twelve years two novels a year regularly: that makes twenty-four. In three different years I have written three stories annually: that makes thirty-three. In five years one a year,—thirty-eight. That is all, isn't it? Yes. Thirty-eight, not forty. I wish I could make them all into one composite story, as Mr. Galton does his faces.

"Hero—heroine—mamma—papa—uncle—sister, and so on. Love—obstacles—misery—tears—despair—glimmer of hope—unexpected solution of difficulties—happy finale.

"Landscape for background according to season Plants of each month got up from botanical calendars.

"I should like much to see the composite novel. Why not apply Mr. Galton's process, and get thirty-eight stories all in one? All the Yankees would resolve into one Yankee, all the P—West Britons—into one Patrick, etc.,—what a saving of time it would be!

"I got along pretty well with my first few stories. I had some characters around me which, a little disguised, answered well enough. There was the minister of the parish, and there was an old schoolmaster: either of them served very satisfactorily for grandfathers and old uncles. All I had to do was to shift some of their leading peculiarities, keeping the rest. The old minister wore knee-breeches. I clapped them on to the schoolmaster. The schoolmaster carried a tall gold-headed cane. I put this in the minister's hands. So with other things,—I shifted them round, and got a set of characters who, taken together, reproduced the chief persons of the village where I lived, but did not copy any individual exactly. Thus it went on for a while; but by and by my stock company began to be rather too familiarly known, in spite of their change of costume, and at last some altogether too sagacious person published what he called a 'key' to several of my earlier stories, in which I found the names of a number of neighbors attached to aliases of my own invention. All the 'types,' as he called them, represented by these personages of my story had come to be recognized, each as standing for one and the same individual of my acquaintance. It had been of no use to change the costume. Even changing the sex did no good. I had a famous old gossip in one of my tales,—a much-babbling Widow Sert-ingly. 'Sho!' they all said, 'that's old Deacon Spinner, the same he told about in that other story of his,—only the deacon's got on a petticoat and a mob-cap,—but it's the same old sixpence.' So I said to myself, I must have some new characters. I had no trouble with young characters; they are all pretty much alike,—dark-haired or light-haired, with the outfits belonging to their complexion, respectively. I had an old great-aunt, who was a tip-top eccentric. I had never seen anything just like her in books. So I said, I will have you, old lady, in one of my stories; and, sure enough, I fitted her out with a first-rate odd-sounding name, which I got from the directory, and sent her forth to the world, disguised, as I supposed, beyond the possibility of recognition. The book sold well, and the eccentric personage was voted a novelty. A few weeks after it was published a lawyer called upon me, as the agent of the person in the directory, whose family name I had used, as he maintained, to his and all his relatives' great damage, wrong, loss, grief, shame, and irreparable injury, for which the sum of blank thousand dollars would be a modest compensation. The story made the book sell, but not enough to pay blank thousand dollars. In the meantime a cousin of mine had sniffed out the resemblance between the character in my book and our great-aunt. We were rivals in her good graces. 'Cousin Pansie' spoke to her of my book and the trouble it was bringing on me,—she was so sorry about it! She liked my story,—only those personalities, you know. 'What personalities?' says old granny-aunt. 'Why, auntie, dear, they do say that he has brought in everybody we know,—didn't anybody tell you about—well,—I suppose you ought to know it,—didn't anybody tell you you were made fun of in that novel?' Somebody—no mat-ter who—happened to hear all this, and told me. She said granny-aunt's withered old face had two red spots come to it, as if she had been painting her cheeks from a pink saucer. No, she said, not a pink saucer, but as if they were two coals of fire. She sent out and got the book, and made her (the somebody that I was speaking of) read it to her. When she had heard as much as she could stand,—for 'Cousin Pansie' explained passages to her,—***explained,*** you know,—she sent for her lawyer, and that same somebody had to be a witness to a new will she had drawn up. It was not to my advantage. 'Cousin Pansie' got the corner lot where the grocery is, and pretty much everything else. The old woman left me a legacy. What do you think it was? An old set of my own books, that looked as if it had been bought out of a bankrupt circulating library!

"After that I grew more careful. I studied my disguises much more diligently. But after all, what could I do? Here I was, writing stories for my living and my reputation. I made a pretty sum enough, and worked hard enough to earn it No tale, no money. Then every story that went from my workshop had to come up to the standard of my reputation, and there was a set of critics,—there *is* a set of critics now and everywhere,—that watch as narrowly for the decline of a man's reputation as ever a village half drowned out by an inundation watched for the falling of the waters. The fame I had won, such as it was, seemed to attend me,—not going before me in the shape of a woman with a trumpet, but rather following me like one of Actæon's hounds, his throat open, ready to pull me down and tear me. What a fierce enemy is that which bays behind us in the voice of our proudest bygone achievement!

"But, as I said above, what could I do? I must write novels, and I must' have characters. 'Then why not invent them?' asks some novice. Oh, yes! Invent them! You can invent a human being that in certain aspects of humanity will answer every purpose for which your invention was intended. A basket of straw, an old coat and pair of breeches, a hat which has been soaked, sat upon, stuffed a broken window, and had a brood of chickens raised in it,—these elements, duly adjusted to each other, will represent humanity so truthfully that the crows will avoid the cornfield when your scarecrow displays his personality. Do you think you can make your heroes and heroines,—nay, even your scrappy supernumeraries,—out of refuse material, as you made your scarecrow? You can't do it. You must study living people and reproduce them. And whom do you know so well as your friends? You will show up your friends, then, one after another. When your friends give out, who is left for you? Why, nobody but your own family, of course. When you have used up your family, there is nothing left for you but to write your autobiography.

"After my experience with my grand-aunt, I became more cautious, very naturally. I kept traits of character, but I mixed ages as well as sexes. In this way I continued to use up a large amount of material, which looked as if it were as dangerous as dynamite to meddle with. Who would have expected to meet my maternal uncle in the guise of a schoolboy? Yet I managed to decant his characteristics as nicely as the old gentleman would have decanted a bottle of Juno Madeira through that long siphon which he always used when the most sacred vintages were summoned from their crypts to render an account of themselves on his hospitable board. It was a nice business, I confess, but I did it, and I drink cheerfully to that good uncle's memory in a glass of wine from his own cellar, which, with many other important tokens of his good will, I call my own since his lamented demise.

"I succeeded so well with my uncle that I thought I would try a course of cousins. I had enough of them to furnish out a whole gallery of portraits. There was cousin 'Creeshy' as we called her; Lucretia, more correctly. She was a cripple. Her left lower limb had had something happen to it, and she walked with a crutch. Her patience under her trial was very pathetic and picturesque, so to speak,—I mean adapted to the tender parts of a story; nothing could work up better in a melting paragraph. But I could not, of course, describe her particular infirmity; that would point her out at once. I thought of shifting the lameness to the *right* lower limb, but even that would be seen through. So I gave the young woman that stood for her in my story a lame *elbow,* and put her arm in a sling, and made her such a model of uncomplaining endurance that my grandmother cried over her as if her poor old heart would break. She cried very easily, my grandmother; in fact, she had such a gift for tears that I availed myself of it, and if you remember old Judy, in my novel *"Honi Soit"* (Honey Sweet, the booksellers called it),—old Judy, the black nurse,—that was my grandmother. She had various other peculiarities, which I brought out one by one, and saddled on to different characters. You see she was a perfect mine of singularities and idiosyncrasies. After I had used her up pretty well, I came down upon my poor relations. They were perfectly fair game; what better use could I put them to? I studied them up very carefully, and as there were a good many of them I helped myself freely. They lasted me, with occasional intermissions, I should say, three or four years. I had to be very careful with my poor relations,—they were as touchy as they could be; and as I felt bound to send a copy of my novel, whatever it might be, to each one of them,—there were as many as a dozen,—I took care to mix their characteristic features, so that, though each might suspect I meant the other, no one should think I meant him or her. I got through all my relations at last except my father and mother. I had treated my brothers and sisters pretty fairly, all except Elisha and Joanna. The truth is they both had lots of odd ways,—family traits, I suppose,—but were just different enough from each other to figure separately in two different stories. These two novels made me some little trouble; for Elisha said he felt sure that I meant Joanna in one of them, and quarrelled with me about it; and Joanna vowed and declared that Elnathan, in the other, stood for brother 'Lisha, and that it was a real mean thing to make fun of folks' own flesh and blood, and treated me to one of her cries. She wasn't handsome when she cried, poor, dear Joanna; in fact, that was one of the personal traits I had made use of in the story that Elisha found fault with.

"So as there was nobody left but my father and mother, you see for yourself I had no choice. There was one great advantage in dealing with them,—I knew them so thoroughly. One naturally feels a certain delicacy in handling from a purely artistic point of view persons who have been so near to him. One's mother, for instance: suppose some of her little ways were so peculiar that the accurate delineation of them would furnish amusement to great numbers of readers; it would not be without hesitation that a writer of delicate sensibility would draw her portrait, with all its whimsicalities, so plainly that it should be generally recognized. One's father is commonly of tougher fibre than one's mother, and one would not feel the same scruples, perhaps, in using him professionally as material in a novel; still, while you are employing him as *bait,*—you see I am honest and plain-spoken, for your characters *are* baits to catch readers with,—I would follow kind Izaak Walton's humane counsel about the frog you are fastening to your fish-hook: fix him artistically, as he directs, but in so doing ' use him as though you loved him.'

"I have at length shown up, in one form and another, all my townsmen who have anything effective in their bodily or mental make-.up, all my friends, all my relatives; that is, all my blood relatives. It has occurred to me that I might open a new field in the family connection of my father-in-law and mother-in-law. We have been thinking of paying them a visit, and I shall have an admirable opportunity of studying them and their relatives and visitors. I have long wanted a good chance for getting acquainted with the social sphere several grades below that to which I am accustomed, and I have no doubt that I shall find matter for half a dozen new stories among those connections of mine. Besides, they live in a Western city, and one doesn't mind much how he cuts up the people of places he doesn't himself live in. I suppose there is not really so much difference in people's feelings, whether they live in Bangor or Omaha, but one's nerves can't be expected to stretch across the continent It is all a matter of greater or less distance. I read this morning that a Chinese fleet was sunk, but I didn't think half so much about it as I did about losing my sleeve button, confound it! People have accused me of want of feeling; they misunderstand the artist-nature,—that is all. I obey that implicitly; I am sorry if people don't like my descriptions, but I have done my best. I have pulled to pieces all the persons I am acquainted with, and put them together again in my characters. The quills I write with come from live geese, I would have you know. I expect to get some first-rate pluckings from those people I was speaking of, and I mean to begin my thirty-ninth novel, as soon as I have got through my visit."

IX.
THE SOCIETY AND ITS NEW SECRETARY.

THERE is no use in trying to hurry the natural course of events, in a narrative like this. June passed away, and July, and August had come, and as yet the enigma which had completely puzzled Arrowhead Village and its visitors remained unsolved. The white canoe still wandered over the lake, alone, ghostly, always avoiding the near approach of the boats which seemed to be coming in its direction. Now and then a circumstance would happen which helped to keep inquiry alive. Good horsemanship was not so common among the young men of the place and its neighborhood that Maurice's accomplishment in that way could be overlooked. If there was a wicked horse or a wild colt whose owner was afraid of him, he would be commended to Maurice's attention. Paolo would lead him to his master with all due precaution,—for he had no idea of risking his neck on the back of any ill-conditioned beast,—and Maurice would fasten on his long spurs, spring into the saddle, and very speedily teach the creature good behavior. There soon got about a story that he was what the fresh-water fisherman called "one o' them whisperers." It is a common legend enough, coming from the Old World, but known in American horse-talking circles, that some persons will whisper certain words in a horse's ear which will tame him if he is as wild and furious as ever Cruiser was. All this added to the mystery which surrounded the young man. A single improbable or absurd story amounts to very little, but when half a dozen such stories are told about the same individual or the same event, they begin to produce the effect of credible evidence. If the year had been 1692 and the place had been Salem Village, Maurice Kirkwood would have run the risk of being treated like the Reverend George Burroughs.

Miss Lurida Vincent's curiosity had been intensely excited with reference to the young man of whom so many stories were told. She had pretty nearly convinced herself that he was the author of the paper on Ocean, Lake, and River, which had been read at one of the meetings of the Pansophian Society. She was very desirous of meeting him, if it were possible. It seemed as if she might, as Secretary of the Society, request the co-operation of any of the visitors, without impropriety. So, after much deliberation, she wrote a careful note, of which the following is an exact copy. Her hand was bold, almost masculine, a curious contrast to that of Euthymia, which was delicately feminine.

ARROWHEAD VILLAGE, *August* 3, 18—

MAURICE KIRKWOOD, ESQ.

DEAR SIR,—You have received, I trust, a card of invitation to the meetings of our Society, but I think we have not yet had the pleasure of seeing you at any of them. We have supposed that we might be indebted to you for a paper read at the last meeting, and listened to with much interest. As it was anonymous, we do not wish to be inquisitive respecting its authorship; but we desire to say that any papers kindly sent us by the temporary residents of our village will be welcome, and if adapted to the wants of our Association will be read at one of its meetings or printed in its records, or perhaps both read and printed. May we not hope for your presence at the meeting, which is to take place next Wednesday evening?

Respectfully yours,

LURIDA VINCENT, *Secretary of the Pansophian Society.*

To this note the Secretary received the following reply:—

ARROWHEAD VILLAGE, *August* 4, 18—.

Miss LURIDA VINCENT, *Secretary of the Pansophian Society:*

DEAR MISS VINCENT,—I have received the ticket you refer to, and desire to express my acknowledgments for the polite attention. I regret that I have not been and I fear shall not be able to attend the meetings of the Society; but if any subject occurs to me on which I feel an inclination to write, it will give me pleasure to send a paper, to be disposed of as the Society may see fit.

Very respectfully yours,

MAURICE KIRKWOOD.

"He says nothing about the authorship of the paper that was read the other evening," the Secretary said to herself. "No matter,—he wrote it,—there is no mistaking his handwriting. We know something about him, now, at any rate. But why doesn't he come to our meetings? What has his *antipathy* to do with his staying away? I must find out what his secret is, and I *will.* I don't believe it's harder than it was to solve that prize problem which puzzled so many teachers, or than beating Crakowitz, the great chess-player."

To this enigma, then, The Terror determined to bend all the faculties which had excited the admiration and sometimes the amazement of those who knew her in her school-days. It was a very delicate piece of business; for though Lurida was an intrepid woman's rights advocate, and believed she was entitled to do almost everything that men dared to, she knew very well there were certain limits which a young woman like herself must not pass.

In the meantime Maurice had received a visit from the young student at the University,—the same whom he had rescued from his dangerous predicament in the rake. With him had called one of the teachers,—an instructor in modern languages, a native of Italy. Maurice and the instructor exchanged a few words in Italian. The young man spoke it with the ease which implied long familiarity with its use.

After they left, the instructor asked many curious questions about him,—who he was, how long he had been in the village, whether anything was known of his history,—all these inquiries with an eagerness which implied some special and peculiar reason for the interest they evinced.

"I feel satisfied," the instructor said, "that I have met that young man in my own country. It was a number of years ago, and of course he has altered in appearance a good deal; but there is a look about him of—what shall I call it ?—apprehension,—as if he were fearing the approach of something or somebody. I think it is the way a man would look that was haunted; you know what I mean,—followed by a spirit or ghost. He does not suggest the idea of a murderer,—very far from it; but if he did, I should think he was every minute in fear of seeing the murdered man's spirit."

The student was curious, in his turn, to know all the instructor could recall He had seen him in Rome, he thought, at the Fountain of Trevi, where so many strangers go before leaving the city. The youth was in the company of a man who looked like a priest. He could not mistake the peculiar expression of his countenance, but that was all he now remembered about his appearance. His attention had been called to this young man by seeing that some of the bystanders were pointing at him, and noticing that they were whispering with each other as if with reference to him. He should say that the youth was at that time fifteen or sixteen years old, and the time was about ten years ago.

After all, this evidence was of little or no value. Suppose the youth were Maurice; what then? We know that he had been in Italy; and had been there a good while,—or at least we infer so much from his familiarity with the language, and are confirmed in the belief by his having an Italian servant, whom he probably brought from Italy when he returned. If he wrote the paper which was read the other evening, that settles it, for the writer says he had lived by the Tiber. We must put this scrap of evidence furnished by the Professor with the other scraps; it may turn out of some consequence, sooner or later. It is like a piece of a dissected map; it means almost nothing by itself, but when we find the pieces it joins with we may discover a very important meaning in it.

In a small, concentrated community like that which centred in and immediately around Arrowhead Village, every day must have its local gossip as well as its general news. The newspaper tells the small community what is going on in the great world, and the busy tongues of male and female, especially the latter, fill in with the occurrences and comments of the ever-stirring microcosm. The fact that the Italian teacher had, or thought he had, seen Maurice ten years before was circulated and made the most of,—turned over and over like a cake, until it was thoroughly done on both sides and all through. It was a very small cake, but better than nothing. Miss Vincent heard this story, as others did, and talked about it with her friend, Miss Tower. Here was one more fact to help along.

The two young ladies who had recently graduated at the Corinna Institute remained, as they had always been, intimate friends. They were the natural complements of each* other. Euthymia represented a complete, symmetrical womanhood. Her outward presence was only an index of a large, wholesome, affluent life. She could not help being courageous, with such a firm organization. She could not help being generous, cheerful, active. She had been told often enough that she was fair to look upon. She knew that she was called The Wonder by the schoolmates who were dazzled by her singular accomplishments, but she did not overvalue them. She rather tended to depreciate her own gifts, in comparison with those of her friend, Miss Lurida Vincent. The two agreed all the better for differing as they did. The octave makes a perfect chord, when shorter intervals jar more or less on the ear. Each admired the other with a heartiness which, if they had been less unlike, would have been impossible.

It was a pleasant thing to observe their dependence on each other. The Terror of the schoolroom was the oracle in her relations with her friend. All the freedom of movement which The Wonder showed in her bodily exercises The Terror manifested in the world of thought She would fling open a book, and decide in a swift glance whether it had any message for her. Her teachers had compared her way of reading to the taking of an instantaneous photograph. When she took up the first book on Physiology which Dr. Butts handed her, it seemed to him that if she only opened at any place, and gave one look, her mind drank its meaning up, as a moist sponge absorbs water. "What can I do with such a creature as this?" he said to himself. "There is only one way to deal with her,—treat her as one treats a silkworm: give it its mulberry leaf, and it will spin its own cocoon. Give her the books, and she will spin her own web of knowledge."

"Do you really think of studying medicine?" said Dr. Butts to her.

"I haven't made up my mind about that," she answered, "but I want to know a little more about this terrible machinery of life and death we are all tangled in. I know something about it, but not enough. I find some very strange beliefs among the women I meet with, and I want to be able to silence them when they attempt to proselyte me to their whims and fancies. Besides, I want to know everything."

"They tell me you do, already," said Dr. Butts.

"I am the most ignorant little wretch that draws the breath of life!" exclaimed The Terror.

The doctor smiled. He knew what it meant. She had reached that stage of education in which the vast domain of the unknown opens its illimitable expanse before the eyes of the student. We never know the extent of darkness until it is partially illuminated.

"You did not leave the Institute with the reputation of being the most ignorant young lady that ever graduated there," said the doctor. "They tell me you got the highest marks of any pupil on their record since the school was founded."

"What a grand thing it was to be the biggest fish in our small aquarium, to be sure!" answered The Terror. "He was six inches long, the monster,—a little too big for bait to catch a pickerel with! What did you hand me that schoolbook for? Did you think I didn't know anything about the human body?"

"You said you were such an ignorant creature I thought I would try you with an easy book, by way of introduction."

The Terror was not confused by her apparent self-contradiction.

"I meant what I said, and I mean what I say. When I talk about my ignorance, I don't measure myself with schoolgirls, doctor. I don't measure myself with my teachers, either. You must talk to me as if I were a man, a grown man, if you mean to teach me anything. Where is your hat, doctor? Let me try it on."

The doctor handed her his wide-awake. The Terror's hair was not naturally abundant, like Euthymia's, and she kept it cut rather short. Her head used to get very hot when she studied hard. She tried to put the hat on.

"Do you see that?" she said. "I couldn't wear it,—it would squeeze my eyes out of my head. The books told me that women's brains were smaller than men's: perhaps they are,—most of them,—I never measured a great many. But when they try to settle what women are good for, by phrenology, I like to have them put their tape round my head. I don't believe in their nonsense, for all that. You might as well tell me that if one horse weighs more than another horse he is worth more,—a cart-horse that weighs twelve or fourteen hundred pounds better than Eclipse, that may have weighed a thousand. Give me a list of the best books you can think of, and turn me loose in your library. I can find what I want, if you have it; and what I don't find there I will get at the Public Library. I shall want to ask you a question now and then."

The doctor looked at her with a kind of admiration, but thoughtfully, as if he feared she was thinking of a task too formidable for her slight constitutional resource.

She returned, instinctively, to the apparent contradiction in her statements about herself.

"I am not a fool, if I am ignorant. Yes, doctor, I sail on a wide sea of ignorance, but I have taken soundings of some of its shallows and some of its depths. Your profession deals with the facts of life that interest me most just now, and I want to know something of it Perhaps I may find it a calling such as would suit me."

"Do you seriously think of becoming a practitioner of medicine?" Said the doctor.

"Certainly, I seriously think of it as a possibility, but I want to know something more about it first. Perhaps I sha'n't believe in medicine enough to practise it. Perhaps I sha'n't like it well enough. No matter about that. I wish to study some of your best books on some of the subjects that most interest me. I know about bones and muscles and all that, and about digestion and respiration and such things. I want to study up the nervous system, and learn all about it. I am of the nervous temperament myself, and perhaps that is the reason. I want to read about insanity and all that relates to it."

A curious expression flitted across the doctor's features as The Terror said this.

"Nervous system. Insanity. She has headaches, I know,—all those large-headed, hard-thinking girls do, as a matter of course; but what has set her off about insanity and the nervous system? I wonder if any of her more remote relatives are subject to mental disorder. Bright people very often have crazy relations. Perhaps some of her friends are in that way. I wonder whether"—the doctor did not speak any of these thoughts, and in fact hardly shaped his "whether," for The Terror interrupted his train of reflection, or rather struck into it in a way which startled him.

"Where is the first volume of this Medical Cyclopædia?" she asked, looking at its empty place on the shelf.

"On my table," the doctor answered. "I have been consulting it."

Lurida flung it open, in her eager way, and turned the pages rapidly until she came to the one she wanted. The doctor cast his eye on the heading of the page, and saw the large letters ANT.

"I thought so," he said to himself. "We shall know everything there is in the books about antipathies now, if we never did before. She has a special object in studying the nervous system, just as I suspected. I think she does not care to mention it at this time; but if she finds out anything of interest she will tell me, if she does anybody. Perhaps she does not mean to tell anybody. It *is* a rather delicate business,—a young girl studying the natural history of a young man. Not quite so safe as botany or palæontology!"

Lurida, lately The Terror, now Miss Vincent, had her own plans, and chose to keep them to herself, for the present, at least. Her hands were full enough, it might seem, without undertaking the solution of the great Arrowhead Village enigma. But she was in the most perfect training, so far as her intelligence was concerned; and the summer rest had restored her bodily vigor, so that her brain was like an overcharged battery which will find conductors somewhere to carry off its crowded energy.

At this time Arrowhead Village was enjoying the most successful season it had ever known. The Pansophian Society flourished to an extraordinary degree under the fostering care of the new Secretary. The rector was a good figure-head as President, but the Secretary was the life of the Society. Communications came in abundantly; some from the village and its neighborhood, some from the University and the Institute, some from distant and unknown sources. The new Secretary was very busy with the work of examining these papers. After a' forenoon so employed, the carpet of her room looked like a barn floor after a husking-match. A glance at the manuscripts strewed about, or lying in heaps, would have frightened any young writer away from the thought of authorship as a business. If the candidate for that fearful calling had seen the process of selection and elimination, he would have felt still more desperately. A paper of twenty pages would come in, with an under-scored request to ***please read through carefully.*** That request alone is commonly sufficient to condemn any paper, and prevent its having any chance of a hearing; but the Secretary was not hardened enough yet for that kind of martial law in dealing with manuscripts. The looker-on might have seen her take up the paper, cast one flashing glance at its title, read the first sentence and the last, dip at a venture into two or three pages, and decide as swiftly as the lightning calculator would add up a column of figures what was to be its destination. If rejected, it went into the heap on the left; if approved, it was laid apart, to be submitted to the Committee for their judgment. The foolish writers who insist on one's reading through their manuscript poems and stories ought to know how fatal the request is to their prospects. It provokes the reader, to begin with. The reading of manuscript is frightful work, at the best; the reading of worthless manuscript—and most of that which one is requested to **read through** is worthless—would add to the terrors of Tartarus, if any infernal deity were ingenious enough to suggest it as a punishment.

If a paper was rejected by the Secretary, it did not come before the Committee, but was returned to the author, if he sent for it, which he commonly did. Its natural course was to try for admission into some one of the popular magazines: into "The Sifter," the most fastidious of them all; if that declined it, into "The Second Best;" and if *that* returned it, into "The Omnivorous." If it was refused admittance at the doors of all the magazines, it might at length find shelter in the corner of a newspaper, where a good deal of very readable verse is to be met with nowadays, some of which has been, no doubt, presented to the Pansophian Society, but was not considered up to its standard.

X.
A NEW ARRIVAL.

THERE was a recent accession to the transient population of the village which gave rise to some speculation. The new-comer was a young fellow, rather careless in his exterior, but apparently as much at home as if he owned Arrowhead Village and everything in it. He commonly had a cigar in his mouth, carried a pocket pistol, of the non-explosive sort, and a stick with a bulldog's head for its knob; wore a soft hat, a coarse check suit, a little baggy, and gaiter-boots which had been half-soled,—a Bohemian-looking personage, altogether.

This individual began making explorations in every direction. He was very curious about the place and all the people in it He was especially interested in the Pansophian Society, concerning which he made all sorts of inquiries. This led him to form a summer acquaintance with the Secretary, who was pleased to give him whatever information he asked for; being proud of the Society, as she had a right to be, and knowing more about it than anybody else.

The visitor could not have been long in the village without hearing something of Maurice If Kirkwood, and the stories, true and false, connected with his name. He questioned everybody who could tell him anything about Maurice, and set down the answers in a little note-book he always had with him.

All this naturally excited the curiosity of the village about this new visitor. Among the rest, Miss Vincent, not wanting in an attribute thought to belong more especially to her sex, became somewhat interested to know more exactly who this inquiring, note-taking personage, who seemed to be everywhere and to know everybody, might himself be. Meeting him at the Public Library at a fortunate moment, when there was nobody but the old Librarian, who was hard of hearing, to interfere with their conversation, the little Secretary had a chance to try to find out something about him.

"This is a very remarkable library for a small village to possess," he remarked to Miss Lurida.

"It is, indeed," she said. "Have you found it well furnished with the books you most want?"

"Oh, yes,—books enough. I don't care so much for the books as I do for the Newspapers. I like a Review well enough,—it tells you all there is in a book; but a good abstract of the Review in a Newspaper saves a fellow the trouble of reading it."

"You find the papers you want, here, I hope," said the young lady.

"Oh, I get along pretty well. It's my off-time, and I don't do much reading or writing. Who is the city correspondent of this place?"

"I don't think we have any one who writes regularly. Now and then, there is a letter, with the gossip of the place in it, or an account of some of the doings at our Society. The city papers are always glad to get the reports of our meetings, and to know what is going on in the village."

"I suppose you write about the Society to the papers, as you are the Secretary."

This was a point-blank shot. She meant to question the young man about his business, and here she was on the witness-stand. She ducked her head, and let the question go over her.

"Oh, there are plenty of members who are willing enough to write,—especially to give an account of their own papers. I think they like to have me put in the applause, when they get any. I do that sometimes." (How much more, she did not say.)

"I have seen some very well written articles, which, from what they tell me of the Secretary, I should have thought she might have written herself."

He looked her straight in the eyes.

"I have transmitted some good papers," she said, without winking, or swallowing, or changing color,—precious little color she had to change; her brain wanted all the blood it could borrow or steal, and more too. "You spoke of Newspapers," she said, without any change of tone or manner: "do you not frequently write for them yourself?"

"I should think I did," answered the young man. "I am a regular correspondent of 'The People's Perennial and Household Inquisitor.' "

"The regular correspondent from where?"

"Where! Oh, anywhere,—the place does not make much difference. I have been writing chiefly from Naples and St. Petersburg, and now and then from Constantinople."

"How long since your return to this country, may I ask?"

"My return? I have never been out of this country. I travel with a gazetteer and some guide-books. It is the cheapest way, and you can get the facts much better from them than by trusting your own observation. I have made the tour of Europe by the help of them and the newspapers. But of late I have taken to interviewing. I find that a very pleasant speciality. It is about as good sport as trout-tickling, and much the same kind of business. I should like to send the Society an account of one of my interviews. Don't you think they would like to hear it?"

"I have no doubt they would. Send it to me, and I will look it over; and if the Committee approve it, we will have it at the next meeting. You know everything has to be examined and voted on by the Committee," said the cautious Secretary.

"Very well,—I will risk it. After it is read, if it *is* read, please send it back to me, as I want to sell it to 'The Sifter,' or' The Second Best,' or some of the paying magazines."

This is the paper, which was read at the next meeting of the Pansophian Society.

"I was ordered by the editor of the newspaper to which I am attached, 'The People's Perennial and Household Inquisitor,' to make a visit to a certain well-known writer, and obtain all the particulars I could concerning him and all that related to him. I have interviewed a good many politicians, who I thought rather liked the process; but I had never tried any of these literary people, and I was not quite sure how this one would feel about it. I said as much to the chief, but he pooh-poohed my scruples. 'It isn't our business whether they like it or not,' said he; 'the public wants it, and what the public wants it's bound to have, and we are bound to furnish it Don't be afraid of your man; he's used to it,—he's been pumped often enough to take it easy, and what you've got to do is to pump him dry. You needn't be modest,—ask him what you like; he isn't bound to answer, you know.'

"As he lived in a rather nice quarter of the town, I smarted myself up a little, put on a fresh collar and cuffs, and got a five-cent shine on my best high-lows. I said to myself, as I was walking towards the house where he lived, that I would keep very shady for a while and pass for a visitor from a distance; one of those 'admiring strangers,' who call in to pay their respects, to get an autograph, and go home and say that they have met the distinguished So and So, which gives ***them*** a certain distinction in the village circle to which they belong.

"My man, the celebrated writer, received me in what was evidently his reception-room. I observed that he managed to get the light full on my face, while his own was in the shade. I had meant to have ***his*** face in the light, but he knew the localities, and had arranged things so as to give him that advantage. It was like two frigates manœuvring,—each trying to get to windward of the other. I never take out my note-book until I and my man have got engaged in artless and earnest conversation,—always about himself and his works, of course, if he is an author.

"I began by saying that he must receive a good many callers. Those who had read his books were naturally curious to see the writer of them.

"He assented, emphatically, to this statement He had, he said, a, ***great*** many callers.

"I remarked that there was a quality in his books which made his readers feel as if they knew him personally, and caused them to cherish a certain attachment to him.

"He smiled, as if pleased. He was himself disposed to think so, he said. In fact, a great many persons, strangers writing to him, had told him so.

"My dear sir, I said, there is nothing wonderful in the fact you mention. You reach a responsive chord in many human breasts.

'One touch of Nature makes the whole world kin.'

Everybody feels as if he, and especially she (his eyes sparkled), were your blood relation. Do they not name their children after you very frequently?

"He blushed perceptibly. 'Sometimes,' he answered. I hope they will all turn out well'

"I am afraid I am taking up too much of your time, I said.

" 'No, not at all,' he replied. 'Come up into my library; it is warmer and pleasanter there.'

"I felt confident that I had him by the right handle then; for an author's library, which is commonly his working-room, is, like a lady's boudoir, a sacred apartment.

"So we went upstairs, and again he got me with the daylight on *my* face, when I wanted it on *his*.

"You have a fine library, I remarked. There were books all round the room, and one of those whirligig square book-cases. I saw *in front* a Bible and a Concordance, Shakespeare and Mrs. Cowden Clarke's book, and other classical works and books of grave aspect. I contrived to give it a turn, and on the side next the wall I got a glimpse of Barnum's Rhyming Dictionary, and several Dictionaries of Quotations and cheap compends of knowledge. Always *twirl* one of those revolving book-cases when you visit a scholar's library. That is the way to find out what books he doesn't want you to see, which of course are the ones you particularly wish to see.

"Some may call all this impertinent and inquisitive. What do you suppose is an interviewer's business? Did you ever see an oyster opened? Yes? Well, an interviewer's business is the same thing. His man is his oyster, which he, not with sword, but with pencil and note-book, must open. Mark how the oysterman's thin blade insinuates itself,—how gently at first, how strenuously when once fairly between the shells!

"And here, I said, you write your books,—those books which have carried your name to all parts of the world, and will convey it down to posterity! Is this the desk at which you write? And is this the pen you write with?

" 'It is the desk and the very pen,' he replied.

"He was pleased with my questions and my way of putting them. I took up the pen as reverentially as if it had been made of the feather which the angel I used to read about in Young's 'Night Thoughts' ought to have dropped, and didn't.

"Would you kindly write your autograph in my notebook, **with that pen?** I asked him. Yes, he would, with great pleasure.

"***So I got out my note-book***.

"It was a spick and span new one, bought on purpose for this interview. I admire your book-cases, said I. Can you tell me just how high they are?

" 'They are about eight feet, with the cornice.'

"I should like to have some like those, if I ever get rich enough, said I. Eight feet,—eight feet, **with the cornice.** I must put that down.

"***So I got out my pencil***.

"I sat there with my pencil and note-book in my hand, all ready, but not using them as yet.

"I have heard it said, I observed, that you began writing poems at a very early age. Is it taking too great a liberty to ask how early you began to write in verse?

"He was getting interested, as people are apt to be when they are themselves the subjects of conversation.

" 'Very early,—I hardly know how early. I can say truly, as Louise Colet said,

"Fe fis mes premiers vers sans savoir les écrire." '

"*I am not a very good French scholar, said I; perhaps you will be kind enough to translate that line for me.*

" '*Certainly. With pleasure.* I made my first verses without knowing how to write them. '

"How interesting! But I never heard of Louise Colet. Who was she?

"My man was pleased to give me a piece of literary information.

" 'Louise the lioness! Never heard of her? You have heard of Alphonse Karr?'

"Why,—yes,—more or less. To tell the truth, I am not very well up in French literature. What had he to do with your lioness?

" 'A good deal. He satirized her, and she waited at his door with a case-knife in her hand, intending to stick him with it. By and by he came down, smoking a cigarette, and was met by this woman flourishing her case-knife. He took it from her, after getting a cut in his dressing-gown, put it in his pocket, and went on with his cigarette. He keeps it with an inscription:—

Donné a Alphonse Karr Par Madame Louise Colet . . . Dans le dos.
Lively little female!'

"I couldn't help thinking that I shouldn't have cared to interview the lively little female. He was evidently tickled with the interest I appeared to take in the story he told me. That made him feel amiably disposed toward me.

"I began with very general questions, but by degrees I got at everything about his family history and the small events of his boyhood. Some of the points touched upon were delicate, but I put a good bold face on my most audacious questions, and so I wormed out a great deal that was new concerning my subject. He had been written about considerably, and the public wouldn't have been satisfied without some new facts; and these I meant to have, and I got. No matter about many of them now, but here are some questions and answers that may be thought worth reading or listening to:—

"How do you enjoy being what they call' a celebrity,' or a celebrated man?

" 'So far as one's vanity is concerned it is well enough. But self-love is a cup without any bottom, and you might pour the Great Lakes all through it, and never fill it up. It breeds an appetite for more of the same kind. It tends to make the celebrity a mere lump of egotism. It generates a craving for high-seasoned personalities which is in danger of becoming slavery, like that following the abuse of alcohol, or opium, or tobacco. Think of a man's having every day, by every post, letters that tell him he is this and that and the other, with epithets and endearments, one tenth part of which would have made him blush red hot before he began to be what you call a celebrity!'

"Are there not some special inconveniences connected with what is called celebrity?

" 'I should think so! Suppose you were obliged every day of your life to stand and shake hands, as the President of the United States has to after his inauguration: how do you think your hand would feel after a few months' practice of that exercise? Suppose you had given you thirty-five millions of money a year, in hundred-dollar coupons, on condition that you cut them all off yourself in the usual manner: how do you think you should like the look of a pair of scissors at the end of a year, in which you had worked ten hours a day every day but Sunday, cutting off a hundred coupons an hour, and found you had not finished your task, after all? You have addressed me as what you are pleased to call "a literary celebrity." I won't dispute with you as to whether or not I deserve that title. I will take it for granted I am what you call me, and give you some few hints of my experience.

" 'You know there was formed a while ago an Association of Authors for Self-Protection. It meant well, and it was hoped that something would come of it in the way of relieving that oppressed class, but I am sorry to say that it has not effected its purpose.'

"I suspected he had a hand in drawing up the Constitution and Laws of that Association. Yes, I said, an admirable Association it was, and as much needed as the one for the Prevention of Cruelty to Animals. I am sorry to hear that it has not proved effectual in putting a stop to the abuse of a deserving class of men. It ought to have done it; it was well conceived, and its public manifesto was a masterpiece. (I saw by his expression that he *was* its author.)

" 'I see I can trust you,' he said. ' I will unbosom myself freely of some of the grievances attaching to the position of the individual to whom you have applied the term "Literary Celebrity."

" 'He is supposed to be a millionaire, in virtue of the immense sales of his books, all the money from which, it is taken for granted, goes into his pocket. Consequently, all subscription papers are handed to him for his signature, and every needy stranger who has heard his name comes to him for assistance.

" 'He is expected to subscribe for all periodicals, and is goaded by receiving blank formulae, which, with their promises to pay, he is expected to fill up.

" 'He receives two or three books daily, with requests to read and give his opinion about each of them, which opinion, if it has a word which can be used as an advertisement, he will find quoted in all the newspapers.

" 'He receives thick masses of manuscript, prose and verse, which he is called upon to examine and pronounce on their merits; these manuscripts having almost invariably been rejected by the editors to whom they have been sent, and having as a rule no literary value whatever.

" 'He is expected to sign petitions, to contribute to journals, to write for fairs, to attend celebrations, to make after-dinner speeches, to send money for objects he does not believe in to places he never heard of.

" 'He is called on to keep up correspondences with unknown admirers, who begin by saying they have no claim upon his time, and then appropriate it by writing page after page, if of the male sex; and sheet after sheet, if of the other.

" 'If a poet, it is taken for granted that he can sit down at any moment and spin off any number of verses on any subject which may be suggested to him; such as congratulations to the writer's great-grandmother on her reaching her hundredth year, an elegy on an infant aged six weeks, an ode for the Fourth of July in a Western township not to be found in Lippincott's last edition, perhaps a valentine for some bucolic lover who believes that wooing in rhyme is the way to win the object of his affections.'

"Isn't it so?" I asked the Celebrity.

" 'I would bet on the prose lover. She will show the verses to him, and they will both have a good laugh over them.'

"I have only reported a small part of the conversation I had with the Literary Celebrity. He was so much taken up with his pleasing self-contemplation, while I made him air his opinions and feelings and spread his characteristics as his laundress spreads and airs his linen on the clothes-line, that I don't believe it ever occurred to him that he had been in the hands of an interviewer until he found himself exposed to the wind and sunshine in full dimensions in the columns of 'The People's Perennial and Household Inquisitor.' "

After the reading of this paper, much curiosity was shown as to who the person spoken of as the "Literary Celebrity" might be. Among the various suppositions the startling idea was suggested that he was neither more nor less than the unexplained personage known in the village as Maurice Kirkwood. Why should that be his real name? Why should not he be the Celebrity, who had taken this name and fled to this retreat to escape from the persecutions of kind friends, who were pricking him and stabbing him nigh to death with their daggers of sugar candy?

The Secretary of the Pansophian Society determined to question the Interviewer the next time she met him at the Library, which happened soon after the meeting when his paper was read.

"I do not know," she said, in the course of a conversation in which she had spoken warmly of his contribution to the literary entertainment of the Society, "that you mentioned the name of the Literary Celebrity whom you interviewed so successfully."

"I did not mention him, Miss Vincent," he answered, "nor do I think it worth while to name him. He might not care to have the whole story told of how he was handled so as to make him communicative. Besides, if I did, it would bring him a new batch of sympathetic letters regretting that he was bothered by those horrid correspondents, full of indignation at the bores who presumed to intrude upon him with their pages of trash, all the writers of which would expect answers to their letters of condolence."

The Secretary asked the Interviewer if he knew the young gentleman who called himself Maurice Kirkwood.

"What," he answered,—"the man that paddles a birch canoe, and rides all the wild horses of the neighborhood? No, I don't know him, but I have met him once or twice, out walking. A mighty shy fellow, they tell me. Do you know anything particular about him?"

"Not much. None of us do, but we should like to. The story is that he has a queer antipathy to something or to somebody, nobody knows what or whom."

"To newspaper correspondents, perhaps," said the Interviewer. "What made you ask me about him? You didn't think he was my 'Literary Celebrity,' did you?"

"I did not know. I thought he might be. Why don't you interview this mysterious personage? He would make a good sensation for your paper, I should think."

"Why, what is there to be interviewed in him? Is there any story of crime, or anything else to spice a column or so, or even a few paragraphs, with? If there is, I am willing to handle him professionally."

"I told you he has what they call an antipathy. I don't know how much wiser you are for that piece of information."

"An antipathy! Why, so have I an antipathy. I hate a spider, and as for a naked caterpillar,—I believe I should go into a fit if I had to touch one. I know I turn pale at the sight of some of those great green caterpillars that come down from the elm-trees in August and early autumn."

"Afraid of them?" asked the young lady.

"Afraid? What should I be afraid of? They can't bite or sting. I can't give any reason. All I know is that when I come across one of these creatures in my path I jump to one side, and cry out,—sometimes using very improper words. The feet is, they make me crazy for the moment."

"I understand what you mean," said Miss Vincent. "I used to have the same feeling about spiders, but I was ashamed of it, and kept a little menagerie of spiders until I had got over the feeling; that is, pretty much got over it, for I don't love the creatures very dearly, though I don't scream when I see one."

"What did you tell me, Miss Vincent, was this fellow s particular antipathy?"

"That is just the question. I told you that we don't know and we can't guess what it is. The people here are tired out with trying to discover some good reason for the young man's keeping out of the way of everybody, as he does. They say he is odd or crazy, and they don't seem to be able to tell which. It would make the old ladies of the village sleep a great deal sounder,—yes, and some of the young ladies, too,—if they could find out what this Mr. Kirkwood has got into his head, that he never comes near any of the people here."

"I think *I* can find out," said the Interviewer, whose professional ambition was beginning to be excited. "I never came across anybody yet that I couldn't get something out of. I am going to stay here a week or two, and before I go I will find out the secret, if there is any, of this Mr. Maurice Kirkwood."

We must leave the Interviewer to his contrivances until they present us with some kind of result, either in the shape of success or failure,

XI.
THE INTERVIEWER ATTACKS THE SPHINX.

WHEN Miss Euthymia Tower sent her oar off in flashing splinters, as she pulled her last stroke in the boat-race, she did not know what a strain she was putting upon it. She did know that she was doing her best, but how great the force of her best was she was not aware until she saw its effects. Unconsciousness belonged to her robust nature, in all its manifestations. She did not pride herself on her knowledge, nor reproach herself for her ignorance. In every way she formed a striking contrast to her friend, Miss Vincent Every word they spoke betrayed the difference between them: the sharp tones of Lurida's head-voice, penetrative, aggressive, sometimes irritating, revealed the corresponding traits of mental and moral character; the quiet, conversational contralto of Euthymia was the index of a nature restful and sympathetic.

The friendships of young girls prefigure the closer relations which will one day come in and dissolve their earlier intimacies. The dependence of two young friends may be mutual, but one will always lean more heavily than the other; the masculine and feminine elements will be as sure to assert themselves as if the friends were of different sexes.

On all common occasions Euthymia looked up to her friend as her superior. She fully appreciated all her varied gifts and knowledge, and deferred to her opinion in every-day matters, not exactly as an oracle, but as riser than herself or any of her other companions. It was a different thing, however, when the graver questions of life came up. Lurida was full of suggestions, plans, projects, which were too liable to run into whims before she knew where they were tending. She would lay out her ideas before Euthymia so fluently and eloquently that she could not help believing them herself, and feeling as if her friend must accept them with an enthusiasm like her own. Then Euthymia would take them up with her sweet, deliberate accents, and bring her calmer judgment to bear on them.

Lurida was in an excited condition, in the midst of all her new interests and occupations. She was constantly on the lookout for papers to be read at the meetings of *her* Society,—for she made it her own in great measure, by her zeal and enthusiasm,—and in the mean time she was reading in various books which Dr. Butts selected for her, all bearing on the profession to which, at least as a possibility, she was looking forward. Privately and in a very still way, she was occupying herself with the problem of the young stranger, the subject of some delusion, or disease, or obliquity of unknown nature, to which the vague name of antipathy had been attached. Euthymia kept an eye upon her, partly in the fear that over-excitement would produce some mental injury, and partly from anxiety lest she should compromise her womanly dignity in her desire to get at the truth of a very puzzling question.

"How do you like the books I see you reading?" said Euthymia to Lurida, one day, as they met at the Library. "Better than all the novels I ever read," she answered. "I have been reading about the nervous system, and it seems to me I have come nearer the springs of life than ever before in all my studies. I feel just as if I were a telegraph operator. I was sure that I had a battery in my head, for I know my brain works like one; but I did not know how many centres of energy there are, and how they are played upon by all sorts of influences, external and internal. Do you know, I believe I could solve the riddle of the 'Arrowhead Village Sphinx,' as the paper called him, if he would only stay here long enough?"

"What paper has had anything about it, Lurida? I have not seen or heard of its being mentioned in any of the papers."

"You know that rather queer-looking young man who has been about here for some time,—the same one who gave the account of his interview with a celebrated author? Well, he has handed me a copy of a paper in which he writes, 'The People's Perennial and Household Inquisitor.' He talks about this village in a very free and easy way. He says there is a Sphinx here, who has mystified us all."

"And you have been chatting with that fellow! Don't you know that he'll have you and all of us in his paper? Don't you know that nothing is safe where one of those fellows gets in with his note-book and pencil? Oh, Lurida, Lurida, do be careful! What with this mysterious young man and this very questionable newspaper-paragraph writer, you will be talked about, if you don't mind, before you know it. You had better let the riddle of the Sphinx alone. If you must deal with such dangerous people, the safest way is to set one of them to find out the other.—I wonder if we can't get this new man to interview the visitor you have so much curiosity about. That might be managed easily enough without your having anything to do with it Let me alone, and I will arrange it. But mind, now, you must not meddle; if you do, you will spoil everything, and get your name in the 'Household Inquisitor,' in a way you won't like."

"Don't be frightened about me, Euthymia. I don't mean to give him a chance to work me into his paper, if I can help it. But if you can get him to try his skill upon this interesting personage and his antipathy, so much the better. I am very curious about it, and therefore about him. I want to know what has produced this strange state of feeling in a young man who ought to have all the common instincts of a social being. I believe there are unexplained facts in the region of sympathies and antipathies which will repay study with a deeper insight into the mysteries of life than we have dreamed of hitherto. I often wonder whether there are not heart-waves and soul-waves as well as brain-waves,' which some have already recognized."

Euthymia wondered, as well she might, to hear this young woman talking the language of science like an adept. The truth is, Lurida was one of those persons who never are young, and who, by way of compensation, will never be old. They are found in both sexes. Two well-known graduates of one of our great universities are living examples of this precocious but enduring intellectual development. If the readers of this narrative cannot pick them out, they need not expect the writer of it to help them. If they guess rightly who they are, they will recognize the fact that just such exceptional individuals as the young woman we are dealing with are met with from time to time in families where intelligence has been cumulative for two or three generations.

Euthymia was very willing that the questioning and questionable visitor should learn all that was known in the village about the nebulous individual whose misty environment all the eyes in the village were trying to penetrate, but that he should learn it from some other informant than Lurida.

The next morning, as the Interviewer took his seat on a bench outside his door, to smoke his after-breakfast cigar, a bright-looking and handsome youth, whose features recalled those of Euthymia so strikingly that one might feel pretty sure he was her brother, took a seat by his side. Presently the two were engaged in conversation. The Interviewer asked all sorts of questions about everybody in the village. When he came to inquire about Maurice, the youth showed a remarkable interest regarding him. The greatest curiosity, he said, existed with reference to this personage. Everybody was trying to find out what his story was,—for a story, and a strange one, he must surely have,—and nobody had succeeded.

The Interviewer began to be unusually attentive. The young man told him the various antipathy stories, about the evil-eye hypothesis, about his horse-taming exploits, his rescuing the student whose boat was overturned, and every occurrence he could recall which would help out the effect of his narrative.

The Interviewer was becoming excited. "Can't find out anything about him, you said, didn't you? How do you know there's anything to find? Do you want to know what I think he is? I'll tell you. I think he is an actor,—a fellow from one of the city theatres. Those fellows go off in their summer vacation, and like to puzzle the country folks. They are the very same chaps, like as not, the visitors have seen in plays at the city theatres; but of course they don't know 'em in plain clothes. Kings and Emperors look pretty shabby off the stage sometimes, I can tell you."

The young man followed the Interviewer's lead. "I shouldn't wonder if you were right," he said. "I remember seeing a young fellow in Romeo that looked a good deal like this one. But I never met the Sphinx, as they call him, face to face. He is as shy as a woodchuck. I believe there are people here that would give a hundred dollars to find out who he is, and where he came from, and what he is here for, and why he doesn't act like other folks. I wonder why some of those newspaper men don't come up here and get hold of this story. It would be just the thing for a sensational writer."

To all this the Interviewer listened with true professional interest. Always on the lookout for something to make up a paragraph or a column about; driven oftentimes to the stalest of repetitions,—to the biggest pumpkin story, the tall cornstalk, the fat ox, the live frog from the human stomach story, the third set of teeth and reading without spectacles at ninety story, and the rest of the marvellous commonplaces which are kept in type with *e o y* or *e* 6 *m* (every other year or every six months) at the foot: always in want of a fresh incident, a new story, an undescribed character, an unexplained mystery, it is no wonder that the Interviewer fastened eagerly upon this most tempting subject for an inventive and emotional correspondent.

He had seen Paolo several times, and knew that he was Maurice's confidential servant, but had never spoken to him. So he said to himself that he must make Paolo's acquaintance, to begin with. In the summer season many kinds of small traffic were always carried on in Arrowhead Village. Among the rest, the sellers of fruits—oranges, bananas, and others, according to the seasons—did an active business. The Interviewer watched one of these fruitsellers, and saw that his hand-cart stopped opposite the house where, as he knew, Maurice Kirkwood was living. Presently Paolo came out of the door, and began examining the contents of the hand-cart The Interviewer saw his opportunity. Here was an introduction to the man, and the man must introduce him to the master.

He knew very well how to ingratiate himself with the man,—there was no difficulty about that. He had learned his name, and that he was an Italian whom Maurice had brought to this country with him.

"Good morning, Mr. Paul," he said. * How do you like the look of these oranges?"

"They pretty fair," said Paolo: "no so good as them las' week; no sweet as them was."

"Why, how do you know without tasting them?" said the Interviewer.

"I know by his look,—I know by his smell,—he no good yaller,—he no smell ripe,—I know orange ever since my head no bigger than he is," and Paolo laughed at his own comparison.

The Interviewer laughed louder than Paolo. "Good!" said he,—"first-rate! Of course you know all about 'em. Why can't you pick me out a couple of what you think are the best of 'em? I shall be greatly obliged to you. I have a sick friend, and I want to get two nice sweet ones for him."

Paolo was pleased. His skill and judgment were recognized. He felt grateful to the stranger, who had given him an opportunity of conferring a favor. He selected two, after careful examination and grave deliberation. The Interviewer had sense and tact enough not to offer him an orange, and so shift the balance of obligation.

"How is Mr. Kirkwood, to-day?" he asked.

"Il Signor? He very well. He always well. Why you ask? Anybody tell you he sick?"

"No, nobody said he was sick. I haven't seen him going about for a day or two, and I thought he might have something the matter with him. Is he in the house now?"

"No: he off riding. He take long, long rides,—sometime gone all day. Sometime he go on lake,—paddle, paddle in the morning, very, very early,—in night when the moon shine; sometime stay in house, and read, and study, and write,—he great scholar, Misser Kirkwood."

"A good many books, hasn't he?"

"He got whole shelfs full of books. Great books, little books, old books, new books, all sorts of books. He great scholar, I tell you."

"Hasn't he some curiosities,—old figures, old jewelry, old coins, or things of that sort?"

Paolo looked at the young man cautiously, almost suspiciously. "He don't keep no jewels nor no money in his chamber. He got some old things,—old jugs, old brass figgers, old money, such as they used to have in old times: she don't pass now." Paolo's genders were apt to be somewhat indiscriminately distributed.

A lucky thought struck the Interviewer. "I wonder if he would examine some old coins of mine?" said he, in a modestly tentative manner.

"I think he like to see anything curious. When he come home I ask him. Who will I tell him wants to ask him about old coin?"

"Tell him a gentleman visiting Arrowhead Village would like to call and show him some old pieces of money, said to be Roman ones."

The Interviewer had just remembered that he had two or three old battered bits of copper which he had picked up at a tollman's, where they had been passed off for cents. He had bought them as curiosities. One had the name of Gallienus upon it, tolerably distinct,—a common little Roman penny; but it would serve his purpose of asking a question, as would two or three others with less legible legends. Paolo told him that if he came the next morning he would stand a fair chance of seeing Mr. Kirkwood. At any rate, he would speak to his master.

The Interviewer presented himself the next morning, after finishing his breakfast and his cigar, feeling reasonably sure of finding Mr. Kirkwood at home, as he proved to be. He had told Paolo to show the stranger up to his library,—or study, as he modestly called it

It was a pleasant room enough, with a lookout on the lake in one direction, and the wooded hill in another. The tenant had fitted it up in scholarly fashion. The books Paolo spoke of were conspicuous, many of them, by their white vellum binding and tasteful gilding, showing that probably they had been bound in Rome, or some other Italian city. With these were older volumes in their dark original leather, and recent ones in cloth or paper. As the Interviewer ran his eye over them, he found that he could make very little out of what their backs taught him. Some of the paper-covered books, some of the cloth-covered ones, had names which he knew; but those on the backs of many of the others were strange to his eyes. The classics of Greek and Latin and Italian literature were there; and he saw enough to feel convinced that he had better not attempt to display his erudition in the company of this young scholar.

The first thing the Interviewer had to do was to account for his visiting a person who had not asked to make his acquaintance, and who was living as a recluse. He took out his battered coppers, and showed them to Maurice.

"I understood that you were very skilful in antiquities, and had a good many yourself. So I took the liberty of calling upon you, hoping that you could tell me something about some ancient coins I have had for a good while." So saying, he pointed to the copper with the name of Gallienus.

"Is this very rare and valuable? I have heard that great prices have been paid for some of these ancient coins,—ever so many guineas, sometimes. I suppose this is as much as a thousand years old."

"More than a thousand years old," said Maurice.

"And worth a great deal of money?" asked the Interviewer.

"No, not a great deal of money," answered Maurice.

"How much should you say?" said the Interviewer.

Maurice smiled. "A little more than the value of its weight in copper,—I am afraid not much more. There are a good many of these coins of Gallienus knocking about. The peddlers and the shopkeepers take such pieces occasionally, and sell them, sometimes for five or ten cents, to young collectors. No, it is not very precious in money value, but as a relic any piece of money that was passed from hand to hand a thousand or fifteen hundred years ago is interesting. The value of such relics is a good deal a matter of imagination."

"And what do you say to these others?" asked the Interviewer. Poor old worn-out things they were, with a letter or two only, and some faint trace of a figure on one or two of them.

"Very interesting, always, if they carry your imagination back to the times when you may suppose they were current. Perhaps Horace tossed one of them to a beggar. Perhaps one of these was the coin that was brought when One said to those about Him, 'Bring me a penny, that I may see it.' But the market price is a different matter. That depends on the beauty and preservation, and above all the rarity of the specimen. Here is a coin, now,"—he opened a small cabinet; and took one from it. "Here is a Syracusan decadrachm with the head of Persephone, which is at once rare, well preserved, and beautiful. I am afraid to tell what I paid for it."

The Interviewer was not an expert in numismatics. He cared very little more for an old coin than he did for an old button, but he had thought his purchase at the tollman's might prove a good speculation. No matter about the battered old pieces: he had found out, at any rate, that Maurice must have money, and could be extravagant, or what he himself considered so; also that he was familiar with ancient coins.

That would do for a beginning.

"May I ask where you picked up the coin you are showing me?" he said.

"That is a question which provokes a negative answer. One does not 'pick up' first-class coins or paintings, very often, in these times. I bought this of a great dealer in Rome."

"Lived in Rome once?" said the Interviewer.

"For some years. Perhaps you have been there yourself?"

The Interviewer said he had never been there yet, but he hoped he should go there one of these years. "I suppose you studied art and antiquities while you were there?" he continued.

"Everybody who goes to Rome must learn something of art and antiquities. Before you go there I advise you to review Roman history and the classic authors. You had better make a study of ancient and modern art, and not have everything to learn while you are going about among ruins, and churches, and galleries. You know your Horace and Virgil well, I take it for granted?"

The Interviewer hesitated. The names sounded as if he had heard them. "Not so well as I mean to before going to Rome," he answered. "May I ask how long you lived in Rome?"

"Long enough to know something of what is to be seen in it. No one should go there without careful preparation beforehand. You are familiar with Vasari, of course?"

The Interviewer felt a slight moisture on his forehead. He took out his hand-kerchief. "It is a warm day," he said. "I have not had time to read all the works I mean to. I have had too much writing to do, myself, to find all the time for reading and study I could have wished."

"In what literary occupation have you been engaged, if you will pardon my inquiry?" said Maurice.

"I am connected with the press. I understood that you were a man of letters, and I hoped I might have the privilege of hearing from your own lips some account of your literary experiences."

"Perhaps that might be interesting, but I think I shall reserve it for my auto-biography. You said you were connected with the press. Do I understand that you are an author?"

By this time the Interviewer had come to the conclusion that it was a ***very*** warm day. He did not seem to be getting hold of his pitcher by the right handle, somehow. But he could not help answering Maurice's very simple question.

"If writing for a newspaper gives one a right to be called an author, I may call myself one. I write for the "People's Perennial and Household Inquisitor.' "

"Are you the literary critic of that well-known journal, or do you manage the political column?"

"I am a correspondent from different places and on various matters of interest."

"Places you have been to, and people you have known?"

"Well, yes,—generally, that is. Sometimes I have to compile my articles."

"Did you write the letter from Rome, published a few weeks ago?"

The Interviewer was in what he would call a tight place. However, he had found that his man was too much for him, and saw that the best thing he could do was to submit to be interviewed himself. He thought that he should be able to pick up something or other which he could work into his report of his visit.

"Well, I—prepared that article for our columns. You know one does not have to see everything he describes. You found it accurate, I hope, in its descriptions?"

"Yes, Murray is generally accurate. Sometimes he makes mistakes, but I can't say how far you have copied them. You got the Ponte Molle—the old Milvian bridge—a good deal too far down the stream, if I remember. I happened to notice that, but I did not read the article carefully. May I ask whether you propose to do me the honor of reporting this visit and the conversation we have had, for the columns of the newspaper with which you are connected?"

The Interviewer thought he saw an opening. "If you have no objections," he said, "I should like very much to ask a few questions." He was recovering his professional audacity.

"You can ask as many questions as you consider proper and discreet,—after you have answered one of two of mine: Who commissioned you to submit me to examination?"

"The curiosity of the public wishes to be gratified, and I am the humble agent of its investigations."

"What has the public to do with my private affairs?"

"I suppose it is a question of majority and minority. That settles everything in this country. You are a minority of one opposed to a large number of curious people that form a majority against you. That is the way I've heard the chief put it."

Maurice could not help smiling at the quiet assumption of the American citizen. The Interviewer smiled, too, and thought he had his man, sure, at last Maurice calmly answered, "There is nothing left for minorities, then, but the right of rebellion. I don't care about being made the subject of an article for your paper. I am here for my pleasure, minding my own business, and content with that occupation. I rebel against your system of forced publicity. Whenever I am ready I shall tell the public all it has any right to know about me. In the meantime I shall request to be spared reading my biography while I am living. I wish you a good-morning."

The Interviewer had not taken out his note-book and pencil. In his next communication from Arrowhead Village he contented himself with a brief mention of the distinguished and accomplished gentleman now visiting the place, whose library and cabinet of coins he had had the privilege of examining, and whose courtesy was equalled only by the modesty that shunned the public notoriety which the organs of popular intelligence would otherwise confer upon him.

The Interviewer had attempted the riddle of the Sphinx, and had failed to get the first hint of its solution.

The many tongues of the village and its visitors could not remain idle. The whole subject of antipathies had been talked over, and the various cases recorded had become more or less familiar to the conversational circles which met every evening in the different centres of social life. The prevalent hypothesis for the moment was that Maurice had a congenital aversion to some color, the effects of which upon him were so painful or disagreeable that he habitually avoided exposure to it. It was known, and it has already been mentioned, that such cases were on record. There had been a great deal of discussion, of late, with reference to a fact long known to a few individuals, but only recently made a matter of careful scientific observation and brought to the notice of the public. This was the now well-known phenomenon of color-blindness. It did not seem very strange that if one person in every score or two could not tell red from green there might be other curious individual peculiarities relating to color. A case has already been referred to where the subject of observation fainted at the sight of any red object. What if this were the trouble with Maurice Kirkwood? It will be seen at once how such a congenital antipathy would tend to isolate the person who was its unfortunate victim. It was an hypothesis not difficult to test, but it was a rather delicate business to be experimenting on an inoffensive stranger. Miss Vincent was thinking it over, but said nothing, even to Euthymia, of any projects she might entertain.

XII.
MISS VINCENT AS A MEDICAL STUDENT.

THE young lady whom we have known as The Terror, as Lurida, as Miss Vincent, Secretary of the Pansophian Society, had been reading various works selected for her by Dr. Butts,—works chiefly relating to the nervous system and its different affections. She thought it was about time to talk over the general subject of the medical profession with her new teacher,—if such a self-directing person as Lurida could be said to recognize anybody as teacher.

She began at the beginning. "What is the first book you would put in a student's hands, doctor?" she said to him one day. They were in his study, and Lurida had just brought back a thick volume on Insanity, one of Bucknill and Tuke's, which she had devoured as if it had been a pamphlet.

"Not that book, certainly," he said. "I am afraid it will put all sorts of notions into your head. Who or what set you to reading that, I should like to know?"

"I found it on one of your shelves, and as I thought I might perhaps be crazy some time or other, I felt as if I should like to know what kind of a condition insanity is. I don't believe they were ever very bright, those insane people, most of them. I hope I am not stupid enough ever to lose my wits."

"There is no telling, my dear, what may happen if you overwork that busy brain of yours. But didn't it make you nervous, reading about so many people possessed with such strange notions?"

"Nervous? Not a bit. I couldn't help thinking, though, how many people I had known that had a little touch of craziness about them. Take that poor woman that says she is Her Majesty's Person,—not Her Majesty, but Her Majesty's Person,—a very important distinction, according to her: how she does remind me of more than one girl I have known ! She would let her skirts down so as to make a kind of train, and pile things on her head like a sort of crown, fold her arms and throw her head back, and feel as grand as a queen. I have seen more than one girl act very much in that way. Are not most of us a little crazy, doctor,—just a little? I think so. It seems to me I never saw but one girl who was free from every hint of craziness."

"And who was that, pray?"

"Why, Euthymia,—nobody else, of course. She never loses her head,—I don't believe she would in an earthquake. Whenever we were at work with our microscopes at the Institute I always told her that her mind was the only achromatic one I ever looked into,—I didn't say looked through.—But I didn't come to talk about that I read in one of your books that when Sydenham was asked by a student what books he should read, the great physician said,' Read "Don Quixote." ' I want you to explain that to me; and then I want you to tell me what is the first book, according to your idea, that a student ought to read."

"What do you say to my taking your question as the subject of a paper to be read before the Society? I think there may be other young ladies at the meeting, besides yourself, who are thinking of pursuing the study of medicine. At any rate, there are a good many who are interested in the subject; in fact, most people listen readily to anything doctors tell them about their calling."

"I wish you would, doctor. I want Euthymia to hear it, and I don't doubt there will be others who will be glad to hear everything you have to say about it. But oh, doctor, if you could only persuade Euthymia to become a physician! What a doctor she would make! So strong, so calm, so full of wisdom! I believe she could take the wheel of a steamboat in a storm, or the hose of a fire-engine in a conflagration, and handle it as well as the captain of the boat or of the fire-company."

"Have you ever talked with her about studying medicine?"

"Indeed I have. Oh, if she would only begin with me! What good times we would have studying together!"

"I don't doubt it. Medicine is a very pleasant study. But how do you think practice would be? How would you like being called up to ride ten miles in a midnight snow-storm, just when one of your raging headaches was racking you?"

"Oh, but we could go into partnership, and Euthymia isn't afraid of storms or anything else. If she would only study medicine with me!"

"Well, what does she say to it?"

"She doesn't like the thought of it She doesn't believe in women doctors. She thinks that now and then a woman may be fitted for it by nature, but she doesn't think there are many who are. She gives me a good many reasons against their practising medicine,—you know what most of them are, doctor,—and ends by saying that the same woman who would be a poor sort of doctor would make a first-rate nurse; and that, she thinks, is a woman's business, if her instinct carries her to the hospital or sick-chamber. I can't argue her ideas out of her."

"Neither can I argue you out of your feeling about the matter; but I am disposed to agree with your friend, that you will often spoil a good nurse to make a poor doctor. Doctors and side-saddles don't seem to me to go together. Riding habits would be awkward things for practitioners. But come, we won't have a controversy just now. I am for giving women every chance for a good education, and if they think medicine is one of their proper callings let them try it. I think they will find that they had better at least limit themselves to certain specialities, and always have an expert of the other sex to fall back upon. The trouble is that they are so impressible and imaginative that they are at the mercy of all sorts of fancy systems. You have only to see what kinds of instruction they very commonly flock to in order to guess whether they would be likely to prove sensible practitioners. Charlatanism always hobbles on two crutches, the tattle of women, and the certificates of clergymen, and I am afraid that half the women doctors will be too much under both those influences."

Lurida believed in Dr. Butts, who, to use the common language of the village, had "carried her through" a fever, brought on by over-excitement and exhausting study. She took no offence at his reference to nursery gossip, which she had learned to hold cheap. Nobody so despises the weaknesses of women as the champion of woman's rights. She accepted the doctor's concession of a fair field and open trial of the fitness of her sex for medical practice, and did not trouble herself about his suggested limitations. As to the imaginative tendencies of women, she knew too well the truth of the doctor's remark relating to them to wish to contradict it.

"Be sure you let me have your paper in season for the next meeting, doctor," she said; and in due season it came, and was of course approved for reading.

XIII.
DR. BUTTS READS A PAPER.

"NEXT to the interest we take in all that relates to our immortal souls is that which we feel for our mortal bodies. I am afraid my very first statement may be open to criticism. The care of the body is the first thought with a great many,—in fact, with the larger part of the world. They send for the physician first, and not until he gives them up do they commonly call in the clergyman. Even the minister himself is not so very different from other people. We must not blame him if he is not always impatient to exchange a world of multiplied interests and ever-changing sources of excitement for that which tradition has delivered to us as one eminently deficient in the stimulus of variety. Besides, these bodily frames, even when worn and disfigured by long years of service, hang about our consciousness like old garments. They are used to us, and we are used to them. And all the accidents of our lives,—the house we dwell in, the living people round us, the landscape we look over, all, up to the sky that covers us like a bell glass,—all these are but looser outside garments which we have worn until they seem a part of us, and we do not like the thought of changing them for a new suit which we have never yet tried on. How well I remember that dear ancient lady, who lived well into the last decade of her century, as she repeated the verse which, if I had but one to choose, I would select from that string of pearls, Gray's 'Elegy'!—

For who to dumb forgetfulness a prey This pleasing, anxious being e'er resigned, Left the warm precincts of the cheerful day, Nor cast one longing, lingering look behind?'

Plotinus was ashamed of his body, we are told. Better so, it may be, than to live solely for it, as so many do. But it may be well doubted if there is any disciple of Plotinus in this Society. On the contrary, there are many who think a great deal of their bodies, many who have come here to regain the health they have lost in the wear and tear of city life, and very few who have not at some time or other of their lives had occasion to call in the services of a physician.

"There is, therefore, no impropriety in my offering to the members some remarks upon the peculiar difficulties which beset the medical practitioner in the discharge of his laborious and important duties.

"A young friend of mine, who has taken an interest in medical studies, happened to meet with a very familiar story about one of the greatest and most celebrated of all English physicians, Thomas Sydenham. The story is that, when a student asked him what books he should read, the great doctor told him to read 'Don Quixote.'

"This piece of advice has been used to throw contempt upon the study of books, and furnishes a convenient shield for ignorant pretenders. But Sydenham left many writings in which he has recorded his medical experience, and he surely would not have published them if he had not thought they would be better reading for the medical student than the story of Cervantes. His own works are esteemed to this day, and he certainly could not have supposed that they contained all the wisdom of all the past. No remedy is good, it was said of old, unless applied at the right time in the right way So we may say of all anecdotes, like this which I have told you about Sydenham and the young man. It is very likely that he carried him to the bedside of some patients, and talked to him about the cases he showed him, instead of putting a Latin volume in his hand. I would as soon begin in that way as any other, with a student who had already mastered the preliminary branches,—who knew enough about the structure and functions of the body in health.

"But if you ask me what reading I would commend to the medical student of a philosophical habit of mind, you may be surprised to hear me say it would be certain passages in 'Rasselas.' They are the ones where the astronomer gives an account to Imlac of his management of the elements, the control of which, as he had persuaded himself, had been committed to him. Let me read you a few sentences from this story, which is commonly bound up with the 'Vicar of Wakefield,' like a woollen lining to a silken mantle, but is full of stately wisdom in processions of paragraphs which sound as if they ought to have a grammatical drum-major to march before their tramping platoons.

"The astronomer has taken Imlac into his confidence, and reveals to him the secret of his wonderful powers:—

" 'Hear, Imlac, what thou wilt not without difficulty credit. I have possessed for five years the regulation of the weather and the distribution of the seasons: the sun has listened to my dictates, and passed from tropic to tropic by my direction; the clouds, at my call, have poured their waters, and the Nile has overflowed at my command; I have restrained the rage of the dog-star, and mitigated the fervors of the crab. The winds alone, of all the elemental powers, have hitherto eluded my authority, and multitudes have perished by equinoctial tempests, which I found myself unable to prohibit or restrain.'

"The reader naturally wishes to know how the astronomer, a sincere, devoted, and most benevolent man, for forty years a student of the heavens, came to the strange belief that he possessed these miraculous powers. This is his account:—

" 'One day, as I was looking on the fields withering with heat, I felt in my mind a sudden wish that I could send rain on the southern mountains, and raise the Nile to an inundation. In the hurry of my imagination I commanded rain to fall, and by comparing the time of my command with that of the inundation I found that the clouds had listened to my lips.'

" 'Might not some other cause,' said I, ' produce this concurrence? The Nile does not always rise on the same day.'

" 'Do not believe,' said he, with impatience, 'that such objections could escape me: I reasoned long against my own conviction, and labored against truth with the utmost obstinacy. I sometimes suspected myself of madness, and should not have dared to impart this secret but to a man like you, capable of distinguishing the wonderful from the impossible and the incredible from the false.'

"The good old astronomer gives his parting directions to Imlac, whom he has adopted as his successor in the government of the elements and the seasons, in these impressive words:—

" 'Do not, in the administration of the year, indulge thy pride by innovation; do not please thyself with thinking that thou canst make thyself renowned to all future ages by disordering the seasons. The memory of mischief is no desirable fame. Much less will it become thee to let kindness or interest prevail. Never rob other countries of rain to pour it on thine own. For us the Nile is sufficient.'

"Do you wonder, my friends, why I have chosen these passages, in which the delusions of an insane astronomer are related with all the pomp of the Johnsonian vocabulary, as the first lesson for the young person about to enter on the study of the science and art of healing? Listen to me while I show you the parallel of the story of the astronomer in the history of medicine.

"This history is luminous with intelligence, radiant with benevolence, but all its wisdom and all its virtue have had to struggle with the ever-rising mists of delusion. The agencies which waste and destroy the race of mankind are vast and resistless as the elemental forces of nature; nay, they are themselves elemental forces. They may be to some extent avoided, to some extent diverted from their aim, to some extent resisted. So may the changes of the seasons, from cold that freezes to heats that strike with sudden death, be guarded against. So may the tides be in some small measure restrained in their inroads. So may the storms be breasted by walls they cannot shake from their foundations. But the seasons and the tides and the tempests work their will on the great scale upon whatever stands in their way; they feed or starve the tillers of the soil; they spare or drown the dwellers by the shore; they waft the seaman to his harbor or bury him in the angry billows.

"The art of the physician can do much to remove its subjects from deadly and dangerous influences, and something to control or arrest the effects of these influences. But look at the records of the life-insurance offices, and see how uniform is the action of nature's destroying agencies. Look at the annual reports of the deaths in any of our great cities, and see how their regularity approaches the uniformity of the tides, and their variations keep pace with those of the seasons. The inundations of the Nile are not more certainly to be predicted than the vast wave of infantile disease which flows in upon all our great cities with the growing heats of July,— than the fevers and dysenteries which visit our rural districts in the months of the falling leaf.

"The physician watches these changes as the astronomer watched the rise of the great river. He longs to rescue individuals, to protect communities from the inroads of these destroying agencies. He uses all the means which experience has approved, tries every rational method which ingenuity can suggest. Some fortunate recovery leads him to believe he has hit upon a preventive or a cure for a malady which had resisted all known remedies. His rescued patient sounds his praises, and a wide circle of his patient's friends joins in a chorus of eulogies. Self-love applauds him for his sagacity. Self-interest congratulates him on his having found the road to fortune; the sense of having proved a benefactor of his race smooths the pillow on which he lays his head to dream of the brilliant future opening before him. If a single coincidence may lead a person of sanguine disposition to believe that he has mastered a disease which had baffled all who were before his time, and on which his contemporaries looked in hopeless impotence, what must be the effect of a series of such coincidences even on a mind of calmer temper! Such series of coincidences will happen, and they may well deceive the very elect Think of Dr. Rush,—you know what a famous man he was, the very head and front of American medical science in his day,—and remember how he spoke about yellow fever, which he thought he had mastered!

"Thus the physician is entangled in the meshes of a wide conspiracy, in, which he and his patient and their friends, and Nature herself, are involved. What wonder that the history of Medicine should be to so great an extent a record of self-delusion!

"If this seems a dangerous concession to the enemies of the true science and art of healing, I will remind you that it is all implied in the first aphorism of Hippocrates, the Father of Medicine. Do not draw a wrong inference from the frank statement of the difficulties which beset the medical practitioner. Think rather, if truth is so hard of attainment, how precious are the results which the consent of the wisest and most experienced among the healers of men agrees in accepting. Think what folly it is to cast them aside in favor of palpable impositions stolen from the records of forgotten charlatanism, or of fantastic speculations spun from the squinting brains of theorists as wild as the Egyptian astronomer.

"Begin your medical studies, then, by reading the fortieth and the following four chapters of 'Rasselas.' Your first lesson will teach you modesty and caution in the pursuit of the most deceptive of all practical branches of knowledge. Faith will come later, when you learn how much medical science and art have actually achieved for the relief of mankind, and how great are the promises it holds out of still larger triumphs over the enemies of human health and happiness."

After the reading of this paper there was a lively discussion, which we have no room to report here, and the Society adjourned.

XIV.
MISS VINCENT'S STARTLING DISCOVERY.

THE sober-minded, sensible, well-instructed Dr. Butts was not a little exercised in mind by the demands made upon his knowledge by his young friend, and for the time being his pupil, Miss Lurida Vincent.

"I don't wonder they called her The Terror," he said to himself. "She is enough to frighten anybody. She has taken down old books from my shelves that I had almost forgotten the backs of, and as to the medical journals, I believe the girl could index them from memory. She is in pursuit of some special point of knowledge, I feel sure, and I cannot doubt what direction she is working in, but her wonderful way of dealing with books amazes me."

What marvels those "first scholars" in the classes of our great universities and colleges are, to be sure! They are not, as a rule, the most distinguished of their class in the long struggle of life. The chances are that "the field" will beat "the favorite" over the long racecourse. Others will develop a longer stride and more staying power. But what fine gifts those "first scholars" have received from nature! How dull we writers, famous or obscure, are in the acquisition of knowledge as compared with them! To lead their classmates they must have quick apprehension, fine memories, thorough control of their mental faculties, strong will power of concentration, facility of expression,—a wonderful equipment of mental faculties. I always want to take my hat off to the first scholar of his year.

Dr. Butts felt somewhat in the same way as he contemplated The Terror. She surprised him so often with her knowledge that he was ready to receive her without astonishment when she burst in upon him one day with a cry of triumph, *"Eureka! Eureka!"*

"And what have you found, my dear?" said the doctor.

Lurida was flushed and panting with the excitement of her new discovery.

"I do believe that I have found the secret of our' strange visitor's dread of all human intercourse!"

The seasoned practitioner was not easily thrown off his balance.

"Wait a minute and get your breath," said the doctor.

"Are you not a little overstating his peculiarity? It is not quite so bad as that. He keeps a man to serve him, he was civil with the people at the Old Tavern, he was affable enough, I understand, with the young fellow he pulled out of the water, or rescued somehow,—I don't believe he avoids the whole human race. He does not look as if he hated them, so far as I have remarked his expression. I passed a few words with him when his man was ailing, and found him polite enough. No, I don't believe it is much more than an extreme case of shyness, connected, perhaps, with some congenital or other personal repugnance to which has been given the name of an antipathy."

Lurida could hardly keep still while the doctor was speaking. When he finished, she began the account of her discovery:—

"I do certainly believe I have found an account of his case in an Italian medical journal of about fourteen years ago. I met with a reference which led me to look over a file of the **Giornale degli Ospitali** lying among the old pamphlets in the medical section of the Library. I have made a translation of it, which you must read and then tell me if you do not agree with me in my conclusion."

"Tell me what your conclusion is, and I will read your paper and see for myself whether I think the evidence justifies the conviction you seem to have reached."

Lurida's large eyes showed their whole rounds like the two halves of a map of the world, as she said,—

"*I believe that Maurice Kirkwood is suffering from the effects of the bite of a* TARANTULA!"

The doctor drew a long breath. He remembered in a vague sort of way the stories which used to be told of the terrible Apulian spider, but he had consigned them to the limbo of medical fable where so many fictions have clothed themselves with a local habitation and a name. He looked into the round eyes and wide pupils a little anxiously, as if he feared that she was in a state of undue excitement. But, true to his professional training, he waited for another symptom, if indeed her mind was in any measure off its balance.

"I know what you are thinking," Lurida said, "but it is not so. 'I am not mad, most noble Festus.' You shall see the evidence and judge for yourself. Read the whole case,—you can read my hand almost as if it were print,—and tell me if you do not agree with me that this young man is in all probability the same person as the boy described in the Italian journal. One thing you might say is against the supposition. The young patient is spoken of as Signorino M . . . Ch. . . . But you must remember that *ch* is pronounced hard in Italian, like *k,* which letter is wanting in the Italian alphabet; and it is natural enough that the initial of the second name should have got changed in the record to its Italian equivalent."

Before inviting the reader to follow the details of this extraordinary case as found in a medical journal, the narrator wishes to be indulged in a few words of explanation, in order that he may not have to apologize for allowing the introduction of a subject which may be thought to belong to the professional student rather than to the readers of this record. There is a great deal in medical books which it is very unbecoming to bring before the general public,—a great deal to repel, to disgust, to alarm, to excite unwholesome curiosity. It is not the men whose duties have made them familiar with this class of subjects who are most likely to offend by scenes and descriptions which belong to the physician's private library, and not to the shelves devoted to polite literature. Goldsmith and even Smollett, both having studied and practised medicine, could not by any possibility have outraged all the natural feelings of delicacy and decency as Swift and Zola have outraged them. But without handling doubtful subjects, there are many curious medical experiences which have interest for every one as extreme illustrations of ordinary conditions with which all are acquainted. No one can study the now familiar history of clairvoyance profitably who has not learned something of the vagaries of hysteria. No one can read understandingly the life of Cowper and that of Carlyle without having some idea of the influence of hypochondriasis and of dyspepsia upon the disposition and intellect of the subjects of these maladies. I need not apologize, therefore, for giving publicity to that part of this narrative which deals with one of the most singular maladies to be found in the records of bodily and mental infirmities.

The following is the account of the case as translated by Miss Vincent. For obvious reasons the whole name was not given in the original paper, and for similar reasons the date of the event and the birth-place of the patient are not precisely indicated here.

[Giornale degli Ospitali, Luglio 21, 18—.]

REMARKABLE CASE OF TARANTISM.

"The great interest attaching to the very singular and exceptional instance of this rare affection induces us to give a full account of the extraordinary example of its occurrence in a patient who was the subject of a recent medical consultation in this city.

"Signorino M . . . Ch . . . is the only son of a gentleman travelling in Italy at this time. He is eleven years of age, of sanguine-nervous temperament, light hair, blue eyes, intelligent countenance, well grown, but rather slight in form, to all appearance in good health, but subject to certain peculiar and anomalous nervous symptoms, of which his father gives this history.

"Nine years ago, the father informs us, he was travelling in Italy with his wife, this child, and a nurse. They were passing a few days in a country village near the city of Bari, capital of the province of the same name in the division (***compartimento***) of Apulia. The child was in perfect health and had never been affected by any serious illness. On the 10th of July he was playing out in the field near the house where the family was staying when he was heard to scream suddenly and violently. The nurse rushing to him found him in great pain, saying that something had bitten him in one of his feet. A laborer, one Tommaso, ran up at the moment and perceived in the grass, near where the boy was standing, 'an enormous spider, which he at once recognized as a tarantula. He managed to catch the creature in a large leaf, from which he was afterwards transferred to a wide-mouthed bottle, where he lived without any food for a month or more. The creature was covered with short hairs, and had a pair of nipper-like jaws, with which he could inflict an ugly wound. His body measured about an inch in length, and from the extremity of one of the longest limbs to the other was between two and three inches. Such was the account given by the physician to whom the peasant carried the great spider.

"The boy who had been bitten continued screaming violently while his stocking was being removed and the foot examined. The place of the bite was easily found and the two marks of the claw-like jaws already showed the effects of the poison, a small livid circle extending around them, with some puffy swelling. The distinguished Dr. Amadei was immediately sent for, and applied cups over the wounds in the hope of drawing forth the poison. In vain all his skill and efforts! Soon, ataxic (irregular) nervous symptoms declared themselves, and it became plain that the system had been infected by the poison.

"The symptoms were very much like those of malignant fever, such as distress about the region of the heart, difficulty of breathing, collapse of all the vital powers, threatening immediate death. From these first symptoms the child rallied, but his entire organism had been profoundly affected by the venom circulating through it. His constitution has never thrown off the malady resulting from this toxic (poisonous) agent. The phenomena which have been observed in this young patient correspond so nearly with those enumerated in the elaborate essay of the celebrated Baglivi that one might think they had been transcribed from his pages.

"He is very fond of solitude,—of wandering about in churchyards and other lonely places. He was once found hiding in an empty tomb, which had been left open. His aversion to certain colors is remarkable. Generally speaking, he prefers bright tints to darker ones, but his likes and dislikes are capricious, and with regard to some colors his antipathy amounts to positive horror. Some shades have such an effect upon him that he cannot remain in the room with them, and if he meets any one whose dress has any of that particular color he will turn away or retreat so as to avoid passing that person. Among these, purple and dark green are the least endurable. He cannot explain the sensations which these obnoxious colors produce except by saying that it is like the deadly feeling from a blow on the epigastrium (pit of the stomach).

"About the same season of the year at which the tarantular poisoning took place he is liable to certain nervous seizures, not exactly like fainting or epilepsy, but reminding the physician of those affections; all the other symptoms are aggravated at this time.

"In other respects than those mentioned the boy is in good health. He is fond of riding, and has a pony on which he takes a great deal of exercise, which seems to do him more good than any other remedy.

"The influence of music, to which so much has been attributed by popular belief and even by the distinguished Professor to whom we shall again refer, has not as yet furnished any satisfactory results. If the graver symptoms recur while the patient is under our observation, we propose to make use of an agency discredited by modern skepticism, but deserving of a fair trial as an exceptional remedy for an exceptional disease. "The following extracts from the work of the celebrated Italian physician of the last century are given by the writer of the paper in the *Giornale* in the original Latin, with a translation into Italian, subjoined. Here are the extracts, or rather here is a selection from them, with a translation of them into English.

"After mentioning the singular aversion to certain colors shown by the subject of Tarantism, Baglivi writes as follows:—

" *'Et si astantes incedant vestibus eo colore diffusis, qui Tarantatis ingratus est, necesse est ut ab illorum aspectu recedant; nam ad intuitum molesti coloris angore cordis, et symptomatum recrudescantia statim corripiuntur.'* (G. Baglivi, Op. Omnia, page 614. Lugduni, 1745.)

"That is, 'if the persons about the patient wear dresses of the color which is offensive to him, he must get away from the sight of them; for on seeing the obnoxious color he is at once seized with distress in the region of the heart, and a renewal of his symptoms.'

"As to the recurrence of the malady, Baglivi says:—

"*'Dum calor solis ardentius exurere incipit, quod contingit circa initia Julii et Augusti, Tarantati lente venientem recrudescentiam veneni percipiunt.'* (Ibid., page 619.)

"Which I render, 'When the heat of the sun begins to burn more fiercely, which happens about the beginning of July and August, the subjects of Tarantism perceive the gradually approaching recrudescence (returning symptoms) of the poisoning.' Among the remedies most valued by this illustrious physician is that mentioned in the following sentence:—

"'Laudo magnopere equitationes in aëre rusticano factas singulis diebus, horâ potissimum matutina, quibus equitationibus morbos chronicos pene incurabiles protinus eliminavi.'

"Or in translation,—

" 'I commend especially riding on horseback in country air, every day, by preference in the morning hours, by the aid of which horseback riding I have driven off chronic diseases which were almost incurable.' "

Miss Vincent read this paper aloud to Dr. Butts, and handed it to him to examine and consider. He listened with a grave countenance and devout attention.

As she finished reading her account, she exclaimed in the passionate tones of the deepest conviction,—

"There, doctor! Haven't I found the true story of this strange visitor? Haven't I solved the riddle of the Sphinx? Who can this man be but the boy of that story? Look at the date of the journal when he was eleven years old; it would make him twenty-five now, and that is just about the age the people here think he must be of. What could account so entirely for his ways and actions as that strange poisoning which produces the state they call Tarantism? I am just as sure it must be that as I am that I am alive. Oh, doctor, doctor, I must be right,—this Signorino M . . . Ch . . . was the boy Maurice Kirkwood, and the story accounts for everything,—his solitary habits, his dread of people,—it must be because they wear the colors he can't bear. His morning rides on horseback, his coming here just as the season was approaching which would aggravate all his symptoms,—doesn't all this prove that I must be right in my conjecture,—no, my conviction?"

The doctor knew too much to interrupt the young enthusiast, and so he let her run on until she ran down. He was more used to the rules of evidence than she was, and could not accept her positive conclusion so readily as she would have liked to have him. He knew that beginners are very apt to make what they think are discoveries. But he had been an angler and knew the meaning of a yielding rod and an easy-running reel. He said quietly,—

"You are a most sagacious young lady, and a very pretty *prima facie* case it is that you make out. I can see no proof that Mr. Kirkwood is not the same person as the M . . . Ch . . . of the medical journal,—that is, if I accept your explanation of the difference in the initials of these two names. Even if there were a difference, that would not disprove their identity, for the initials of patients whose cases are reported by their physicians are often altered for the purpose of concealment. I do not know, however, that Mr. Kirkwood has shown any special aversion to any particular color. It might be interesting to inquire whether it is so, but it is a delicate matter. I don't exactly see whose business it is to investigate Mr. Maurice Kirkwood's idiosyncrasies and constitutional history. If he should have occasion to send for me at any time, he might tell me all about himself,—in confidence, you know. These old accounts from Baglivi are curious and interesting, but I am cautious about receiving any stories a hundred years old, if they involve an improbability, as his stories about the cure of the tarantula bite by music certainly do. I am disposed to wait for future developments, bearing in mind, of course, the very singular case you have unearthed. It wouldn't be very strange if our young gentleman had to send for me before the season is over. He is out a good deal before the dew is off the grass, which is rather risky in this neighborhood as autumn comes on. I am somewhat curious, I confess, about the young man, but I do not meddle where I am not asked for or wanted, and I have found that eggs hatch just as well if you let them alone in the nest as if you take them out and shake them every day. This is a wonderfully interesting supposition of yours, and may prove to be strictly in accordance with the facts. But I do not think we have all the facts in this young man's case. If it were proved that he had an aversion to any color, it would greatly strengthen your case. His 'antipatia,' as his man called it, must be one which covers a wide ground, to account for his self-isolation,—and the color hypothesis seems as plausible as any. But, my dear Miss Vincent, I think you had better leave your singular and striking hypothesis in my keeping for a while, rather than let it get abroad in a community like this, where so many tongues are in active exercise. I will carefully study this paper, if you will leave it with me, and we will talk the whole matter over. It is a fair subject for speculation, only we must keep quiet about it."

This long speech gave Lurida's perfervid brain time to cool off a little. She left the paper with the doctor, telling him she would come for it the next day, and went off to tell the result of this visit to her bosom friend, Miss Euthymia Tower.

XV.
DR. BUTTS CALLS ON EUTHYMIA.

THE doctor was troubled in thinking over his interview with the young lady. She was fully possessed with the idea that she had discovered the secret which had defied the most sagacious heads of the village. It was of no use to oppose her while her mind was in an excited state. But he felt it his duty to guard her against any possible results of indiscretion into which her eagerness and her theory of the equality, almost the identity of the sexes might betray her. Too much of the woman in a daughter of our race leads her to forget danger. Too little of the woman prompts her to defy it. Fortunately for this last class of women, they are not quite so likely to be perilously seductive as their more emphatically feminine sisters.

Dr. Butts had known Lurida and her friend from the days of their infancy. He had watched the development of Lurida's intelligence from its precocious nursery-life to the full vigor of its trained faculties. He had looked with admiration on the childish beauty of Euthymia, and had seen her grow up to womanhood, every year making her more attractive. He knew that if anything was to be done with his self-willed young scholar and friend, it would be more easily effected through the medium of Euthymia than by direct advice to the young lady herself. So the thoughtful doctor made up his mind to have a good talk with Euthymia, and put her on her guard, if Lurida showed any tendency to forget the conventionalities in her eager pursuit of knowledge.

For the doctor's horse and chaise to stop at the door of Miss Euthymia Tower's parental home was an event strange enough to set all the tongues in the village going. This was one of those families where illness was hardly looked for among the possibilities of life. There were other families where a call from the doctor was hardly more thought of than a call from the baker. But here he was a stranger, at least on his professional rounds, and when he asked for Miss Euthymia the servant, who knew his face well, stared as if he had held in his hand a warrant for her apprehension.

Euthymia did not keep the doctor waiting very long while she made ready to meet him. One look at her glass to make sure that a lock had not run astray, or a ribbon got out of place, and her toilet for a morning call was finished. Perhaps if Mr. Maurice Kirkwood had been announced, she might have taken a second look, but with the good middle-aged, married doctor, one was enough for a young lady who had the gift of making all the dresses she wore look well, and had no occasion to treat her chamber like the laboratory where an actress compounds herself.

Euthymia welcomed the doctor very heartily. She could not help suspecting his errand, and she was very glad to have a chance to talk over her friend's schemes and fancies with him.

The doctor began without any roundabout prelude.

"I want to confer with you about our friend Lurida. Does she tell you all her plans and projects?"

"Why, as to that, doctor, I can hardly say, positively, but I do not believe she keeps back anything of importance from me. I know what she has been busy with lately, and the queer idea she has got into her head. What do you think of the Tarantula business? She has shown you the paper she has written, I suppose."

"Indeed she has. It is a very curious case she has got hold of, and I do not wonder at all that she should have felt convinced that she had come at the true solution of the village riddle. It may be that this young man is the same person as the boy mentioned in the Italian medical journal. But it is very far from clear that he is so. You know all her reasons, of course, as you have read the story. The times seem to agree well enough. It is easy to conceive that *Ch* might be substituted for *K* in the report. The singular solitary habits of this young man entirely coincide with the story. If we could only find out whether he has any of those feelings with reference to certain colors, we might guess with more chance of guessing right than we have at present. But I don't see exactly how we are going to submit him to examination on this point. If he were only a chemical compound, we could analyze him. If he were only a bird or a quadruped, we could find out his likes and dislikes. But being, as he is, a young man, with ways of his own, and a will of his own, which he may not choose to have interfered with, the problem becomes more complicated. I hear that a newspaper correspondent has visited him so as to make a report to his paper,—-do you know what he found out?"

"Certainly I do, very well. My brother has heard his own story, which was this: He found out he had got hold of the wrong person to interview. The young gentleman, he says, interviewed *him,* so that he did not learn much about the Sphinx. But the newspaper man told Willy about the Sphinx's library and a cabinet of coins he had; and said he should make an article out of him, anyhow. I wish the man would take himself off. I am afraid Lurida's love of knowledge will get her into trouble!"

"*Which* of the men do you wish would take himself off?"

"I was thinking of the newspaper man."

She blushed a little as she said, "I can't help feeling a strange sort of interest about the other, Mr. Kirk wood. Do you know that I met him this morning, and had a good look at him, full in the face?"

"Well, to be sure ! That *was* an interesting experience. And how did you like his looks?"

"I thought his face a very remarkable one. But he looked very pale as he passed me, and I noticed that he put his hand to his left side as if he had a twinge of pain, or something of that sort,—spasm or neuralgia,—I don't know what. I wondered whether he had what you call **angina pectoris.** It was the same kind of look and movement, I remember, as you must, too, in my uncle who died with that complaint."

The doctor was silent for a moment. Then he asked, "Were you dressed as you are now?"

"Yes, I was, except that I had a thin mantle over my shoulders. I was out early, and I have always remembered your caution."

"What color was your mantle?"

"It was black. I have been over all this with Lurida. A black mantle on a white dress. A straw hat with an old faded ribbon. There can't be much in those colors to trouble him, I should think, for his man wears a black coat and white linen,—more or less white, as you must have noticed, and he must have seen ribbons of all colors often enough. But Lurida believes it was the ribbon, or something in the combination of colors. Her head is full of Tarantulas and Tarantism. I fear that she will never be easy until the question is settled by actual trial. And will you believe it? the girl is determined in some way to test her supposition!"

"Believe it, Euthymia! I can believe almost anything of Lurida. She is the most irrepressible creature I ever knew. You know as well as I do what a complete possession any ruling idea takes of her whole nature. I have had some fears lest her zeal might run away with her discretion. It is a great deal easier to get into a false position than to get out of it."

"I know it well enough. I want you to tell me what you think about the whole business. I don't like the look of it at all, and yet I can do nothing with the girl except let her follow her fancy, until I can show her plainly that she will get herself into trouble in some way or other. But she is ingenious,—full of all sorts of devices, innocent enough in themselves, but liable to be misconstrued. You remember how she won us the boat-race?" "To be sure I do. It was rather sharp practice, but she felt she was paying off an old score. The classical story of Atalanta, told, like that of Eve, as illustrating the weakness of woman, provoked her to make trial of the powers of resistance in the other sex. But it was audacious. I hope her audacity will not go too far. You must watch her. ***Keep an eye on her correspondence.***"

The doctor had great confidence in the good sense of Lurida's friend. He felt sure that she would not let Lurida commit herself by writing foolish letters to the subject of her speculations, or similar indiscreet performances. The boldness of young girls, who think no evil, in opening correspondence with idealized personages is something quite astonishing to those who have had an opportunity of knowing the facts. Lurida had passed the most dangerous age, but her theory of the equality of the sexes made her indifferent to the by-laws of social usage. She required watching, and her two guardians were ready to check her, in case of need.

XVI.
MISS VINCENT WRITES A LETTER.

EUTHYMIA noticed that her friend had been very much preoccupied for two or three days. She found her more than once busy at her desk, with a manuscript before her, which she turned over and placed inside the desk, as Euthymia entered.

This desire of concealment was not what either of the friends expected to see in the other. It showed that some project was under way, which, at least in its present stage, the Machiavellian young lady did not wish to disclose. It had cost her a good deal of thought and care, apparently, for her waste-basket was full of scraps of paper, which looked as if they were the remains of a manuscript like that at which she was at work. "Copying and recopying, probably," thought Euthymia, but she was willing to wait to learn what Lurida was busy about, though she had a suspicion that it was something in which she might feel called upon to interest herself.

"Do you know what I think?" said Euthymia to the doctor, meeting him as he left his door. "I believe Lurida is writing to this man, and I don't like the thought of her doing such a thing. Of course she is not like other girls in many respects, but other people will judge her by the common rules of life."

"I am glad that you spoke of it," answered the doctor; "she would write to him just as quickly as to any woman of his age. Besides, under the cover of her office, she has got into the way of writing to anybody. I think she has already written to Mr. Kirkwood, asking rim to contribute a paper for the Society. She can find a pretext easily enough if she has made up her mind to write. In fact, I doubt if she would trouble herself for any pretext at all if she decided to write. Watch her well. Don't let any letter go without seeing it, if you can help it."

Young women are much given to writing letters to persons whom they only know indirectly, for the most part through their books, and especially to romancers and poets. Nothing can be more innocent and simple-hearted than most of these letters. They are the spontaneous outflow of young hearts easily excited to gratitude for the pleasure which some story or poem has given them, and recognizing their own thoughts, their own feelings, in those expressed by the author, as if on purpose for them to read. Undoubtedly they give great relief to solitary young persons, who must have some ideal reflection of themselves, and know not where to look since Protestantism has taken away the crucifix and the Madonna. The recipient of these letters sometimes wonders, after reading through one of them, how it is that his young correspondent has managed to fill so much space with her simple message of admiration or of sympathy.

Lurida did not belong to this particular class of correspondents, but she could not resist the law of her sex, whose thoughts naturally surround themselves with superabundant drapery of language, as their persons float in a wide superfluity of woven tissues. Was she indeed writing to this unknown gentleman? Euthymia questioned her point-blank.

"Are you going to open a correspondence with Mr. Maurice Kirkwood, Lurida? You seem to be so busy writing, I can think of nothing else. Or are you going to write a novel, or a paper for the Society,—do tell me what you are so much taken up with."

"I will tell you, Euthymia, if you will promise not to find fault with me for carrying out my plan as I have made up my mind to do. You may read this letter before I seal it, and if you find anything in it you don't like you can suggest any change that you think will improve it. I hope you will see that it explains itself. I don't believe that yon will find anything to frighten you in it."

This is the letter, as submitted to Miss Tower by her friend. The bold handwriting made it look like a man's letter, and gave it consequently a less dangerous expression than that which belongs to the tinted and often fragrant sheet with its delicate thready characters, which slant across the page like an April shower with a south wind chasing it.

ARROWHEAD VILLAGE, *August*—, 18—.

MY DEAR SIR,—You will doubtless be surprised at the sight of a letter like this from one whom you only know as the Secretary of the Pansophian Society. There is a very common feeling that it is unbecoming in one of my sex to address one of your own with whom she is unacquainted, unless she has some special claim upon his attention. I am by no means disposed to concede to the vulgar prejudice on this point. If one human being has anything to communicate to another,—anything which deserves being communicated,—I see no occasion for bringing in the question of sex. I do not think the ***homo sum*** of Terence can be claimed for the male sex as its private property on general any more than on grammatical grounds.

I have sometimes thought of devoting myself to the noble art of healing. If I did so, it would be with the fixed purpose of giving my whole powers to the service of humanity. And if I should carry out that idea, should I refuse my care and skill to a suffering fellow-mortal because that mortal happened to be a brother, and not a sister? My whole nature protests against such one-sided humanity! No! I am blind to all distinctions when my eyes are opened to any form of suffering, to any spectacle of want. You may ask me why I address ***you,*** whom I know little or nothing of, and to whom such an advance may seem presumptuous and intrusive. It is because I was deeply impressed by the paper which I attributed to you,—that on Ocean, River, and Lake, which was read at one of our meetings. I say that I was deeply impressed, but I do not mean this as a compliment to that paper. I am not bandying compliments now, but thinking of better things than praises or phrases. I was interested in the paper, partly because I recognized some of the feelings expressed in it as my own,—partly because there was an undertone of sadness in all the voices of nature as you echoed them which made me sad to hear, and which I could not help longing to cheer and enliven. I said to myself, I should like to hold communion with the writer of that paper. I have had my lonely hours and days, as he has had. I have had some of his experiences in my intercourse with nature. And oh! if I could draw him into those better human relations which await us all, if we come with the right dispositions, I should blush if I stopped to inquire whether I violated any conventional rule or not.

You will understand me, I feel sure. You believe, do you not? in the insignificance of the barrier which divides the sisterhood from the brotherhood of mankind. You believe, do you not? that they should be educated side by side, that they should share the same pursuits, due regard being had to the fitness of the particular individual for hard or light work, as it must always be, whether we are dealing with the "stronger" or the "weaker" sex. I mark these words because, notwithstanding their common use, they involve so much that is not true. Stronger! Yes, to lift a barrel of flour, or a barrel of cider,—though there have been women who could do that, and though when John Wesley was mobbed in Staffordshire a woman knocked down three or four men, one after another, until she was at last overpowered and nearly murdered. Talk about the weaker sex! Go and see Miss Euthymia Tower at the gymnasium! But no matter about which sex has the strongest muscles. Which has most to suffer, and which has most endurance and vitality? We go through many ordeals which you are spared, but we outlast you in mind and body. I have been led away into one of my accustomed trains of thought, but not so far away from it as you might at first suppose.

My brother! Are you not ready to recognize in me a friend, an equal, a sister, who can speak to you as if she had been reared under the same roof? And is not the sky that covers us one roof, which makes us all one family? You are lonely, you must be longing for some human fellowship. Take me into your confidence. What is there that you can tell me to which I cannot respond with sympathy? What saddest note in your spiritual dirges which will not find its chord in mine?

I long to know what influence has cast its shadow over your existence. I myself have known what it is to carry a brain that never rests in a body that is always tired. I have defied its infirmities, and forced it to do my bidding. You have no such hindrance, if we may judge by your aspect and habits. You deal with horses like a Homeric hero. No wild Indian could handle his bark canoe more dexterously or more vigorously than we have seen you handling yours. There must be some reason for your seclusion which curiosity has not reached, and into which it is not the province of curiosity to inquire. But in the irresistible desire which I have to bring you into kindly relations with those around you, I must run the risk of giving offence that I may know in what direction to look for those restorative influences which the sympathy of a friend and sister can offer to a brother in need of some kindly impulse to change the course of a life which is not, which cannot be, in accordance with his true nature.

I have thought that there may be something in the conditions with which you are here surrounded which is repugnant to your feelings,—something which can be avoided only by keeping yourself apart from the people whose acquaintance you would naturally have formed. There can hardly be anything in the place itself, or you would not have voluntarily sought it as a residence, even for a single season. There might be individuals here whom you would not care to meet,—there must be such, but you cannot have a personal aversion to everybody. I have heard of cases in which certain sights and sounds, which have no particular significance for most persons, produced feelings of distress or aversion that made them unbearable to the subjects of the constitutional dislike. It has occurred to me that possibly you might have some such natural aversion to the sounds of the street, or such as are heard in most houses, especially where a piano is kept, as it is in fact in almost all of those in the village. Or it might be, I imagined, that some color in the dresses of women or the furniture of our rooms affected you unpleasantly. I know that instances of such antipathy have been recorded, and they would account for the seclusion of those who are subject to it.

If there is any removable condition which interferes with your free entrance into and enjoyment of the social life around you, tell me, I beg of you, tell me what it is, and it shall be eliminated. Think it not strange, O my brother, that I thus venture to introduce myself into the hidden chambers of your life. I will never suffer myself to be frightened from the carrying out of any thought which promises to be of use to a fellow-mortal by a fear lest it should be considered "unfeminine." I can bear to be considered unfeminine, but I cannot endure to think of myself as inhuman. Can I help you, my brother?

Believe me your most sincere well-wisher,

LURIDA VINCENT.

Euthymia had carried off this letter and read it by herself. As she finished it, her feelings found expression in an old phrase of her grandmother's, which came up of itself, as such survivals of early days are apt to do, on great occasions.

"Well, I never!"

Then she loosened some button or string that was too tight, and went to the window for a breath of outdoor air. Then she began at the beginning and read the whole letter all over again.

What should she do about it? She could not let this young girl send a letter like that to a stranger of whose character little was known except by inference,—to a young man, who would consider it a most extraordinary advance on the part of the sender. She would have liked to tear it into a thousand pieces, but she had no right to treat it in that way. Lurida meant to send it the next morning, and in the meantime Euthymia had the night to think over what she should do about it.

There is nothing like the pillow for an oracle. There is no voice like that which breaks the silence of the stagnant hours of the night with its sudden suggestions and luminous counsels. When Euthymia awoke in the morning, her course of action was as clear before her as if it had been dictated by her guardian angel. She went straight over to the home of Lurida, who was just dressed for breakfast.

She was naturally a little surprised at this early visit. She was struck with the excited look of Euthymia, being herself quite calm, and contemplating her project with entire complacency.

Euthymia began, in tones that expressed deep anxiety.

"I have read your letter, my dear, and admired its spirit and force. It is a fine letter, and does you great credit as an expression of the truest human feeling. But it must not be sent to Mr. Kirkwood. If you were sixty years old, perhaps if you were fifty, it might be admissible to send it. But if you were forty, I should question its propriety; if you were thirty, I should veto it, and you are but a little more than twenty. How do you know that this stranger will not show your letter to anybody or everybody? How do you know that he will not send it to one of the gossiping journals like the 'Household Inquisitor'? But supposing he keeps it to himself, which is more than you have a right to expect, what opinion is he likely to form of a young lady who invades his privacy with such freedom? Ten to one he will think curiosity is at the bottom of it,—and,—come, don't be angry at me for suggesting it,—may there not be a little of that same motive mingled with the others? No, don't interrupt me quite yet; you *do* want to know whether your hypothesis is correct. You are full of the best and kindest feelings in the world, but your desire for knowledge is the ferment under them just now, perhaps more than you know."

Lurida's pale cheeks flushed and whitened more than once while her friend was speaking. She loved her too sincerely and respected her intelligence too much to take offence at her advice, but she could not give up her humane and sisterly intentions merely from the fear of some awkward consequences to herself. She had persuaded herself that she was playing the part of a Protestant sister of charity, and that the fact of her not wearing the costume of these ministering angels made no difference in her relations to those who needed her aid.

"I cannot see your objections in the light in which they appear to you," she said gravely. "It seems to me that I give up everything when I hesitate to help a fellow-creature because I am a woman. I am not afraid to send this letter and take all the consequences."

"Will you go with me to the doctor's, and let him read it in our presence? And will you agree to abide by his opinion, if it coincides with mine?"

Lurida winced a little at this proposal. "I don't quite like," she said, "showing this letter to—to"—she hesitated, but it had to come out—"to a man,—that is, to another man than the one for whom it was intended."

The neuter gender business had got a pretty damaging side-hit.

"Well, never mind about letting him read the letter. Will you go over to his house with me at noon, when he comes back after his morning visits, and have a talk over the whole matter with him? You know I have sometimes had to say *must* to you, Lurida, and now I say you *must* go to the doctor's with me and carry that letter."

There was no resisting the potent monosyllable as the sweet but firm voice delivered it. At noon the two maidens rang at the doctor's door. The servant said he had been at the house after his morning visits, but found a hasty summons to Mr. Kirkwood, who had been taken suddenly ill and wished to see him at once. Was the illness dangerous? The servant-maid didn't know, but thought it was pretty bad, for Mr. Paul came in as white as a sheet, and talked all sorts of languages which she couldn't understand, and took on as if he thought Mr. Kirkwood was going to die right off.

And so the hazardous question about sending the letter was disposed of, at least for the present

XVII.
DR. BUTTS'S PATIENT.

THE physician found Maurice just regaining his heat after a chill of a somewhat severe character. He knew too well what this meant, and the probable series of symptoms of which it was the prelude. His patient was not the only one in the neighborhood who was attacked in this way. The autumnal fevers to which our country towns are subject, in the place of those "agues," or intermittents, so largely prevalent in the South and West, were already beginning, and Maurice, who had exposed himself in the early and late hours of the dangerous season, must be expected to go through the regular stages of this always serious and not rarely fatal disease.

Paolo, his faithful servant, would fain have taken the sole charge of his master during his illness. But the doctor insisted that he must have a nurse to help him in his task, which was likely to be long and exhausting.

At the mention of the word "nurse" Paolo turned white, and exclaimed in an agitated and thoroughly frightened way,—

"No! no nuss! no woman! She kill him! I stay by him day and night, but don' let no woman come near him,—if you do, he die!"

The doctor explained that he intended to send a *man* who was used to taking care of sick people, and with no little effort at last succeeded in convincing Paolo that, as he could not be awake day and night for a fortnight or three weeks, it was absolutely necessary to call in some assistance from without. And so Mr. Maurice Kirkwood was to play the leading part in that drama of nature's composing called a typhoid fever, with its regular bedchamber scenery, its properties of phials and pillboxes, its little company of stock actors, its gradual evolution of a very simple plot, its familiar incidents, its emotional alternations, and its denouement, sometimes tragic, oftener happy.

It is needless to say that the sympathies of all the good people of the village, residents and strangers, were actively awakened for the young man about whom they knew so little and conjectured so much. Tokens of their kindness came to him daily: flowers from the woods and from the gardens; choice fruit grown in the open air or under glass, for there were some fine houses surrounded by well-kept grounds, and greenhouses and graperies were not unknown in the small but favored settlement.

On all these luxuries Maurice looked with dull and languid eyes. A faint smile of gratitude sometimes struggled through the stillness of his features, or a murmured word of thanks found its way through his parched lips, and he would relapse into the partial stupor or the fitful sleep in which, with intervals of slight wandering, the slow hours dragged along the sluggish days one after another. With no violent symptoms, but with steady persistency, the disease moved on in its accustomed course. It was at no time immediately threatening, but the experienced physician knew its uncertainties only too well. He had known fever patients suddenly seized with violent internal inflammation, and carried off with frightful rapidity. He remembered the case of a convalescent, a young woman who had been attacked while in apparently vigorous general health, who, on being lifted too suddenly to a sitting position, while still confined to her bed, fainted, and in a few moments ceased to breathe. It may well be supposed that he took every possible precaution to avert the accidents which tend to throw from its track a disease the regular course of which is arranged by nature as carefully as the route of a railroad from one city to another. The most natural interpretation which the common observer would put upon the manifestations of one of these autumnal maladies would be that some noxious combustible element had found its way into the system which must be burned to ashes before the heat which pervades the whole body can subside. Sometimes the fire may smoulder and seem as if it were going out, or were quite extinguished, and again it will find some new material to seize upon, and flame up as fiercely as ever. Its coming on most frequently at the season when the brush fires which are consuming the dead branches, and withered leaves, and all the refuse of vegetation are sending up their smoke is suggestive. Sometimes it seems as if the body, relieved of its effete materials, renewed its youth after one of these quiet, expurgating, internal fractional cremations. Lean, pallid students have found themselves plump and blooming, and it has happened that one whose hair was straight as that of an Indian has been startled to behold himself in his mirror with a fringe of hyacinthine curls about his rejuvenated countenance.

There was nothing of what medical men call malignity in the case of Maurice Kirkwood. The most alarming symptom was a profound prostration, which at last reached such a point that he lay utterly helpless, at unable to move without aid as the feeblest of paralytics. In this state he lay for many days, not suffering pain, but with the sense of great weariness, and the feeling that he should never rise from his bed again. For the most part his intellect was unclouded when his attention was aroused. He spoke only in whispers, a few words at a time. The doctor felt sure, by the expression which passed over his features from time to time, that something was worrying and oppressing him; something which he wished to communicate, and had not the force, or the tenacity of purpose, to make perfectly clear. His eyes often wandered to a certain desk, and once he had found strength to lift his emaciated arm and point to it. The doctor went towards it as if to fetch it to him, but he slowly shook his head. He had not the power to say at that time what he wished. The next day he felt a little less prostrated, and succeeded in explaining to the doctor what he wanted. His words, so far as the physician could make them out, were these which follow. Dr. Butts looked upon them as possibly expressing wishes which would be his last, and noted them down carefully immediately after leaving his chamber.

"I commit the secret of my life to your charge. My whole story is told in a paper locked in that desk. The key is—put your hand under my pillow. If I die, let the story be known. It will show that I was—human—and save my memory from reproach."

He was silent for a little time. A single tear stole down his hollow cheek. The doctor turned his head away, for his own eyes were full. But he said to himself, "It is a good sign; I begin to feel strong hopes that he will recover."

Maurice spoke once more. "Doctor, I put full trust in you. You are wise and kind. Do what you will with this paper, but open it at once and read. I want you to know the story of my life before it is finished—if the end is at hand. Take it with you and read it before you sleep." He was exhausted and presently his eyes closed, but the doctor saw a tranquil look on his features which added encouragement to his hopes.

I AM an American by birth, but a large part of my life has been passed in foreign lands. My father was a man of education, possessed of an ample fortune; my mother was considered a very accomplished and amiable woman. I was their first and only child. She died while I was yet an infant. If I remember her at all it is as a vision, more like a glimpse of a pre-natal existence than as a part of my earthly life. At the death of my mother I was left in the charge of the old nurse who had enjoyed her perfect confidence. She was devoted to me, and I became absolutely dependent on her, who had for me all the love and all the care of a mother. I was naturally the object of the attentions and caresses of the family relatives. I have been told that I was a pleasant, smiling infant, with nothing to indicate any peculiar nervous susceptibility; not afraid of strangers, but on the contrary ready to make their acquaintance. My father was devoted to me and did all in his power to promote my health and comfort.

I was still a babe, often carried in arms, when the event happened which changed my whole future, and destined me to a strange and lonely existence. I cannot relate it even now without a sense of terror. I must force myself to recall the circumstances as told me and vaguely remembered, for I am not willing that my doomed and wholly exceptional life should pass away unrecorded, unexplained, unvindicated. My nature is, I feel sure, a kind and social one, but I have lived apart, as if my heart were filled with hatred of my fellow-creatures. If there are any readers who look without pity, without sympathy, upon those who shun the fellowship of their fellow men and women, who show by their downcast or averted eyes that they dread companionship and long for solitude, I pray them, it this paper ever reaches them, to stop at this point Follow me no further, for you will not believe my story, nor enter into the feelings which I am about to reveal. But if there are any to whom all that is human is of interest, who have felt in their own consciousness some stirrings of invincible attraction to one individual and equally invincible repugnance to another, who know by their own experience that elective affinities have as their necessary counterpart, and, as it were, their polar opposites, currents not less strong of elective repulsions, let them read with unquestioning faith the story of a blighted life I am about to relate, much of it, of course, received from the lips of others.

My cousin Laura, a girl of seventeen, lately returned from Europe, was considered eminently beautiful. It was in my second summer that she visited my father's house, where he was living with his servants and my old nurse, my mother having but recently left him a widower. Laura was full of vivacity, impulsive, quick in her movements, thoughtless occasionally, as it is not strange that a young girl of her age should be. It was a beautiful summer day when she saw me for the first time. My nurse had me in her arms, walking back and forward on a balcony with a low railing, upon which opened the windows of the second story of my father's house. While the nurse was thus carrying me, Laura came suddenly upon the balcony. She no sooner saw me than with all the delighted eagerness of her youthful nature she rushed toward me, and, catching me from the nurse's arms, began tossing me after the fashion of young girls who have been so lately playing with dolls that they feel as if babies were very much of the same nature. The abrupt seizure frightened me; I sprang from her arms in my terror, and fell over the railing of the balcony. I should probably enough have been killed on the spot but for the fact that a low thorn-bush grew just beneath the balcony, into which I fell and thus had the violence of the shock broken. But the thorns tore my tender flesh, and I bear to this day marks of the deep wounds they inflicted.

That dreadful experience is burned deep into my memory. The sudden apparition of the girl; the sense of being torn away from the protecting arms around me; the frantic effort to escape; the shriek that accompanied my fall through what must have seemed unmeasurable space; the cruel lacerations of the piercing and rending thorns,—all these fearful impressions blended in one paralyzing terror.

When I was taken up I was thought to be dead. I was perfectly white, and the physician who first saw me said that no pulse was perceptible. But after a time consciousness returned; the wounds, though painful, were none of them dangerous, and the most alarming effects of the accident passed away. My old nurse cared for me tenderly day and night, and my father, who had almost been distracted in the first hours which followed the injury, hoped and believed that no permanent evil results would be found to result from it. My cousin Laura was of course deeply distressed to feel that her thoughtlessness had been the cause of so grave an accident. As soon as I had somewhat recovered are came to see me, very penitent very anxious to make me forget the alarm she had caused me, with all its consequences. I was in the nursery sitting up in my bed, bandaged, but not in any pain, as it seemed, for I was quiet and to all appearance in a perfectly natural state of feeling. As Laura came near me I shrieked and instantly changed color. I put my hand upon my heart as if I had been stabbed, and fell over, unconscious. It was very much the same state as that in which I was found immediately after my fall.

The cause of this violent and appalling seizure was but too obvious. The approach of the young girl and the dread that she was about to lay her hand upon me had called up the same train of effects which the moment of terror and pain had already occasioned. The old nurse saw this in a moment. "Go! Go!" she cried to Laura,—"go, or the child will die!" Her command did not have to be repeated. After Laura had gone I lay senseless, white and cold as marble, for some time. The doctor soon came, and by the use of smart rubbing and stimulants the color came back slowly to my cheeks and the arrested circulation was again set in motion.

It was hard to believe that this was anything more than a temporary effect of the accident There could be little doubt, it was thought by the doctor and by my father, that after a few days I should recover from this morbid sensibility and receive my cousin as other infants receive pleasant-looking young persons. The old nurse shook her head. "The girl will be the death of the child," she said, "if she touches him or comes near him. His heart stopped beating just as when the girl snatched him out of my arms, and he fell over the balcony railing" Once more the experiment was tried, cautiously, almost insidiously. The same alarming consequences followed. It was too evident that a chain of nervous disturbances had been set up in my system which repeated itself whenever the original impression gave the first impulse. I never saw my cousin Laura after this last trial. Its result had so distressed her that she never ventured again to show herself to me.

If the effect of the nervous shock had stopped there, it would have been a misfortune for my cousin and myself, but hardly a calamity. The world is wide, and a cousin or two more or less can hardly be considered an essential of existence. I often heard Laura's name mentioned, but never by any one who was acquainted with all the circumstances, for it was noticed that I changed color and caught at my breast as if I wanted to grasp my heart in my hand whenever that fatal name was mentioned.

Alas! this was not all. While I was suffering from the effects of my fall among the thorns I was attended by my old nurse, assisted by another old woman, by a physician, and my father, who would take his share in caring for me. It was thought best to keep me perfectly quiet, and strangers and friends were alike excluded from my nursery, with one exception, that my old grandmother came in now and then. With her it seems that I was somewhat timid and shy, following her with rather anxious eyes, as if not quite certain whether or not she was dangerous. But one day, when I was far advanced towards recovery, my father brought in a young lady, a relative of his, who had expressed a great desire to see me. She was, as I have been told, a very handsome girl, of about the same age as my cousin Laura, but bearing no personal resemblance to her in form, features, or complexion. She had no sooner entered the room than the same sudden changes which had followed my cousin's visit began to show themselves, and before she had reached my bedside I was in a state of deadly collapse, as on the occasions already mentioned.

Some time passed before any recurrence of these terrifying seizures. A little girl of five or six years old was allowed to come into the nursery one day and bring me some flowers. I took them from her hand, but turned away and shut my eyes. There was no seizure, but there was a certain dread and aversion, nothing more than a feeling which it might be hoped that time would overcome. Those around me were gradually finding out the circumstances which brought on the deadly attack to which was subject.

The daughter of one of our near neighbors was considered the prettiest girl of the village where we were passing the summer. She was very anxious to see me, and as I was now nearly well it was determined that she should be permitted to pay me a short visit. I had always delighted in seeing her and being caressed by her. I was sleeping when she entered the nursery and came and took a seat at my side in perfect silence. Presently I became restless, and a moment later I opened my eyes, and saw her stooping over me. My hand went to my left breast,—the color faded from my cheeks,—I was again the cold marble image so like death that it had well-nigh been mistaken for it.

Could it be possible that the fright which had chilled my blood had left me with an unconquerable fear of woman at the period when she is most attractive not only to adolescents, but to children of tender age, who feel the fascination of her flowing locks, her bright eyes, her blooming cheeks, and that mysterious magnetism of sex which draws all life into its warm and potently vitalized atmosphere? So it did indeed seem. The dangerous experiment could not be repeated indefinitely.

It was not intentionally tried again, but accident brought about more than one renewal of it during the following years, until it became fully recognized that I was the unhappy subject of a mortal dread of woman,—not absolutely of the human female, for I had no fear of my old nurse or of my grandmother, or of any old wrinkled face, and I had become accustomed to the occasional meeting of a little girl or two, whom I nevertheless regarded with a certain ill-defined feeling that there was danger in their presence. I was sent to a boy's school very early, and during the first ten or twelve years of my life I had rarely any occasion to be reminded of my strange idiosyncrasy.

As I grew out of boyhood into youth, a change came over the feelings which had so long held complete possession of me. This was what my father and his advisers had always anticipated, and was the ground of their confident hope in my return to natural conditions before I should have grown to mature manhood.

How shall I describe the conflicts of those dreamy, bewildering, dreadful years? Visions of loveliness haunted me sleeping and waking. Sometimes a graceful girlish figure would so draw my eyes towards it that I lost sight of all else, and was ready to forget all my fears and find myself at her side, like other youths by the side of young maidens,—happy in their cheerful companionship, while I,—I, under the curse of one blighting moment, looked on, hopeless. Sometimes the glimpse of a fair face or the tone of a sweet voice stirred within me all the instincts that make the morning of life beautiful to adolescence. I reasoned with myself:—

Why should I not have outgrown that idle apprehension which had been the nightmare of my earlier years? Why should not the rising tide of life have drowned out the feeble growths that infested the shallows of childhood? How many children there are who tremble at being left alone in the dark, but who, a few years later, will smile at their foolish terrors and brave all the ghosts of a haunted chamber! Why should I any longer be the slave of a foolish fancy that has grown into a half insane habit of mind? I was familiarly acquainted with all the stories of the strange antipathies and invincible repugnances to which others, some of them famous men, had been subject. I said to myself, Why should not I overcome this dread of woman as Peter the Great fought down his dread of wheels rolling over a bridge? Was I, alone of all mankind, to be doomed to perpetual exclusion from the society which, as it seemed to me, was all that rendered existence worth the trouble and fatigue of slavery to the vulgar need of supplying the waste of the system and working at the task of respiration like the daughters of Danaus,—toiling day and night as the worn-out sailor labors at the pump of his sinking vessel?

Why did I not brave the risk of meeting squarely, and without regard to any possible danger, some one of those fair maidens whose far-off smile, whose graceful movements, at once attracted and agitated me? I can only answer this question to the satisfaction of any really inquiring reader by giving him the true interpretation of the singular phenomenon of which I was the subject For this I shall have to refer to a paper of which I have made a copy, and which will be found included with this manuscript It is enough to say here, without entering into the explanation of the fact, which will be found simple enough as seen by the light of modern physiological science, that the "nervous disturbance" which the presence of a woman in the flower of her age produced in my system was *a sense of impending death,* sudden, overwhelming, unconquerable, appalling. It was a reversed action of the nervous centres,—the opposite of that which flushes the young lover's cheek and hurries his bounding pulses as he comes into the presence of the object of his passion. No one who has ever felt the sensation can have failed to recognize it as an imperative summons, which commands instant and terrified submission.

It was at this period of my life that my father determined to try the effect of travel and residence in different localities upon my bodily and mental condition. I say bodily as well as mental, for I was too slender for my height and subject to some nervous symptoms which were a cause of anxiety. That the mind was largely concerned in these there was no doubt, but the mutual interactions of mind and body are often too complex to admit of satisfactory analysis. Each is in part cause and each also in part effect.

We passed some years in Italy, chiefly in Rome, where I was placed in a school conducted by priests, I and where of course I met only those of my own sex. There I had the opportunity of seeing the influences under which certain young Catholics destined forth & priesthood, are led to separate themselves from all communion with the sex associated in their minds with the most subtle dangers to which the human soul can be exposed. I became in some degree reconciled to the thought of exclusion from the society of women by seeing around me so many who were self-devoted to celibacy. The thought sometimes occurred to me whether I should not find the best and the only natural solution of the problem of existence, as submitted to myself, in taking upon me the vows which settle the whole question and raise an impassable barrier between the devotee and the object of his dangerous attraction.

How often I talked this whole matter over with the young priest who was at once my special instructor and my favorite companion! But accustomed as I had become to the forms of the Roman Church, and impressed as I was with the purity and excellence of many of its young members with whom I was acquainted, my early training rendered it impossible for me to accept the credentials which it offered me as authoritative. My friend and instructor had to set me down as a case of "invincible ignorance." This was the loop-hole through which he crept out of the prison-house of his creed, and was enabled to look upon me without the feeling of absolute despair with which his sterner brethren would, I fear, have regarded me.

I have said that accident exposed me at times to the influence which I had such reasons for dreading. Here is one example of such an occurrence, which I relate as simply as possible, vividly as it is impressed upon my memory. A young friend whose acquaintance I had made in Rome asked me one day to come to his rooms and look at a cabinet of gems and medals which he had collected. I had been but a short time in his library when a vague sense of uneasiness came over me. My heart became restless,—I could feel it stirring irregularly, as if it were some frightened creature caged in my breast. There was nothing that I could see to account for it. A door was partly open, but not so that I could see into the next room. The feeling grew upon me of some influence which was paralyzing my circulation. I begged my friend to open a window. As he did so, the door swung in the draught, and I saw a blooming young woman,—it was my friend's sister, who had been sitting with a book in her hand, and who rose at the opening of the door. Something had warned me of the presence of a woman,—that occult and potent *aura* of individuality, call it personal magnetism, spiritual effluence, or reduce it to a simpler expression if you will; whatever it was, it had warned me of the nearness of the dread attraction which allured at a distance and revealed itself with all the terrors of the *lorelei* if approached too recklessly.

A sign from her brother caused her to withdraw at once, but not before I had felt the impression which betrayed itself in my change of color, anxiety about the region of the heart, and sudden failure as if about to fall in a deadly fainting-fit.

Does all this seem strange and incredible to the reader of my manuscript? Nothing in the history of life is so strange or exceptional as it seems to those who have not made a long study of its mysteries. I have never known just such a case as my own, and yet there must have been such, and if the whole history of mankind were unfolded I cannot doubt that there have been many like it. Let my reader suspend his judgment until he has read the paper I have referred to, which was drawn up by a Committee of the Royal Academy of the Biological Sciences. In this paper the mechanism of the series of nervous derangements to which I have been subject since the fatal shock experienced in my infancy is explained in language not hard to understand. It will be seen that such a change of polarity in the nervous centres is only a permanent form and an extreme degree of an emotional disturbance, which as a temporary and comparatively unimportant personal accident is far from being uncommon,—is so frequent, in fact, that every one must have known instances of it, and not a few must have had more or less serious experiences of it in their own private history.

It must not be supposed that my imagination dealt with me as I am now dealing with the reader. I was full of strange fancies and wild superstitions. One of my Catholic friends gave me a silver medal which had been blessed by the Pope, and which I was to wear next my body. I was told that this would turn black after a time, in virtue of a power which it possessed of drawing out original sin, or certain portions of it, together with the evil and morbid tendencies which have been engrafted on the corrupt nature. I wore the medal faithfully, as directed, and watched it carefully. It became tarnished and after a time darkened, but it wrought no change in my unnatural condition.

There was an old gypsy who had the reputation of knowing more of futurity than she had any right to know. The story was that she foretold the assassination of Count Rossi and the death of Cavour. However that may have been, I was persuaded to let her try her black art upon my future. I shall never forget the strange, wild look of the wrinkled hag as she took my hand and studied its lines and fixed her wicked old eyes on my young countenance. After this examination she shook her head and muttered some words, which as nearly as I could get them would be in English like these:—

Fair lady cast a spell on thee, Fair lady's hand shall set thee free.

Strange as it may seem, these words of a withered old creature, whose palm had to be crossed with silver to bring forth her oracular response, have always clung to my memory as if they were destined to fulfillment. The extraordinary nature of the affliction to which I was subject disposed me to believe the incredible with reference to all that relates to it. I have never ceased to have the feeling that, sooner or later, I should find myself freed from the blight laid upon me in my infancy. It seems as if it would naturally come through the influence of some young and fair woman, to whom that merciful errand should be assigned by the Providence that governs our destiny. With strange hopes, with trembling fears, with mingled belief and doubt, wherever I have found myself I have sought with longing yet half-averted eyes for the "elect lady," as I have learned to call her, who was to lift the curse from my ruined life.

Three times I have been led to the hope, if not the belief, that I had found the object of my superstitious belief. Singularly enough it was always on the water that the phantom of my hope appeared before my bewildered vision. Once it was an English girl who was a fellow passenger with me in one of my ocean voyages. I need not say that she was beautiful, for she was my dream realized. I heard her singing, I saw her walking the deck on some of the fair days when sea-sickness was forgotten. The passengers were a social company enough, but I had kept myself apart, as was my wont. At last the attraction became too strong to resist any longer. "I will venture into the charmed circle if it kills me," I said to my father. I did venture, and it did not kill me, or I should not be telling this story. But there was a repetition of the old experiences. I need not relate the series of alarming consequences of my venture. The English girl was very lovely, and I have no doubt has made some one supremely happy before this, but she was not the "elect lady" of the prophecy and of my dreams.

A second time I thought myself for a moment in the presence of the destined deliverer who was to restore me to my natural place among my fellow men and women. It was on the Tiber that I met the young maiden who drew me once more into that inner circle which surrounded young womanhood with deadly peril for me, if I dared to pass its limits. I was floating with the stream in the little boat in which I passed many long hours of reverie when I saw another small boat with a boy and a young girl in it. The boy had been rowing, and one of his oars had slipped from his grasp. He did not know how to paddle with a single oar, and was hopelessly rowing round and round, his oar all the time floating farther away from him. I could not refuse my assistance. I picked up the oar and brought my skiff alongside of the boat. When I handed the oar to the boy the young girl lifted her veil and thanked me in the exquisite music of the language which

"Sounds as if it should be writ on satin."

She was a type of Italian beauty,—a ***nocturne*** in flesh and blood, if I may borrow a term certain artists are fond of; but it was her voice which captivated me and for a moment made me believe that I was no longer shut off from all relations with the social life of my race. An hour later I was found lying insensible on the floor of my boat, white, cold, almost pulseless. It cost much patient labor to bring me back to consciousness. Had not such extreme efforts been made, it seems probable that I should never have waked from a slumber which was hardly distinguishable from that of death.

Why should I provoke a catastrophe which appears inevitable if I invite it by exposing myself to its too well ascertained cause? The habit of these deadly seizures has become a second nature. The strongest and the ablest men have found it impossible to resist the impression produced by the most insignificant object, by the most harmless sight or sound to which they had a congenital or acquired antipathy. What prospect have I of ever being rid of this long and deep-seated infirmity? I may well ask myself these questions, but my answer is that I will never give up the hope that time will yet bring its remedy. It may be that the wild prediction which so haunts me shall find itself fulfilled. I have had of late strange premonitions, to which if I were superstitious I could not help giving heed. But I have seen too much of the faith that deals in miracles to accept the supernatural in any shape,—assuredly when it comes from an old witch-like creature who takes pay for her revelations of the future. Be it so: though I am not superstitious, I have a right to be imaginative, and my imagination will hold to those words of the old zingara with an irresistible feeling that, sooner or later, they will prove true.

Can it be possible that her prediction is not far from its realization? I have had both waking and sleeping visions within these last months and weeks which have taken possession of me and filled my life with new thoughts, new hopes, new resolves.

Sometimes on the bosom of the lake by which I am dreaming away this season of bloom and fragrance, sometimes in the fields or woods in a distant glimpse, once in a nearer glance, which left me pale and tremulous, yet was followed by a swift reaction, so that my cheeks flushed and my pulse bounded, I have seen her who—how do I dare to tell it so that my own eyes can read it?—I cannot help believing is to be my deliverer, my saviour.

I have been warned in the most solemn and impressive language by the experts most deeply read in the laws of life and the history of its disturbing and destroying influences, that it would be at the imminent risk of my existence if I should expose myself to the repetition of my former experiences. I was reminded that unexplained sudden deaths were of constant, of daily occurrence; that any emotion is liable to arrest the movements of life; terror, joy, good news or bad news,—anything that reaches the deeper nervous centres. I had already died once, as Sir Charles Napier said of himself; yes, more than once, died and been resuscitated. The next time, I might very probably fail to get my return ticket after my visit to Hades. It was a rather grim stroke of humor, but I understood its meaning full well, and felt the force of its menace.

After all, what had I to live for if the great primal instinct which strives to make whole the half life of lonely manhood is defeated, suppressed, crushed out of existence? Why not as well die in the attempt to break up a wretched servitude to a perverted nervous movement as in any other way? I am alone in these world,—alone save for my faithful servant, through whom I seem to hold to the human race as it were by a single filament. My father, who was my instructor, my companion, my dearest and best friend through all my later youth and my earlier manhood, died three years ago and left me my own master, with the means of living as might best please my fancy. This season shall decide my fate. One more experiment, and I shall find myself restored to my place among my fellow-beings, or, as I devoutly hope, in a sphere where all our mortal infirmities are past and forgotten.

I have told the story of a blighted life without reserve, so that there shall not remain any mystery or any dark suspicion connected with my memory if I should be taken away unexpectedly. It has cost me an effort to do it, but now that my life is on record I feel more reconciled to my lot, with all its possibilities,—and among these possibilities is a gleam of a better future. I have been told by my advisers, some of them wise, deeply instructed, and kind-hearted men, that such a life-destiny should be related by the subject of it for the instruction of others, and especially for the light it throws on certain peculiarities of human character often wrongly interpreted as due to moral perversion, when they are in reality the results of misdirected or reversed actions in some of the closely connected nervous centres.

For myself I can truly say that I have very little morbid sensibility left with reference to the destiny which has been allotted to me. I have passed through different stages of feeling with reference to it, as I have developed from infancy to manhood. At first it was mere blind instinct about which I had no thought, living like other infants the life of impressions without language to connect them in series. In my boyhood I began to be deeply conscious of the infirmity which separated me from those around me. In youth began that conflict of emotions and impulses with the antagonistic influence of which I have already spoken, a conflict which has never ceased, but to which I have necessarily become to a certain degree accustomed, and against the dangers of which I have learned to guard myself habitually. That is the meaning of my isolation. You, young man,—if at any time your eyes shall look upon my melancholy record,—you at least will understand me. Does not your heart throb, in the presence of budding or blooming womanhood, sometimes as if it "were ready to crack" with its own excess of strain? What if instead of throbbing it should falter, flutter, and stop as if never to beat again? You, young woman, who with ready belief and tender sympathy will look upon these pages, if they are ever spread before you, know what it is when your breast heaves with uncontrollable emotion and the grip of the bodice seems unendurable as the embrace of the iron virgin of the Inquisition. Think what it would be if the grasp were tightened so that no breath of air could enter your panting chest!

Does your heart beat in the same way, young man, when your honored friend, a venerable matron of seventy years, greets you with her kindly smile as it does in the presence of youthful loveliness? When a pretty child brings you her doll and looks into your eyes with artless grace and trustful simplicity, does your pulse quicken, do you tremble, does life palpitate through your whole being, as when the maiden of seventeen meets your enamored sight in the glow of her rosebud beauty? Wonder not, then, if the period of mystic attraction for you should be that of agitation, terror, danger, to one in whom the natural current of the instincts has had its course changed as that of a stream is changed by a convulsion of nature, so that the impression which is new life to you is death to him.

I am now twenty-five years old. I have reached the time of life which I have dreamed, nay even ventured to hope, might be the limit of the sentence which was pronounced upon me in my infancy. I can assign no good reason for this anticipation. But in writing this paper I feel as if I were preparing to begin a renewed existence. There is nothing for me to be ashamed of in the story I have told. There is no man living who would not have yielded to the sense of instantly impending death which seized upon me under the conditions I have mentioned. Martyrs have gone singing to their flaming shrouds, but never a man could hold his breath long enough to kill himself; he must have rope or water, or some mechanical help, or nature will make him draw in a breath of air, and would make him do so though he knew the salvation of the human race would be forfeited by that one gasp.

This paper may never reach the eye of anyone afflicted in the same way that I have been. It probably never will; but for all that, there are many shy natures which will recognize tendencies in themselves in the direction of my unhappy susceptibility. Others, to whom such weakness seems inconceivable, will find their scepticism shaken, if not removed, by the calm, judicial statement of the Report drawn up for the Royal Academy. It will make little difference to me whether my story is accepted unhesitatingly or looked upon as largely a product of the imagination. I am but a bird of passage that lights on the boughs of different nationalities. I belong to no flock; my home may be among the palms of Syria, the olives of Italy, the oaks of England, the elms that shadow the Hudson or the Connecticut; I build no nest; to-day I am here, to-morrow on the wing.

If I quit my native land before the trees have dropped their leaves I shall place this manuscript in the safe hands of one whom I feel sure that I can trust, to do with it as he shall see fit. If it is only curious and has no bearing on human welfare, he may think it well to let it remain unread until I shall have passed away. If in his judgment it throws any light on one of the deeper mysteries of our nature,—the repulsions which play such a formidable part in social life, and which must be recognized as the correlatives of the affinities that distribute the individuals governed by them in the face of impediments which seem to be impossibilities,—then it may be freely given to the world.

But if I am here when the leaves are all fallen, the programme of my life will have changed, and this story of the dead past will be illuminated by the light of a living present which will irradiate all its saddening features. Who would not pray that my last gleam of light and hope may be that of dawn and not of departing day?

The reader who finds it hard to accept the reality of a story so far from the common range of experience is once more requested to suspend his judgment until he has read the paper which will next be offered for his consideration.

THE REPORT OF THE BIOLOGICAL COMMITTEE.

PERHAPS it is too much to expect a reader who wishes to be entertained, excited, amused, and does not want to work his passage through pages which he cannot understand without some effort of his own, to read the paper which follows and Dr. Butts's reflections upon it. If he has no curiosity in the direction of these chapters, he can afford to leave them to such as relish a slight flavor of science. But if he does so leave them he will very probably remain sceptical as to the truth of the story to which they are meant to furnish him with a key.

Of course the case of Maurice Kirkwood is a remarkable and exceptional one, and it is hardly probable that any reader's experience will furnish him with its parallel. But let him look back over all his acquaintances, if he has reached middle life, and see if he cannot recall more than one who, for some reason or other, shunned the society of young women, as if they had a deadly fear of their company. If he remembers any such, he can understand the simple statements and natural reflections which are laid before him.

One of the most singular facts connected with the history of Maurice Kirkwood was the philosophical equanimity with which he submitted to the fate which had fallen upon him. He did not choose to be pumped by the Interviewer, who would show him up in the sensational columns of his prying newspaper. He lived chiefly by himself, as the easiest mode of avoiding those meetings to which he would be exposed in almost every society into which he might venture. But he had learned to look upon himself very much as he would upon an intimate *not* himself,—upon a different personality. A young man will naturally enough be ashamed of his shyness. It is something which others believe, and perhaps he himself thinks, he might overcome. But in the case of Maurice Kirkwood there was no room for doubt as to the reality and gravity of the long enduring effects of his first convulsive terror. He had accepted the fact as he would have accepted the calamity of losing his sight or his hearing. When he was questioned by the experts to whom his case was submitted, he told them all that he knew about it almost without a sign of emotion. Nature was so peremptory with him,—saying in language that had no double meaning: "If you violate the condition on which you hold' my gift of existence I slay you on the spot,"—that he became as decisive in his obedience as she was in her command, and accepted his fate without repining.

Yet it must not be thought for a moment,—it cannot be supposed,—that he was insensible because he looked upon himself with the coolness of an enforced philosophy. He bore his burden manfully, hard as it was to live under it, for he lived, as we have seen, in hope. The thought of throwing it off with his life, as too grievous to be borne, was familiar to his lonely hours, but he rejected it as unworthy of his manhood. How he had speculated and dreamed about it is plain enough from the paper the reader may remember on Ocean, River, and Lake.

With these preliminary hints the paper promised is submitted to such as may find any interest in them.

ACCOUNT OF A CASE OF GYNOPHOBIA.

WITH REMARKS.

Being the Substance of a Report to the Royal Academy of the Biological Sciences by a Committee of that Institution.

"The singular nature of the case we are about to narrate and comment upon will, we feel confident, arrest the attention of those who have learned the great fact that Nature often throws the strongest light upon her laws by the apparent exceptions and anomalies which from time to time are observed. We have done with the lusus naturœ of earlier generations. We pay little attention to the stories of 'miracles,' except so far as we receive them ready-made at the hands of the churches which still hold to them. Not the less do we meet with strange and surprising facts, which a century or two ago would have been handled by the clergy and the courts, but to-day are calmly recorded and judged by the best light our knowledge of the laws of life can throw upon them. It must be owned that there are stories which we can hardly dispute, so clear and full is the evidence in their support, which do, notwithstanding, tax our faith and sometimes leave us sceptical in spite of all the testimony which supports them.

"In this category many will be disposed to place the case we commend to the candid attention of the Academy. If one were told that a young man, a gentleman by birth and training, well formed, in apparently perfect health, of agreeable physiognomy and manners, could not endure the presence of the most attractive young woman, but was seized with deadly terror and sudden collapse of all the powers of life, if he came into her immediate presence; if it were added that this same young man did not shrink from the presence of an old withered crone; that he had a certain timid liking for little maidens who had not yet outgrown the company of their dolls, the listener would be apt to smile, if he did not laugh, at the absurdity of the fable. Surely, he would say, this must be the fiction of some fanciful brain, the whim of some romancer, the trick of some playwright. It would make a capital farce, this idea, carried out. A young man slighting the lovely heroine of the little comedy and making love to her grandmother! This would, of course, be overstating the truth of the story, but to such a misinterpretation the plain facts lend themselves too easily. We will relate the leading circumstances of the case, as they were told us with perfect simplicity and frankness by the subject of an affection which, if classified, would come under the general head of Antipathy, but to which, if we give it a name, we shall have to apply the term Gynophobia, or Fear of Woman"

[Here follows the account furnished to the writer of the paper, which is in all essentials identical with that already laid before the reader.]

"Such is the case offered to our consideration. Assuming its truthfulness in all its particulars, it remains to see in the first place whether or not it is as entirely exceptional and anomalous as it seems at first sight, or whether it is only the last term of a series of cases which in their less formidable aspect are well known to us in literature, in the records of science, and even in our common experience.

"To most of those among us the explanations we are now about to give are entirely superfluous. But there are some whose chief studies have been in different directions, and who will not complain if certain facts are mentioned which to the expert will seem rudimentary, and which hardly require recapitulation to those who are familiarly acquainted with the common text-books.

"The heart is the centre of every living movement in the higher animals, and in man, furnishing in varying amount, or withholding to a greater or less extent, the needful supplies to all parts of the system. If its action is diminished to a certain degree, faintness is the immediate consequence; if it is arrested, loss of consciousness; if its action is not soon restored, death, of which fainting plants the white flag, remains in possession of the system.

"How closely the heart is under the influence of the emotions we need not go to science to learn, for all human experience and all literature are overflowing with evidence that shows the extent of this relation. Scripture is full of it; the heart in Hebrew poetry represents the entire life, we might almost say. Not less forcible is the language of Shakespeare, as for instance, in 'Measure for Measure:'—

'Why does my blood thus muster to my heart, Making it both unable for itself And dispossessing all my other parts Of necessary fitness?'

More especially is the heart associated in every literature with the passion of love. A famous old story is that of Galen, who was called to the case of a young lady long ailing, and wasting away from some cause the physicians who had already seen her were unable to make out. The shrewd old practitioner suspected that love was at the bottom of the young lady's malady. Many relatives and friends of both sexes, all of them ready with their sympathy, came to see her. The physician sat by her bedside during one of these visits, and in an easy, natural way took her hand and placed a finger on her pulse. It beat quietly enough until a certain comely young gentleman entered the apartment, when it suddenly rose in frequency, and at the same moment her hurried breathing, her changing color, pale and flushed by turns, betrayed the profound agitation his presence excited. This was enough for the sagacious Greek; love was the disease, the cure of which by its like may be claimed as an anticipation of homœopathy. In the frontispiece to the fine old 'Junta' edition of the works of Galen, you may find among the wood-cuts a representation of the interesting scene, with the title **Amantis Dignotio,**—the diagnosis, or recognition, of the lover.

"Love has many languages, but the heart talks through all of them. The pallid or burning cheek tells of the failing or leaping fountain which gives it color. The lovers at the 'Brookside' could hear each other's hearts beating. When Genevieve, in Coleridge's poem, forgot herself, and was beforehand with her suitor in her sudden embrace,—

''Twas partly love and partly fear, And partly 'twas a bashful art, That I might rather feel than see The swelling of her heart.'

Always the heart, whether its hurried action is seen, or heard, or felt. But it is not always in this way that the 'deceitful' organ treats the lover.

'Faint heart never won fair lady.'

This saying was not meant, perhaps, to be taken literally, but it has its literal truth. Many a lover has found his heart' sink within him,'—lose all its force, and leave him weak as a child in his emotion at the sight of the object of his affections. When Porphyro looked upon Madeline at her prayers in the chapel, it was too much for him:—

'She seemed a splendid angel, newly drest, Save wings, for heaven:—*Porphyro grew faint,* She knelt, so pure a thing, so free from earthly taint.'

And in Balzac's novel, 'César Birotteau,' the hero of the story, *'fainted away for joy* at the moment when, under a linden-tree, at Sceaux, Constance-Barbe-Josephine accepted him as her future husband.'

"One who faints is *dead* if he does not 'come to,' and nothing is more likely than that too susceptible lovers have actually gone off in this way. Everything depends on how the heart behaves itself in these and similar trying moments. The mechanism of its actions becomes an interesting subject, therefore, to lovers of both sexes, and to all who are capable of intense emotions.

"The heart is a great reservoir, which distributes food, drink, air, and heat to every part of the system, in exchange for its waste material. It knocks at the gate of every organ seventy or eighty times in a minute, calling upon it to receive its supplies and unload its refuse. Between it and the brain there is the closest relation. The emotions, which act upon it as we have seen, govern it by a mechanism only of late years thoroughly understood. This mechanism can be made plain enough to the reader who is not afraid to believe that he can understand it.

"The brain, as all know, is the seat of ideas, emotions, volition. It is the great central telegraphic station with which many lesser centres are in close relation, from which they receive, and to which they transmit, their messages. The heart has its own little brains, so to speak,—small collections of nervous substance which govern its rythmical motions under ordinary conditions. But these lesser nervous centres are to a large extent dominated by influences transmitted from certain groups of nerve-cells in the brain and its immediate dependencies.

"There are two among the special groups of nerve-cells which produce directly opposite effects. One of these has the power of accelerating the action of the heart, while the other has the power of retarding or arresting this action. One acts as the spur, the other as the bridle. According as one or the other predominates, the action of the heart will be stimulated or restrained. Among the great modern discoveries in physiology is that of the existence of a distinct centre of ***inhibition,*** as the re-straining influence over the heart is called.

"The centre of inhibition plays a terrible part in the history of cowardice and of unsuccessful love. No man can be brave without blood to sustain his courage, any more than he can think, as the German materialist says, not absurdly, without phosphorus. The fainting lover must recover his circulation, or his lady will lend him her smelling-salts and take a gallant with blood in his cheeks. Porphyro got over his faintness before he ran away with Madeline, and César Birotteau was an accepted lover when he swooned with happiness: but many an officer has been cashiered, and many a suitor has been rejected, because the centre of inhibition has got the upper hand of the centre of stimulation.

"In the well-known cases of deadly antipathy which have been recorded, the most frequent cause has been the disturbed and depressing influence of the centre of inhibition. Fainting at the sight of blood is one of the commonest examples of this influence. A single impression, in a very early period of atmospheric existence,—perhaps, indirectly, before that period, as was said to have happened in the case of James the First of England,—may establish a communication between this centre and the heart which will remain open ever afterwards. How does a footpath across a field establish itself? Its curves are arbitrary, and what we call accidental, but one after another follows it as if he were guided by a chart on which it was laid down. So it is with this dangerous transit between the centre of inhibition and the great organ of life. If once the path is opened by the track of some profound impression, that same impression, if repeated or a similar one, is likely to find the old foot-marks and follow them. Habit only makes the path easier to traverse, and thus the unreasoning terror of a child, of an infant, may perpetuate itself in a timidity which shames the manhood of its subject.

"The case before us is an exceptional and most remarkable example of the effect of inhibition on the heart.

"We will not say that we believe it to be unique in the history of the human race; on the contrary, we do not doubt that there have been similar cases, and that in some rare instances sudden death has been the consequence of seizures like that of the subject of this Report. The case most like it is that of Colonel Townsend, which is too well known to require any lengthened description in this paper. It is enough to recall the main facts. He could by a voluntary effort suspend the action of his heart for a considerable period, during which he lay like one dead, pulseless, and without motion. After a time the circulation returned, and he does not seem to have been the worse for his dangerous, or seemingly dangerous, experiment. But in his case it was by an act of the will that the heart's action was suspended. In the case before us it is an involuntary impulse transmitted from the brain to the inhibiting centre, which arrests the cardiac movements.

"What is like to be the further history of the case?

"The subject of this anomalous affliction is now more than twenty years old. The chain of nervous actions has become firmly established. It might have been hoped that the changes of adolescence would have effected a transformation of the perverted instinct. On the contrary, the whole force of this instinct throws itself on the centre of inhibition, instead of quickening the heart-beats, and sending the rush of youthful blood with fresh life through the entire system to the throbbing finger-tips.

"Is it probable that time and circumstances will alter a habit of nervous inter-actions so long established? We are disposed to think that there is a chance of its being broken up. And we are not afraid to say that we suspect the old gypsy woman, whose prophecy took such hold of the patient's imagination, has hit upon the way in which the 'spell,' as she called it, is to be dissolved. She must, in all probability, have had a hint of the *'antipatia'* to which the youth before her was a victim, and its cause, and if so, her guess as to the probable mode in which the young man would obtain relief from his unfortunate condition was the one which would natu-rally suggest itself.

"If once the nervous impression which falls on the centre of inhibition can be made to change its course, so as to follow its natural channel, it will probably keep to that channel ever afterwards. And this will, it is most likely, be effected by some sudden, unexpected impression. If he were drowning, and a young woman should rescue him, it is by no means impossible that the change in the nervous current we have referred to might be brought about as rapidly, as easily, as the reversal of the poles in a magnet, which is effected in an instant. But he cannot be expected to throw himself into the water just at the right moment when the 'fair lady' of the gitana's prophecy is passing on the shore. Accident may effect the cure which art seems incompetent to perform. It would not be strange if in some future seizure he should never come back to consciousness. But it is quite conceivable, on the other hand, that a happier event may occur,—that in a single moment the nervous polarity may be reversed, the whole course of his life changed, and his past terrible experiences be to him like a scarce remembered dream.

"This is one of those cases in which it is very hard to determine the wisest course to be pursued. The question is not unlike that which arises in certain cases of dislocation of the bones of the neck. Shall the unfortunate sufferer go all his days with his face turned far round to the right or the left, or shall an attempt be made to replace the dislocated bones?—an attempt which may succeed, or may cause instant death. The patient must be consulted as to whether he will take the chance. The practitioner may be unwilling to risk it, if the patient consents. Each case must be judged on its own special grounds. We cannot think that this young man is doomed to perpetual separation from the society of womanhood during the period of its bloom and attraction. But to provoke another seizure after his past experiences would be too much like committing suicide. We fear that we must trust to the chapter of accidents. The strange malady—for such it is—has become a second nature, and may require as energetic a shock to displace it as it did to bring it into existence. Time alone car solve this question, on which depends the well-being and, it may be, the existence of a young man every way fitted to be happy, and to give happiness if restored to his true nature."

DR. BUTTS REFLECTS.

DR. BUTTS sat up late at night reading these papers and reflecting upon them. He was profoundly impressed and tenderly affected by the entire frankness, the absence of all attempt at concealment, which Maurice showed in placing these papers at his disposal. He believed that his patient would recover from this illness for which he had been taking care of him. He thought deeply and earnestly of what he could do for him after he should have regained his health and strength.

There were references, in Maurice's own account of himself, which the doctor called to mind with great interest after reading his brief autobiography. Some one person—some young woman, it must be—had produced a singular impression upon him since those earlier perilous experiences through which he had passed. The doctor could not help thinking of that meeting with Euthymia of which she had spoken to him. Maurice, as she said, turned pale,—he clapped his hand to his breast. He might have done so if he had met her chambermaid, or any straggling damsel of the village. But Euthymia was not a young woman to be looked upon with indifference. She held herself like a queen, and walked like one,—not a stage queen, but one born and bred to self-reliance, and command of herself as well as others. One could not pass her without being struck with her noble bearing and spirited features. If she had known how Maurice trembled as he looked upon her, in that conflict of attraction and uncontrollable dread,—if she had known it! But what, even then, could she have done? Nothing but get away from him as fast as she could. As it was, it was a long time before his agitation subsided, and his heart beat with its common force and frequency.

Dr. Butts was not a male gossip nor a match-making go-between. But he could not help thinking what a pity it was that these two young persons could not come together as other young people do in the pairing season, and find out whether they cared for and were fitted for each other. He did not pretend to settle this question in his own mind, but the thought was a natural one. And here was a gulf between them as deep and wide as that between Lazarus and Dives. Would it ever be bridged over? This thought took possession of the doctor's mind, and he imagined all sorts of ways of effecting some experimental approximation between Maurice and Euthymia. From this delicate subject he glanced off to certain general considerations suggested by the extraordinary history he had been reading. He began by speculating as to the possibility of the personal presence of an individual making itself perceived by some channel other than any of the five senses. The study of the natural sciences teaches those who are devoted to them that the most insignificant facts may lead the way to the discovery of the most important, all-pervading laws of the universe. From the kick of a frog's hind leg to the amazing triumphs which began with that seemingly trivial incident is a long, a very long stride. If Madam Galvani had not been in delicate health, which was the occasion of her having some frog-broth prepared for her, the world of to-day might not be in possession of the electric telegraph and the light which blazes like the sun at high noon. A common looking occurrence, one seemingly unimportant, which had hitherto passed un-noticed with the ordinary course of things, was the means of introducing us to a new and vast realm of closely related phenomena. It was like a key that we might have picked up, looking so simple that it could hardly fit any lock but one of like simplicity, but which should all at once throw back the bolts of the one lock which had defied the most ingenious of our complex implements and open our way into a hitherto unexplored territory.

It certainly was not through the eye alone that Maurice felt the paralyzing influence. He could contemplate Euthymia from a distance, as he did on the day of the boat-race, without any nervous disturbance. A certain proximity was necessary for the influence to be felt, as in the case of magnetism and electricity. An atmosphere of danger surrounded every woman he approached during the period when her sex exercises its most powerful attractions. How far did that atmosphere extend, and through what channel did it act?

The key to the phenomena of this case, he believed, was to be found in a fact as humble as that which gave birth to the science of galvanism and its practical applications. The circumstances connected with the very common antipathy to ***cats*** were as remarkable in many points of view as the similar circumstances in the case of Maurice Kirkwood. The subjects of that antipathy could not tell what it was which disturbed their nervous system. All they knew was that a sense of uneasiness, restlessness, oppression, came over them in the presence of one of these animals. He remembered the fact already mentioned, that persons sensitive to this impression can tell by their feelings if a cat is concealed in the apartment in which they may happen to be. It may be through some emanation. It may be through the medium of some electrical disturbance. What if the nerve-thrills passing through the whole system of the animal propagate themselves to a certain distance without any more regard to intervening solids than is shown by magnetism? A sieve lets sand pass through it; a filter arrests sand, but lets fluids pass; glass holds fluids, but lets light through; wood shuts out light, but magnetic attraction goes through it as sand went through the sieve. No good reasons can be given why the presence of a cat should not betray itself to certain organizations, at a distance, through the walls of a box in which the animal is shut up. We need not disbelieve the stories which allege such an occurrence as a fact and not a very infrequent one.

If the presence of a cat can produce its effects under these circumstances, why should not that of a human being under similar conditions, acting on certain constitutions, exercise its specific influence? The doctor recalled a story told him by one of his friends, a story which the friend himself heard from the lips of the distinguished actor, the late Mr. Fechter. The actor maintained that Rachel had no **genius** as an actress. It was all Samson's training and study, according to him, which explained the secret of her wonderful effectiveness on the stage. But **magnetism,** he said,— **magnetism,** she was full of. He declared that he was made aware of her presence on the stage, when he could not see her or know of her presence otherwise, by this magnetic emanation. The doctor took the story for what it was worth. There might very probably be exaggeration, perhaps high imaginative coloring about it, but it was not a whit more unlikely than the cat-stories, accepted as authentic. He continued this train of thought into further developments. Into this series of reflections we will try to follow him.

What is the meaning of the **halo** with which artists have surrounded the heads of their pictured saints,—of the **aureola** which wraps them like a luminous cloud? Is it not a recognition of the fact that these holy personages diffuse their personality in the form of a visible emanation, which reminds us of Milton's definition of light:—

"Bright effluence of bright essence increate"?

The common use of the term influence would seem to imply the existence of its correlative, effluence. There is no good reason that I can see, the doctor said to himself, why among the forces which work upon the nervous centres there should not be one which acts at various distances from its source. It may not be visible like the "glory" of the painters, it may not be appreciable by any one of the five senses, and yet it may be felt by the person reached by it as much as if it were a palpable presence,—more powerfully, perhaps, from the mystery which belongs to its mode of action.

Why should not Maurice have been rendered restless and anxious by the unseen nearness of a young woman who was in the next room to him, just as the persons who have the dread of cats are made conscious of their presence through some unknown channel? Is it anything strange that the larger and more powerful organism should diffuse a consciousness of its presence to some distance as well as the slighter and feebler one? Is it strange that this mysterious influence or effluence should belong especially or exclusively to the period of complete womanhood in distinction from that of immaturity or decadence? On the contrary, it seems to be in accordance with all the analogies of nature,—analogies too often cruel in the sentence they pass upon the human female.

Among the many curious thoughts which came up in the doctor's mind was this, which made him smile as if it were a jest, but which he felt very strongly had its serious side, and was involved with the happiness or suffering of multitudes of youthful persons who die without telling their secret:—

How many young men have a mortal fear of woman, as woman, which they never overcome, and in consequence of which the attraction which draws man towards her, as strong in them as in others,—oftentimes, in virtue of their pecularily sensitive organizations, more potent in them than in others of like age and conditions,—in consequence of which fear, this attraction is completely neutralized, and all the possibilities of doubled and indefinitely extended life depending upon it are left unrealized! Think what numbers of young men in Catholic countries devote themselves to lives of celibacy. Think how many young men lose all their confidence in the presence of the young woman to whom they are most attracted, and at last steal away from a companionship which is rapture to dream of and torture to endure, so does the presence of the beloved object paralyze all the powers of expression. Sorcerers have in all time and countries played on the hopes and terrors of lovers. Once let loose a strong impulse on the centre of inhibition, and the warrior who had faced bayonets and batteries becomes a coward whom the well-dressed hero of the ball-room and leader of the German will put to ignominious flight in five minutes of easy, audacious familiarity with his lady-love.

Yes, the doctor went on with his reflections, I do not know that I have seen the term **Gynophobia** before I opened this manuscript, but I have seen the malady many times. Only one word has stood between many a pair of young people and their life-long happiness, and that word has got as far as the lips,—but the lips trembled and would not, could not, shape that little word All young women are not like Coleridge's Genevieve, who knew how to help her lover out of his difficulty, and said yes before he had asked for an answer. So the wave which was to have wafted them on to the shore of Elysium has just failed of landing them, and back they have been drawn into the desolate ocean to meet no more on earth.

Love is the master-key, he went on thinking,—love is the master-key that opens the gates of happiness, of hatred, of jealousy, and, most easily of all, the gate of *fear.* How terrible is the one fact of beauty!—not only the historic wonder of beauty, that "burnt the topless towers of Ilium" for the smile of Helen, and fired the palaces of Babylon by the hand of Thais, but the beauty which springs up in all times and places, and carries a torch and wears a serpent for a wreath as truly as any of the Eumenides. Paint Beauty with her foot upon a skull and a dragon coiled around her.

The doctor smiled at his own imposing classical allusions and pictorial imagery. Drifting along from thought to thought, he reflected on the probable consequences of the general knowledge of Maurice Kirkwood's story, if it came before the public.

What a piece of work it would make among the lively youths of the village, to be sure! What scoffing, what ridicule, what embellishments, what fables, would follow in the trail of the story! If the Interviewer got hold of it, how "The People's Perennial and Household Inquisitor "would blaze with capitals in its next issue! The young fellows of the place would be disposed to make fun of the whole matter. The young girls—the doctor hardly dared to think what would happen when the story got about among them. "The Sachem" of the solitary canoe, the bold horseman, the handsome hermit,—handsome so far as the glimpses they had got of him went,—must needs be a subject of tender interest among them, now that he was ailing, suffering, in danger of his life, away from friends,—poor fellow! Little tokens of their regard had reached his sick-chamber; bunches of flowers with dainty little notes, some of them pinkish, some three-cornered, some of them with brief messages, others "criss-crossed," were growing more frequent as it was understood that the patient was likely to be convalescent before many days had passed. If it should come to be understood that there was a deadly obstacle to their coming into any personal relations with him, the doctor had his doubts whether there were not those who would subject him to the risk; for there were coquettes in the village,—strangers, visitors, let us hope,—who would sacrifice anything or anybody to their vanity and love of conquest

AN INTIMATE CONVERSATION.

THE illness from which Maurice had suffered left him in a state of profound prostration. The doctor, who remembered the extreme danger of any over-exertion in such cases, hardly allowed him to lift his head from the pillow. But his mind was gradually recovering its balance, and he was able to hold some conversation with those about him. His faithful Paolo had grown so thin in waiting upon him and watching with him that the village children had to take a second look at his face when they passed him to make sure that it was indeed their old friend and no other. But as his master advanced towards convalescence and the doctor assured him that he was going in all probability to get well, Paolo's face began to recover something of its old look and expression, and once more his pockets filled themselves with comfits for his little circle of worshipping three and four year old followers.

"How is Mr Kirkwood?" was the question with which he was always greeted. In the worst periods of the fever he rarely left his master. When he did, and the question was put to him, he would shake his head sadly, sometimes without a word, sometimes with tears and sobs and faltering words,—more like a broken-hearted child than a stalwart man as he was, such a man as soldiers are made of in the great Continental armies.

"He very bad,—he no eat nothing,—he no say nothing,—he never be no better," and all his Southern nature betrayed itself in a passionate burst of lamentation. But now that he began to feel easy about his master, his ready optimism declared itself no less transparently.

"He better every day now. He get well in few weeks, sure. You see him on hoss in little while." The kind-hearted creature's life was bound up in that of his "master," as he loved to call him, in sovereign disregard of the comments of the natives, who held themselves too high for any such recognition of another as their better. They could not understand how he, so much their superior in bodily presence, in air and manner, could speak of the man who employed him in any other way than as "Kirkwood," without even demeaning himself so far as to prefix a "Mr." to it But "my master" Maurice remained for Paolo in spite of the fact that all men are born free and equal And never was a servant more devoted to a master than was Paolo to Maurice during the days of doubt and danger. Since his improvement Maurice insisted upon his leaving his chamber and getting out of the house, so as to breathe the fresh air of which he was in so much need. It worried him to see his servant returning after too short an absence. The attendant who had helped him in the care of the patient was within call, and Paolo was almost driven out of the house by the urgency of his master's command that he should take plenty of exercise in the open air.

Notwithstanding the fact of Maurice's improved condition, although the force of the disease had spent itself, the state of weakness to which he had been reduced was a cause of some anxiety, and required great precautions to be taken. He lay in bed, wasted, enfeebled to such a degree that he had to be cared for very much as a child is tended. Gradually his voice was coming back to him, so that he could hold some conversation, as was before mentioned, with those about him. The doctor waited for the right moment to make mention of the manuscript which Maurice had submitted to him. Up to this time, although it had been alluded to and the doctor had told him of the intense interest with which he had read it, he had never ventured to make it the subject of any long talk, such as would be liable to fatigue his patient. But now he thought the time had come.

"I have been thinking," the doctor said, "of the singular seizures to which you are liable, and as it is my business not merely to think about such cases, but to do what I can to help any who may be capable of receiving aid from my art, I wish to have some additional facts about your history. And in the first place, will you allow me to ask what led you to this particular place? It is so much less known to the public at large than many other resorts that we naturally ask, What brings this or that new visitor among us? We have no ill-tasting, natural spring of bad water to be analyzed by the state chemist and proclaimed as a specific. We have no great gambling-houses, no racecourse (except that for boats on the lake); we have no coaching-club, no great balls, few lions of any kind,—so we ask, What brings this or that stranger here? And I think I may venture to ask you whether any special motive brought you among us, or whether it was accident that determined your coming to this place."

"Certainly, doctor," Maurice answered, "I will tell you with great pleasure. Last year I passed on the border of a great river. The year before I lived in a lonely cottage at the side of the ocean. I wanted this year to be by a lake. You heard the paper read at the meeting of your society, or at least you heard of it,—for such matters are always talked over in a village like this. You can judge by that paper, or could, if it were before you, of the frame of mind in which I came here. I was tired of the sullen indifference of the ocean and the babbling egotism of the river, always hurrying along on its own private business. I wanted the dreamy stillness of a large, tranquil sheet of water that had nothing in particular to do, and would leave me to myself and my thoughts. I had read somewhere about the place, and the old Anchor Tavern, with its paternal landlord and motherly landlady and old-fashioned household, and that, though it was no longer open as a tavern, I could find a resting-place there early in the season, at least for a few days, while I looked about me for a quiet place in which I might pass my summer. I have found this a pleasant residence. By being up early and out late I have kept myself mainly in the solitude which has become my enforced habit of life. The season has gone by too swiftly for me since my dream has become a vision."

The doctor was sitting with his hand round Maurice's wrist three fingers on his pulse. As he spoke these last words he noticed that the pulse fluttered a little,—beat irregularly a few times; intermitted; became feeble and thready; while his cheek grew whiter than the pallid bloodlessness of his long illness had left it.

"No more talk, now," he said. "You are too tired to be using your voice. I will hear all the rest another time."

The doctor had interrupted Maurice at an interesting point. What did he mean by saying that his dream had become a vision? This is what the doctor was naturally curious, and professionally anxious, to know. But his hand was still on his patient's pulse, which told him unmistakably that the heart had taken the alarm and was losing its energy under the depressing nervous influence. Presently, however, it recovered its natural force and rhythm, and a faint flush came back to the pale cheek. The doctor remembered the story of Galen, and the young maiden whose complaint had puzzled the physicians.

The next day his patient was well enough to enter once more into conversation.

"You said something about a dream of yours which had become a vision," said the doctor, with his fingers on his patient's wrist, as before. He felt the artery leap, under his pressure, falter a little, stop, then begin again, growing fuller in its beat. The heart had felt the pull of the bridle, but the spur had roused it to swift reaction.

"You know the story of my past life, doctor," Maurice answered; "and I will tell you what is the vision which has taken the place of my dreams. You remember the boat-race? I watched it from a distance, but I held a powerful opera-glass in my hand, which brought the whole crew of the young ladies' boat so close to me that I could see the features, the figures, the movements, of every one of the rowers. I saw the little coxswain fling her bouquet in the track of the other boat,—you remember how the race was lost and won,—but I saw one face among those young girls which drew me away from all the rest It was that of the young lady who pulled the bow oar, the captain of the boat's crew. I have since learned her name,—you know it well,—I need not name her. Since that day I have had many distant glimpses of her; and once I met her so squarely that the deadly sensation came over me, and I felt that in another moment I should fall senseless at her feet. But she passed on her way and I on mine, and the spasm which had clutched my heart gradually left it, and I was as well as before. You know that young lady, doctor?"

"I do; and she is a very noble creature. You are not the first young man who has been fascinated, almost at a glance, by Miss Euthymia Tower. And she is well worth knowing more intimately."

The doctor gave him a full account of the young lady, of her early days, her character, her accomplishments. To all this he listened devoutly, and when the doctor left him he said to himself,—

"I will see her and speak with her, if it costs me my life."

EUTHYMIA.

"THE Wonder" of the Corinna Institute had never willingly made a show of her gymnastic accomplishments. Her feats, which were so much admired, were only her natural exercise. Gradually the dumb-bells others used became too light for her, the ropes she climbed too short, the clubs she exercised with seemed as if they were made of cork instead of being heavy wood, and all the tests and meters of strength and agility had been strained beyond the standards which the records of the school had marked as their historic maxima. It was not her fault that she broke a dynamometer one day; she apologized for it, but the teacher said he wished he could have a dozen broken every year in the same way. The consciousness of her bodily strength had made her very careful in her movements. The pressure of her hand was never too hard for the tenderest little maiden whose palm was against her own. So far from priding herself on her special gifts, she was disposed to be ashamed of them. There were times and places in which she could give full play to her muscles without fear or reproach. She had her special costume for the boat and for the woods. She would climb the rugged old hemlocks now and then for the sake of a wide outlook, or to peep into the large nest where a hawk, or it may be an eagle, was raising her little brood of air-pirates.

There were those who spoke of her wanderings in lonely places as an unsafe exposure. One sometimes met doubtful characters about the neighborhood, and stories were told of occurrences which might well frighten a young girl, and make her cautious of trusting herself alone in the wild solitudes which surrounded the little village. Those who knew Euthymia thought her quite equal to taking care of herself. Her very look was enough to ensure the respect of any vagabond who might cross her path, and if matters came to the worst she would prove as dangerous as a panther.

But it was a pity to associate this class of thoughts with a noble specimen of true womanhood. Health, beauty, strength, were fine qualities, and in all these she was rich. She enjoyed all her natural gifts, and thought little about them. Unwillingly, but over-persuaded by some of her friends, she had allowed her arm and hand to be modelled. The artists who saw the cast wondered if it would be possible to get the bust of the maiden from whom it was taken. Nobody would have dared to suggest such an idea to her except Lurida. For Lurida sex was a trifling accident, to be disregarded not only in the interests of humanity, but for the sake of art.

"It is a shame," she said to Euthymia, "that you will not let your exquisitely moulded form be perpetuated in marble. You have no right to withhold such a model from the contemplation of your fellow-creatures. Think how rare it is to see a woman who truly represents the divine idea! You belong to your race, and not to yourself,—at least, your beauty is a gift not to be considered as a piece of private property. Look at the so-called Venus of Milo. Do you suppose the noble woman who was the original of that divinely chaste statue felt any scruple about allowing the sculptor to reproduce her pure, unblemished perfections?"

Euthymia was always patient with her imaginative friend. She listened to her eloquent discourse, but she could not help blushing, used as she was to Lurida's audacities. "The Terror's" brain had run away with a large share of the blood which ought to have gone to the nourishment of her general system. She could not help admiring, almost worshipping, a companion whose being was rich in the womanly developments with which nature had so economically endowed herself. An impoverished organization carries with it certain neutral qualities which make its subject appear, in the presence of complete manhood and womanhood, like a deaf-mute among speaking persons. The deep blush which crimsoned Euthymia's cheek at Lurida's suggestion was in a strange contrast to her own undisturbed expression. There was a range of sensibilities of which Lurida knew far less than she did of those many and difficult studies which had absorbed her vital forces. She was startled to see what an effect her proposal had produced, for Euthymia was not only blushing, but there was a flame in her eyes which she had hardly ever seen before.

"Is this only your own suggestion?" Euthymia said, "or has some one been putting the idea into your head?" The truth was that she had happened to meet the Interviewer at the Library, one day, and she was offended by the long, searching stare with which that individual had honored her. It occurred to her that he, or some such visitor to the place, might have spoken of her to Lurida, or to some other person who had repeated what was said to Lurida, as a good subject for the art of the sculptor, and she felt all her maiden sensibilities offended by the proposition. Lurida could not understand her excitement, but she was startled by it. Natures which are complementary of each other are liable to these accidental collisions of feeling. They get along very well together, none the worse for their differences, until all at once the tender spot of one or the other is carelessly handled in utter unconsciousness on the part of the aggressor, and the exclamation, the outcry, or the explosion explains the situation altogether too emphatically. Such scenes did not frequently occur between the two friends, and this little flurry was soon over; but it served to warn Lurida that Miss Euthymia Tower was not of that class of self-conscious beauties who would be ready to dispute the empire of the Venus of Milo on her own ground, in defences as scanty and insufficient as those of the marble divinity.

Euthymia had had admirers enough, at a distance, while at school, and in the long vacations, near enough to find out that she was anything but easy to make love to. She fairly frightened more than one rash youth who was disposed to be too sentimental in her company. They overdid flattery, which she was used to and tolerated, but which cheapened the admirer in her estimation, and now and then betrayed her into an expression which made him aware of the fact, and was a discouragement to aggressive amiability. The real difficulty was that not one of her adorers had ever greatly interested her. It could not be that nature had made her insensible. It must have been because the man who was made for her had never yet shown himself. She was not easy to please, that was certain; and she was one of those young women who will not accept as a lover one who but half pleases them. She could not pick up the first stick that fell in her way and take it to shape her ideal out of. Many of the good people of the village doubted whether Euthymia would ever be married.

"There's nothing good enough for her in this village," said the old landlord of what had been the Anchor Tavern.

"She must wait till a prince comes along," the old landlady said in reply. "She'd make as pretty a queen as any of them that's born to it. Wouldn't she be splendid with a gold crown on her head, and di'monds a glitterin' all over her! D' you remember how handsome she looked in the tableau, when the fair was held for the Dorcas Society? She had on an old dress of her grandma's,—they don't make anything half so handsome nowadays,—and she was just as pretty as a pictur' But what's the use of good looks if they scare away folks? The young fellows think that such a handsome girl as that would cost ten times as much to keep as a plain one. She must be dressed up like an empress,—so they seem to think. It ain't so with Euthymy: she'd look like a great lady dressed anyhow, and she hasn't got any more notions than the homeliest girl that ever stood before a glass to look at herself."

In the humbler walks of Arrowhead Village society, similar opinions were entertained of Miss Euthymia. The fresh-water fisherman represented pretty well the average estimate of the class to which he belonged. "I tell ye," said he to another gentleman of leisure, whose chief occupation was to watch the coming and going of the visitors to Arrowhead Village,—"I tell ye that girl ain't a gon to put up with any o' them slab-sided fellahs that you see hangin' raound to look at her every Sunday when she comes aout o' meetin'. It's one o' them big gents from Boston or New York that'll step up an' kerry her off."

In the meantime nothing could be further from the thoughts of Euthymia than the prospect of an ambitious worldly alliance. The ideals of young women cost them many and great disappointments, but they save them very often from those lifelong companionships which accident is constantly trying to force upon them, in spite of their obvious unfitness. The higher the ideal, the less likely is the commonplace neighbor who has the great advantage of easy access, or the boarding-house acquaintance who can profit by those vacant hours when the least interesting of visitors is better than absolute loneliness,—the less likely are these undesirable personages to be endured, pitied, and, if not embraced, accepted, for want of something better. Euthymia found so much pleasure in the intellectual companionship of Lurida, and felt her own prudence and reserve so necessary to that independent young lady, that she had been contented, so far, with friendship, and thought of love only in an abstract sort of way. Beneath her abstractions there was a capacity of loving which might have been inferred from the expression of her features, the light that shone in her eyes, the tones of her voice, all of which were full of the language which belongs to susceptible natures. How many women never say to themselves that they were born to love, until all at once the discovery opens upon them, as the sense that he was born a painter is said to have dawned suddenly upon Correggio!

Like all the rest of the village and its visitors, she could not help thinking a good deal about the young man lying ill amongst strangers. She was not one of those who had sent him the three-cornered notes or even a bunch of flowers. She knew that he was receiving abounding tokens of kindness and sympathy from different quarters, and a certain inward feeling restrained her from joining in these demonstrations. If he had been suffering from some deadly and contagious malady she would have risked her life to help him, without a thought that there was any wonderful heroism in such self-devotion. Her friend Lurida might have been capable of the same sacrifice, but it would be after reasoning with herself as to the obligations which her sense of human rights and duties laid upon her, and fortifying her courage with the memory of noble deeds recorded of women in ancient and modern history. With

Euthymia the primary human instincts took precedence of all reasoning or reflection about them. All her sympathies were excited by the thought of this forlorn stranger in his solitude, but she felt the impossibility of giving any complete expression to them. She thought of Mungo Park in the African desert, and she envied the poor negress who not only pitied him, but had the blessed opportunity of helping and consoling him. How near were these two human creatures, each needing the other! How near in bodily presence, how far apart in their lives, with a barrier seemingly impassable between them!

THE MEETING OF MAURICE AND EUTHYMIA.

THESE autumnal fevers, which carry off a large number of our young people every year, are treacherous and deceptive diseases. Not only are they liable, as has been mentioned, to various accidental complications which may prove suddenly fatal, but too often, after convalescence seems to be established, relapses occur which are more serious than the disease had appeared to be in its previous course. One morning Dr. Butts found Maurice worse instead of better, as he had hoped and expected to find him. Weak as he was, there was every reason to fear the issue of this return of his threatening symptoms. There was not much to do besides keeping up the little strength which still remained. It was all needed.

Does the reader of these pages ever think of the work a sick man as much as a well one has to perform while he is lying on his back and taking what we call his "rest"? More than a thousand times an hour, between a hundred and fifty and two hundred thousand times a week, he has to lift the bars of the cage in which his breathing organs are confined, to save himself from asphyxia. Rest! There is no rest until the last long sigh tells those who look upon the dying that the ceaseless daily task, to rest from which is death, is at last finished. We are all galley-slaves, pulling at the levers of respiration,—which, rising and falling like so many oars, drive us across an unfathomable ocean from one unknown shore to another. No! Never was a galley-slave so chained as we are to these four and twenty oars at which we must tug day and night all our life long!

The doctor could not find any accidental cause to account for this relapse. It presently occurred to him that there might be some local source of infection which had brought on the complaint, and was still keeping up the symptoms which were the ground of alarm. He determined to remove Maurice to his own house, where he could be sure of pure air, and where he himself could give more constant attention to his patient during this critical period of his disease. It was a risk to take, but he could be carried on a litter by careful men, and remain wholly passive during the removal. Maurice signified his assent, as he could hardly help doing,—for the doctor's suggestion took pretty nearly the form of a command. He thought it a matter of life and death, and was gently urgent for his patient's immediate change of residence. The doctor insisted on having Maurice's books and other movable articles carried to his own house, so that he should be surrounded by familiar sights, and not worry himself about what might happen to objects which he valued, if they were left behind him.

All these dispositions were quickly and quietly made, and everything was ready for the transfer of the patient to the house of the hospitable physician. Paolo was at the doctor's, superintending the arrangement of Maurice's effects and making all ready for his master. The nurse in attendance, a trustworthy man enough in the main, finding his patient in a tranquil sleep, left his bedside for a little fresh air. While he was at the door he heard a shouting which excited his curiosity, and he followed the sound until he found himself at the border of the lake. It was nothing very wonderful that had caused the shouting. A Newfoundland dog had been showing off his accomplishments, and some of the idlers were betting as to the time it would take him to bring back to his master the various floating objects which had been thrown as far from the shore as possible. He watched the dog a few minutes, when his attention was drawn to a light wherry, pulled by one young lady and steered by another. It was making for the shore, which it would soon reach. The attendant remembered all at once that he had left his charge, and just before the boat came to land he turned and hurried back to the patient Exactly how long he had been absent he could not have said,—perhaps a quarter of an hour, perhaps longer; the time appeared short to him, wearied with long sitting and watching.

It had seemed, when he stole away from Maurice's bedside, that he was not in the least needed. The patient was lying perfectly quiet, and to all appearance wanted nothing more than letting alone. It was such a comfort to look at something besides the worn features of a sick man, to hear something besides his labored breathing and faint, half-whispered words, that the temptation to indulge in these luxuries for a few minutes had proved irresistible.

Unfortunately, Maurice's slumbers did not remain tranquil during the absence of the nurse. He very soon fell into a dream, which began quietly enough, but in the course of the sudden transitions which dreams are in the habit of undergoing became successively anxious, distressing, terrifying. His earlier and later experiences came up before him, fragmentary, incoherent, chaotic even, but vivid as reality. He was at the bottom of a coal-mine in one of those long, narrow galleries, or rather worm-holes, in which human beings pass a large part of their lives, like so many larvæ boring their way into the beams and rafters of some old building. How close the air was in the stifling passage through which he was crawling! The scene changed, and he was climbing a slippery sheet of ice with desperate effort, his foot on the floor of a shallow niche, his hold an icicle ready to snap in an instant, an abyss below him waiting for his foot to slip or the icicle to break. How thin the air seemed, how desperately hard to breathe! He was thinking of Mont Blanc, it may be, and the fearfully rarefied atmosphere which he remembered well as one of the great trials in his mountain ascents. No, it was not Mont Blanc,—it was not any one of the frozen Alpine summits; it was not that he was climbing! The smoke of the burning mountain was wrapping itself around him; he was choking with its dense fumes; he heard the flames roaring around him, he felt the hot lava beneath his feet, he uttered a faint cry, and awoke.

The room was full of smoke. He was gasping for breath, strangling in the smothering oven which his chamber had become.

The house was on fire!

He tried to call for help, but his voice failed him, and died away in a whisper. He made a desperate effort, and rose so as to sit up in the bed for an instant, but the effort was too much for him, and he sank back upon his pillow, helpless. He felt that his hour had come, for he could not live in this dreadful atmosphere, and he was left alone. He could hear the crackle of fire as the flame crept along from one partition to another. It was a cruel fate to be left to perish in that way,—the fate that many a martyr had had to face,—to be first strangled and then burned. Death had not the terror for him that it has for most young persons. He was accustomed to thinking of it calmly, sometimes wistfully, even to such a degree that the thought of self-destruction had come upon him as a temptation. But here was death in an unexpected and appalling shape. He did not know before how much he cared to live. All his old recollections came before him as it were in one long, vivid flash. The closed vista of memory opened to its far horizon-line, and past and present were pictured in a single instant of clear vision. The dread moment which had blighted his life returned in all its terror. He felt the convulsive spring in the form of a faint, impotent spasm,—the rush of air,—the thorns of the stinging and lacerating cradle into which he was precipitated. One after another those paralyzing seizures which had been like deadening blows on the naked heart seemed to repeat themselves, as real as at the moment of their occurrence. The pictures passed in succession with such rapidity that they appeared almost as if simultaneous. The vision of the "inward eye" was so intensified in this moment of peril that an instant was like an hour of common existence. Those who have been very near drowning know well what this description means. The development of a photograph may not explain it, but it illustrates the curious and familiar fact of the revived recollections of the drowning man's experience. The sensitive plate has taken one look at a scene, and remembers it all. Every little circumstance is there,—the hoof in air, the wing in flight, the leaf as it falls, the wave as it breaks. All there, but invisible; potentially present, but impalpable, inappreciable, as if not existing at all. A wash is poured over it, and the whole scene comes out in all its perfection of detail. In those supreme moments when death stares a man suddenly in the face the rush of unwonted emotion floods the undeveloped pictures of vanished years, stored away in the memory, the vast panorama of a lifetime, and in one swift instant the past comes out as vividly as if it were again the present. So it was at this moment with the sick man, as he lay helpless and felt that he was left to die. For he saw no hope of relief: the smoke was drifting in clouds into the room; the flames were very near; if he was not reached and rescued immediately it was all over with him.

His past life had flashed before him. Then all at once rose the thought of his future,—of all its possibilities, of the vague hopes which he had cherished of late that his mysterious doom would be lifted from him. There was something, then, to be lived for,—something! There was a new life, it might be, in store for him, and such a new life! He thought of all he was losing. Oh, could he but have lived to know the meaning of love! And the passionate desire of life came over him,—not the dread of death, but the longing for what the future might yet have of happiness for him.

All this took place in the course of a very few moments. Dreams and visions have little to do with measured time, and ten minutes, possibly fifteen or twenty, were all that had passed since the beginning of those nightmare terrors which were evidently suggested by the suffocating air he was breathing.

What had happened? In the confusion of moving books and other articles to the doctor's house, doors and windows had been forgotten. Among the rest a window opening into the cellar, where some old furniture had been left by a former occupant, had been left unclosed. One of the lazy natives, who had lounged by the house smoking a bad cigar, had thrown the burning stump in at this open window. He had no particular intention of doing mischief, but he had that indifference to consequences which is the next step above the inclination to crime. The burning stump happened to fall among the straw of an old mattress which had been ripped open. The smoker went his way without looking behind him, and it so chanced that no other person passed the house for some time. Presently the straw was in a blaze, and from this the fire extended to the furniture, to the stairway leading up from the cellar, and was working its way along the entry under the stairs leading up to the apartment where Maurice was lying.

The blaze was fierce and swift, as it could not help being with such a mass of combustibles,—loose straw from the mattress, dry old furniture, and old warped floors which had been parching and shrinking for a score or two of years. The whole house was, in the common language of the newspaper reports, "a perfect tinder-box," and would probably be a heap of ashes in half an hour. And there was this unfortunate deserted sick man lying between life and death, beyond all help unless some unexpected assistance should come to his rescue.

As the attendant drew near the house where Maurice was lying, he was horror-struck to see dense volumes of smoke pouring out of the lower windows. It was beginning to make its way through the upper windows, also, and presently a tongue of fire shot out and streamed upward along the side of the house. The man shrieked Fire! Fire! with all his might, and rushed to the door of the building to make his way to Maurice's room and save him. He penetrated but a short distance when, blinded and choking with the smoke, he rushed headlong down the stairs with a cry of despair that roused every man, woman, and child within reach of a human voice. Out they came from their houses in every quarter of the village. The shout of Fire! Fire! was the chief aid lent by many of the young and old. Some caught up pails and buckets: the more thoughtful ones filling them; the hastier snatching them up empty, trusting to find water nearer the burning building.

Is the sick man moved?

This was the awful question first asked,—for in the little village all knew that Maurice was about being transferred to the doctor's house. The attendant, white as death, pointed to the chamber where he had left him, and gasped out,—

"He is there!"

A ladder! A ladder! was the general cry, and men and boys rushed off in search of one. But a single minute was an age now, and there was no ladder to be had without a delay of many minutes. The sick man was going to be swallowed up in the flames before it could possibly arrive. Some were going for a blanket or a coverlet, in the hope that the young man might have strength enough to leap from the window and be safely caught in it. The attendant shook his head, and said faintly,—

"He cannot move from his bed."

One of the visitors at the village,—a millionaire, it was said,—a kind-hearted man, spoke in hoarse, broken tones:—

"A thousand dollars to the man that will bring him from his chamber!"

The fresh-water fisherman muttered, "I should like to save the man and to see the money, but it ain't a thaousan' dollars, nor ten thaousan' dollars, that'll pay a fellah for burnin' to death,—or even chokin' to death, anyhaow."

The carpenter, who knew the framework of every house in the village, recent or old, shook his head.

"The stairs have been shored up," he said, "and when the j'ists that holds 'em up goes, down they'll come. It ain't safe for no man to go over them stairs. Hurry along your ladder,—that's your only chance."

All was wild confusion around the burning house. The ladder they had gone for was missing from its case,—a neighbor had carried it off for the workmen who were shingling his roof. It would never get there in time. There was a fire-engine, but it was nearly half a mile from the lakeside settlement. Some were throwing on water in an aimless, useless way; one was sending a thin stream through a garden syringe: it seemed like doing something, at least. But all hope of saving Maurice was fast giving way, so rapid was the progress of the flames, so thick the cloud of smoke that filled the house and poured from the windows. Nothing was heard but confused cries, shriek of women, all sorts of orders to do this and that, no one knowing what was to be done. The ladder! The ladder! Five minutes more and it will be too late!

In the mean time the alarm of fire had reached Paolo, and he had stopped his work of arranging Maurice's books in the same way as that in which they had stood in his apartment, and followed in the direction of the sound, little thinking that his master was lying helpless in the burning house. "Some chimney afire," he said to himself; but he would go and take a look, at any rate.

Before Paolo had reached the scene of destruction and impending death, two young women, in boating dresses of decidedly Bloomerish aspect, had suddenly joined the throng. "The Wonder" and "The Terror" of their school-days—Miss Euthymia Tower and Miss Lurida Vincent—had just come from the shore, where they had left their wherry. A few hurried words told them the fearful story. Maurice Kirkwood was lying in the chamber to which every eye was turned, unable to move, doomed to a dreadful death. All that could be hoped was that he would perish by suffocation rather than by the flames, which would soon be upon him. The man who had attended him had just tried to reach his chamber, but had reeled back out of the door, almost strangled by the smoke. A thousand dollars had been offered to any one who would rescue the sick man, but no one had dared to make the attempt; for the stairs might fall at any moment, if the smoke did not blind and smother the man who passed them before they fell.

The two young women looked each other in the face for one swift moment.

"How can he be reached?" asked Lurida. "Is there nobody that will venture his life to save a brother like that?"

"I will venture mine," said Euthymia.

"No! no!" shrieked Lurida,—"not you! not you! It is a man's work, not yours! You shall not go!"

Poor Lurida had forgotten all her theories in this supreme moment. But Euthymia was not to be held back. Taking a handkerchief from her neck, she dipped it in a pail of water and bound it about her head. Then she took several deep breaths of air and filled her lungs as full as they would hold. She knew she must not take a single breath in the choking atmosphere if she could possibly help it, and Euthymia was noted for her power of staying under water so long that more than once those who saw her dive thought she would never come up again. So rapid were her movements that they paralyzed the bystanders, who would forcibly have prevented her from carrying out her purpose. Her imperious determination was not to be resisted. And so Euthymia, a willing martyr, if martyr she was to be, and not saviour, passed within the veil that hid the sufferer.

Lurida turned deadly pale, and sank fainting to the ground. She was the first, but not the only one, of her sex that fainted as Euthymia disappeared in the smoke of the burning building. Even the rector grew very white in the face,—so white that one of his vestry-men begged him to sit down at once, and sprinkled a few drops of water on his forehead, to his great disgust and manifest advantage. The old landlady was crying and moaning, and her husband was wiping his eyes and shaking his head sadly.

"She will never come out alive," he said solemnly.

"Nor dead neither," added the carpenter. "Ther' won't be nothing left of neither of 'em but ashes." And the carpenter hid his face in his hands.

The fresh-water fisherman had pulled out a rag which he called a "hangkercher,"—it had served to carry bait that morning,—and was making use of its best corner to dry the tears which were running down his cheeks. The whole village was proud of Euthymia, and with these more quiet signs of grief were mingled loud lamentations, coming alike from old and young.

All this was not so much like a succession of events as it was like a tableau. The lookers-on were stunned with its suddenness, and before they had time to recover their bewildered senses all was lost, or seemed lost. They felt that they should never look again on either of those young faces.

The rector, not unfeeling by nature, but inveterately professional by habit, had already recovered enough to be thinking of a text for the funeral sermon. The first that occurred to him was this,—vaguely, of course, in the background of consciousness:—

"Then Shadrach, Meshach, and Abed-nego came forth of the midst of the fire."

The village undertaker was of naturally sober aspect and reflective disposition.

He had always been opposed to cremation, and here was a funeral pile blazing before his eyes. He, too, had his human sympathies, but in the distance his imagination pictured the final ceremony, and how he himself should figure in a spectacle where the usual centre piece of attraction would be wanting,—perhaps his own services uncalled for.

Blame him not, you whose garden-patch is not watered with the tears of mourners. The string of self-interest answers with its chord to every sound; it vibrates with the funeral-bell, it finds itself trembling to the wail of the De Profundis. Not always,—not always; let us not be cynical in our judgments, but common human nature, we may safely say, is subject to those secondary vibrations under the most solemn and soul-subduing influences.

It seems as if we were doing great wrong to the scene we are contemplating in delaying it by the description of little circumstances and individual thoughts and feelings. But linger as we may, we cannot compress into a chapter—we could not crowd into a volume—all that passed through the minds and stirred the emotions of the awestruck company which was gathered about the scene of danger and of terror. We are dealing with an impossibility: consciousness is a surface; narrative is a line.

Maurice had given himself up for lost. His breathing was becoming every moment more difficult, and he felt that his strength could hold out but a few minutes longer.

"Robert!" he called in faint accents. But the attendant was not there to answer.

"Paolo! Paolo!" But the faithful servant, who would have given his life for his master, had not yet reached the place where the crowd was gathered.

"Oh, for a breath of air! Oh, for an arm to lift me from this bed! Too late! Too late!" he gasped, with what might have seemed his dying expiration.

"Not too late!" The soft voice reached his obscured consciousness as if it had come down to him from heaven.

In a single instant he found hsimself rolled in a blanket and in the arms of—a woman!

Out of the stifling chamber,—over the burning stairs,—close by the tongues of fire that were lapping up all they could reach,—out into the open air, he was borne swiftly and safely,—carried as easily as if he had been a babe, in the strong arms of "The Wonder" of the gymnasium, the captain of the Atalanta, who had little dreamed of the use she was to make of her natural gifts and her school-girl accomplishments.

Such a cry as arose from the crowd of on-lookers! It was a sound that none of them had ever heard before or could expect ever to hear again, unless he should be one of the last boat-load rescued from a sinking vessel Then, those who had resisted the overflow of their emotion, who had stood in white despair as they thought of these two young lives soon to be wrapped in their burning shroud,—those stern men—the old sea-captain, the hard-faced, money-making, cast-iron tradesmen of the city counting-room—sobbed like hysteric women; it was like a convulsion that overcame natures unused to those deeper emotions which many who are capable of experiencing die without ever knowing.

This was the scene upon which the doctor and Paolo suddenly appeared at the same moment.

As the fresh breeze passed over the face of the rescued patient, his eyes opened wide, and his consciousness returned in almost supernatural lucidity. Euthymia had sat down upon a bank, and was still supporting him. His head was resting on her bosom. Through his awakening senses stole the murmurs of the living cradle which rocked him with the wave-like movements of respiration, the soft *susurrus* of the air that entered with every breath, the double beat of the heart which throbbed close to his ear. And every sense, and every instinct, and every reviving pulse told him in language like a revelation from another world that a woman's arms were around him, and that it was life, and not death, which her embrace had brought him.

She would have disengaged him from her protecting hold, but the doctor made her a peremptory sign, which he followed by a sharp command:

"Do not move him a hair's breadth," he said. "Wait until the litter comes. Any sudden movement might be dangerous. Has anybody a brandy flask about him?"

One or two members of the local temperance society looked rather awkward, but did not come forward.

The fresh-water fisherman was the first who spoke.

"I han't got no brandy," he said, "but there's a drop or two of old Medford rum in this here that you're welcome to, if it'll be of any help. I alliz kerry a little on't in case o' gettin' wet 'n' chilled."

So saying he held forth a flat bottle with the word **Sarsaparilla** stamped on the green glass, but which contained half a pint or more of the specific on which he relied in those very frequent exposures which happen to persons of his calling.

The doctor motioned back Paolo, who would have rushed at once to the aid of Maurice, and who was not wanted at that moment. So poor Paolo, in an agony of fear for his master, was kept as quiet as possible, and had to content himself with asking all sorts of questions and repeating all the prayers he could think of to Our Lady and to his holy namesake the Apostle.

The doctor wiped the mouth of the fisherman's bottle very carefully. "Take a few drops of this cordial," he said, as he held it to his patient's lips. "Hold him just so, Euthymia, without stirring. I will watch him, and say when he is ready to be moved. The litter is near by, waiting." Dr Butts watched Maurice's pulse and color. The "old Medford" knew its business. It had knocked over its tens of thousands; it had its redeeming virtue, and helped to set up a poor fellow now and then. It did this for Maurice very effectively. When he seemed somewhat restored, the doctor had the litter brought to his side, and Euthymia softly resigned her helpless burden, which Paolo and the attendant Robert lifted with the aid of the doctor, who walked by the patient as he was borne to the home where Mrs. But had made all ready for his reception.

As for poor Lurida, who had thought herself equal to the sanguinary duties of the surgeon, she was left lying on the grass with an old woman over her, working hard with fan and smelling-salts to bring her back from her long fainting fit

THE INEVITABLE.

WHY should human nature not be the same in Arrowhead Village as else-where? It could not seem strange to the good people of that place and their visitors that these two young persons, brought together under circumstances that stirred up the deepest emotions of which the human soul is capable, should become attached to each other. But the bond between them was stronger than any knew, except the good doctor, who had learned the great secret of Maurice's life. For the first time since his infancy he had fully felt the charm which the immediate presence of youthful womanhood carries with it. He could hardly believe the fact when he found himself no longer the subject of the terrifying seizures of which he had many and threatening experiences.

It was the doctor's business to save his patient's life, if he could possibly do it. Maurice had been reduced to the most perilous state of debility by the relapse which had interrupted his convalescence. Only by what seemed almost a miracle had he survived the exposure to suffocation and the mental anguish through which he had passed. It was perfectly clear to Dr. Butts that if Maurice could see the young woman to whom he owed his life, and, as the doctor felt assured, the revolution in his nervous system, which would be the beginning of a new existence, it would be of far more value as a restorative agency than any or all of the drugs in the pharmacopœia. He told this to Euthymia, and explained the matter to her parents and friends. She must go with him on some of his visits. Her mother should go with her, or her sister; but this was a case of life and death, and no maidenly scruples must keep her from doing her duty.

The first of her visits to the sick, perhaps dying, man presented a scene not unlike the picture before spoken of on the title-page of the old edition of Galen. The doctor was perhaps the most agitated of the little group. He went before the others, took his seat by the bedside, and held the patient's wrist with his finger on the pulse. As Euthymia entered it gave a single bound, fluttered for an instant as if with a faint memory of its old habit, then throbbed full and strong, comparatively, as if under the spur of some powerful stimulus. Euthymia's task was a delicate one, but she knew how to disguise its difficulty.

"Here is a flower I have brought you, Mr. Kirkwood," she said, and handed him a white chrysanthemum. He took it from her hand, and before she knew it he took her hand into his own, and held it with a gentle constraint. What could she do? Here was the young man whose life she had saved, at least for the moment, and who was yet in danger from the disease which had almost worn out his powers of resistance.

"Sit down by Kirkwood's side," said the doctor.

"He wants to thank you, if he has strength to do it, for saving him from the death which seemed inevitavle."

Not many words could Maurice command. He was weak enough for womanly tears, but their fountains no longer flowed; it was with him as with the dying, whose eyes may light up, but rarely shed a tear.

The river which has found a new channel widens and deepens it; it lets the old water-course fill up, and never returns to its forsaken bed. The tyrannous habit was broken. The prophecy of the gitana had verified itself, and the ill a fair woman had wrought a fairer woman had conquered and abolished.

The history of Maurice Kirkwood loses its exceptional character from the time of his restoration to his natural conditions. His convalescence was very slow and gradual, but no further accident interrupted its even progress. The season was over, the summer visitors had left Arrowhead Village; the chrysanthemums were going out of flower, the frosts had come, and Maurice was still beneath the roof of the kind physician. The relation between him and his preserver were so entirely apart from all common acquaintances and friendships that no ordinary rules could apply to it. Euthymia visited him often during the period of his extreme prostration.

"You *must* come every day," the doctor said. "He gains with every visit you make him; he pines if you miss him for a single day." So she came and sat by him, the doctor or good Mrs. Butts keeping her company in his presence. He grew stronger,—began to sit up in bed; and at last Euthymia found him dressed as in health, and beginning to walk about the room. She was startled. She had thought of herself as a kind of nurse, but the young gentleman could hardly be said to need a nurse any longer. She had scruples about making any further visits. She asked Lurida what she thought about it.

"Think about it?" said Lurida. "Why shouldn't you go to see a brother as well as a sister, I should like to know? If you are afraid to go to see Maurice Kirkwood, *I* am not afraid, at any rate. If you would rather have me go than go yourself, I will do it, and let people talk just as much as they want to. Shall I go instead of you?"

Euthymia was not quite sure that this would be the best thing for the patient. The doctor had told her he thought there were special reasons for her own course in coming daily to see him. "I am afraid," she said, "you are too bright to be safe for him in his weak state. Your mind is such a stimulating one, you know. A dull sort of person like myself is better for him just now. I will continue visiting him as long as the doctor says it is important that I should; but you must defend me, Lurida,—I know you can explain it all so that people will not blame me."

Euthymia knew full well what the effect of Lurida's penetrating head-voice would be in a convalescent's chamber. She knew how that active mind of hers would set the young man's thoughts at work, when what he wanted was rest of every faculty. Were not these good and sufficient reasons for her decision? What others could there be?

So Euthymia kept on with her visits, until she blushed to see that she was continuing her charitable office for one who was beginning to look too well to be called an invalid. It was a dangerous condition of affairs, and the busy tongues of the village gossips were free in their comments. Free, but kindly, for the story of the rescue had melted every heart; and what could be more natural than that these two young people whom God had brought together in the dread moment of peril should find it hard to tear themselves asunder after the hour of danger was past? When gratitude is a bankrupt, love only can pay his debts; and if Maurice gave his heart to Euthymia, would not she receive it as payment in full?

The change which had taken place in the vital currents of Maurice Kirkwood's system was as simple and solid a fact as the change in a magnetic needle when the boreal becomes the austral pole, and the austral the boreal. It was well, perhaps, that this change took place while he was enfeebled by the wasting effects of long illness. For all the long-defeated, disturbed, perverted instincts had found their natural channel from the centre of consciousness to the organ which throbs in response to every profound emotion. As his health gradually returned, Euthymia could not help perceiving a flush in his cheek, a glitter in his eyes, a something in the tone of his voice, which altogether were a warning to the young maiden that the highway of friendly intercourse was fast narrowing to a lane, at the head of which her woman's eye could read plainly enough, "Dangerous passing."

"You look so much better to-day, Mr. Kirkwood," she said, "that I think I had better not play Sister of Charity any longer. The next time we meet I hope you will be strong enough to call on me."

She was frightened to see how pale he turned,—he was weaker than she thought. There was a silence so profound and so long that Mrs. Butts looked up from the stocking she was knitting. They had forgotten the good woman's presence.

Presently Maurice spoke,—very faintly, but Mrs. Butts dropped a stitch at the first word, and her knitting fell into her lap as she listened to what followed.

"No! you must not leave me. You must never leave me. You saved my life. But you have done more than that,—more than you know or can ever know. To you I owe it that I am living; with you I live henceforth, if I am to live at all. All I am, all I hope,—will you take this poor offering from one who owes you everything, whose lips never touched those of woman or breathed a word of love before you taught him the meaning of that word?"

What could Euthymia reply to this question, uttered with all the depth of a passion which had never before found expression?

Not one syllable of answer did listening Mrs. Butts overhear. But she told her husband afterwards that there was nothing in the tableaux they had had in September to compare with what she then saw. It was indeed a pleasing picture which those two young heads presented as Euthymia gave her inarticulate but infinitely expressive answer to the question of Maurice Kirkwood. The good-hearted woman thought it time to leave the young people. Down went the stocking with the needles in it; out of her lap tumbled the ball of worsted, rolling along the floor with its yarn trailing after it, like some village matron who goes about circulating from hearth to hearth, leaving all along her track the story of the new engagement or of the arrival of the last "little stranger."

Not many suns had set before it was told all through Arrowhead Village that Maurice Kirkwood was the accepted lover of Euthymia Tower.

POSTSCRIPT: AFTER-GLIMPSES.

MISS LURIDA VINCENT TO MRS. EUTHYMIA KIRKWOOD.

ARROWHEAD VILLAGE, *May* 18.

MY DEAREST EUTHYMIA,—Who would have thought, when you broke your oar as the Atalanta flashed by the Algonquin, last June, that before the roses came again you would find yourself the wife of a fine scholar and grand gentleman, and the head of a household such as that of which you are the mistress? You must not forget your old Arrowhead Village friends. What am I saying?—*you* forget them! No, dearest, I know your heart too well for that! You are not one of those who lay aside their old friendships as they do last year's bonnet when they get a new one.

You have told me all about yourself and your happiness, and now you want me to tell you about myself and what is going on in our little place.

And first about myself. I have given up the idea of becoming a doctor. I have studied mathematics so much that I have grown fond of certainties, of demonstrations, and medicine deals chiefly in probabilities. The practice of the art is so mixed up with the deepest human interests that it is hard to pursue it with that even poise of the intellect which is demanded by science. I want knowledge pure and simple,—I do not fancy having it mixed. Neither do I like the thought of passing my life in going from one scene of suffering to another; I am not saintly enough for such a daily martyrdom, nor callous enough to make it an easy occupation. I fainted at the first operation I saw, and I have never wanted to see another. I don't say that I wouldn't *marry* a physician, if the right one asked me, but the young doctor is not forthcoming at present. Yes, I think I might make a pretty good doctor's wife. I could teach him a good deal about headaches and backaches and all sorts of nervous *revolutions* as the doctor says the French women call their tantrums. I don't know but I should be willing to let him try his new medicines on me. If he were a homœopath, I know I should; for if a billionth of a grain of sugar won't begin to sweeten my tea or coffee, I don't feel afraid that a billionth of a grain of anything would poison me,—no, not if it were snake-venom; and if it were not disgusting, I would swallow a handful of his *lachesis* globules, to please my husband. But if I ever become a doctor's wife, my husband will not be one of that kind of practitioners, you may be sure of that, nor an "eclectic," nor a "faith-cure man." On the whole, I don't think I want to be married at all. I don't like the male animal very well (except such noble specimens as your husband). They are all tyrants,—almost all—so far as our sex is concerned, and I often think we could get on better without them.

However, the creatures are useful in the Society. They send us papers, some of them well worth reading. You have told me so often that you would like to know how the Society is getting on, and to read some of the papers sent to it if they happened to be interesting, that I have laid aside one or two manuscripts expressly for your perusal. You will get them by and by.

I am delighted to know that you keep Paolo with you. Arrowhead Village misses him dreadfully, I can tell you. What is the reason people become so attached to these servants with Southern sunlight in their natures?

I suppose life is not long enough to cool their blood down to our Northern standard. Then they are so childlike, whereas the native of these latitudes is never young after he is ten or twelve years old. Mother says,—you know mother's old-fashioned notions, and how shrewd and sensible she is in spite of them,—mother says that when she was a girl families used to import young men and young women from the country towns, who called themselves "helps," not servants,—no, that was Scriptural; "but they didn't know everything down in Judee," and it is not good American language. She says that these people would live in the same household until they were married, and the women often remain in the same service until they died or were old and worn out, and then, what with the money they had saved and the care and assistance they got from their former employers, would pass a decent and comfortable old age, and be buried in the family lot. Mother has made up her mind to the change, but grandmother is bitter about it. She says there never was a country yet where the population was made up of "ladies" and "gentlemen," and she doesn't believe there can be; nor that putting a spread eagle on a copper makes a gold dollar of it. She is a pessimist after her own fashion. She thinks all sentiment is dying out of our people. No loyalty for the sovereign, the king-post of the political edifice, she says; no deep attachment between employer and employed; no reverence of the humbler members of a household for its heads; and to make sure of continued corruption and misery, what she calls "*universal* suffrage" emptying all the sewers into the great aqueduct we all must drink from. "*Universal* suffrage!" I suppose we women don't belong to the universe! Wait until we get a chance at the ballot-box, I tell grandma, and see if we don't wash out the sewers before they reach the aqueduct! But my pen has run away with me. I was thinking of Paolo, and what a pleasant thing it is to have one of those child-like, warm-hearted, attachable, cheerful, contented, humble, faithful, companionable, but never presuming grown-up children of the South waiting on one, as if everything he could do for one was a pleasure, and carrying a look of content in his face which makes every one who meets him happier for a glimpse of his features.

It does seem a shame that the charming relation of master and servant, intelligent authority and cheerful obedience, mutual interest in each other's welfare, thankful recognition of all the advantages which belong to domestic service in the better class of families, should be almost wholly confined to aliens and their immediate descendants. Why should Hannah think herself so much better than Bridget? When they meet at the polls together, as they will before long, they will begin to feel more of an equality than is recognized at present. The native female turns her nose up at the idea of "living out;" does she think herself so much superior to the women of other nationalities? Our women will have to come to it,—so grandmother says,—in another generation or two, and in a hundred years, according to her prophecy, there will be a new set of old "Miss Pollys" and "Miss Betseys" who have lived half a century in the same families, respectful and respected, cherished, cared for in time of need (citizens as well as servants, holding a ballot as well as a broom, I tell her), and bringing back to us the lowly, underfoot virtues of contentment and humility, which we do so need to carpet the barren and hungry thoroughfare of our unstratified existence.

There, I have got a-going, and am forgetting all the news I have to tell you. There is an engagement you will want to know all about. It came to pass through our famous boat-race, which you and I remember, and shall never forget as long as we live. It seems that the young fellow who pulled the bow oar of that men's college boat which we had the pleasure of beating got some glimpses of Georgina, our handsome stroke oar. I believe he took it into his head that it was she who threw the bouquet that won the race for us. He was, as you know, greatly mistaken, and ought to have made love to me, only he didn't. Well, it seems he came posting down to the Institute just before the vacation was over, and there got a sight of Georgina. I wonder whether she told him she didn't fling the bouquet! Anyhow, the acquaintance began in that way, and now it seems that this young fellow, good-looking and a bright scholar, but with a good many months more to pass in college, is her captive. It was too bad. Just think of my bouquet's going to another girl's credit! No matter,—the old Atalanta story was paid off, at any rate.

You want to know all about dear Dr. Butts. They say he has just been offered a Professorship in one of the great medical colleges. I asked him about it, and he did not say that he had or had not. "But," said he, "suppose that I had been offered such a place; do you think I ought to accept it and leave Arrowhead Village? Let us talk it over," said he, "just as if I had had such an offer." I told him he ought to stay. There are plenty of men that can get into a Professor's chair, I said, and talk like Solomons to a class of wondering pupils: but once get a really good doctor in a place, a man who knows all about everybody, whether they have this or that tendency, whether when they are sick they have a way of dying or a way of getting well, what medicines agree with them and what drugs they cannot take, whether they are of the sort that think nothing is the matter with them until they are dead as smoked herring, or of the sort that send for the minister if they get a stomach-ache from eating too many cucumbers,—who knows all about all the people within half a dozen miles (all the sensible ones, that is, who employ a regular practitioner),—such a man as that, I say, is not to be replaced like a missing piece out of a Springfield musket or a Waltham watch. Don't go! said I. Stay here and save our precious lives, if you can, or at least put us through in the proper way, so that we needn't be ashamed of ourselves for dying, if we must die. Well, Dr. Butts is **not** going to leave us. I hope you will have no unwelcome occasion for his services,—you are never ill, you know,—but, anyhow, he is going to be here, and no matter what happens he will be on hand.

The village news is not of a very exciting character. Item 1. A new house is put up over the ashes of the one in which your husband lived while he was here. It was planned by one of the autochthonous inhabitants with the most ingenious combination of inconveniences that the natural man could educe from his original perversity of intellect. To get at any one room you must pass through every other. It is blind, or nearly so, on the only side which has a good prospect, and commands a fine view of the barn and pig-sty through numerous windows. Item 2. We have a small fire-engine near the new house which can be worked by a man or two, and would be equal to the emergency of putting out a bunch of fire-crackers. Item 3. We have a new ladder, in a box, close to the new fire-engine, so if the new house catches fire, like its predecessor, and there should happen to be a sick man on an upper floor, he can be got out without running the risk of going up and down a burning staircase. What a blessed thing it was that there was no fire-engine near by and no ladder at hand on the day of the great rescue! If there had been, what a change in your programme of life! You remember that "cup of tea spilt on Mrs. Masham's apron," which we used to read of in one of Everett's Orations, and all its wide reaching consequences in the affairs of Europe. I hunted up that cup of tea as diligently as ever a Boston matron sought for the last leaves in her old caddy after the tea-chests had been flung overboard at Griffin's wharf,—but no matter about that, now. That is the way things come about in this world. I must write a lecture on lucky mishaps, or, more elegantly, fortunate calamities. It will be just the converse of that odd essay of Swift's we read together,—the awkward and stupid things done with the best intentions. Perhaps I shall deliver the lecture in your city: you will come and hear it, and bring *him,* won't you, dearest? Always, your loving LURIDA.

MISS LURIDA VINCENT TO MRS. EUTHYMIA KIRKWOOD.

It seems forever since you left us, dearest Euthymia! And are you, and is your husband, and Paolo,—good Paolo,—are you all as well and happy as you have been and as you ought to be? I suppose our small village seems a very quiet sort of place to pass the winter in, now that you have become accustomed to the noise and gayety of a great city. For all that, it is a pretty busy place this winter, I can tell you. We have sleighing parties,—I never go to them, myself, because I can't keep warm, and my mind freezes up when my blood cools down below 95° or 96° Fahrenheit. I had a great deal rather sit by a good fire and read about Arctic discoveries. But I like very well to hear the bells jingling and to see the young people trying to have a good time as hard as they do at a picnic. It may be that they do, but to me a picnic is purgatory and a sleigh-ride that other place, where, as my favorite Milton says, "frost performs the effect of fire." I believe I have quoted him correctly; I ought to, for I could repeat half his poems from memory once, if I cannot now.

You must have plenty of excitement in your city life. I suppose you recognized yourself in one of the society columns of the "Household Inquisitor:" "Mrs. E. K., very beautiful, in an elegant," etc., etc, "with pearls," etc, etc,—as if you were not the ornament of all that you wear, no matter what it is!

I am so glad that you have married a scholar! Why should not Maurice—you both tell me to call him so—take the diplomatic office which has been offered him? It seems to me that he would find himself in exactly the right place. He can talk in two or three languages, has good manners, and a wife who—well, what shall I say of Mrs Kirkwood but that "she would be good company for a queen," as our old friend the quondam landlady of the Anchor Tavern used to say? I should so like to see you presented at Court! It seems to me that I should be willing to hold your train for the sake of seeing you in your court feathers and things.

As for myself, I have been thinking of late that I would become either a professional lecturer or head mistress of a great school or college for girls. I have tried the first business a little. Last month I delivered a lecture on Quaternions. I got three for my audience; two came over from the Institute, and one from that men's college which they try to make out to be a university, and where no female is admitted unless she belongs among the quadrupeds. I enjoyed lecturing, but the subject is a difficult one, and I don't *think* any one of them had any very clear notion of what I was talking about, except Rhodora,—and I *know* she didn't. To tell the truth, I was lecturing to instruct myself. I mean to try something easier next time. I have thought of the Basque language and literature. What do you say to that?

The Society goes on famously. We have had a paper presented and read lately which has greatly amused some of us and provoked a few of the weaker sort. The writer is that crabbed old Professor of Belles-Lettres at that men's college over there. He is dreadfully hard on the poor "poets," as they call themselves. It seems that a great many young persons, and more especially a great many young girls, of whom the Institute has furnished a considerable proportion, have taken to sending him their rhymed productions to be criticised,—expecting to be praised, no doubt, every one of them. I must give you one of the sauciest extracts from his paper in his own words:—

"It takes half my time to read the 'poems' sent me by young people of both sexes. They would be more shy of doing it if they knew that I recognize a tendency to rhyming as a common form of mental weakness, and the publication of a thin volume of verse as *prima facie* evidence of ambitious mediocrity, if not inferiority. Of course there are exceptions to this rule of judgment, but I maintain that the presumption is always against the rhymester as compared with the less pretentious persons about him or her, busy with some useful calling,—too busy to be tagging rhymed commonplaces together. Just now there seems to be an epidemic of rhyming as bad as the dancing mania, or the sweating sickness. After reading a certain amount of manuscript verse one is disposed to anathematize the inventor of homophonous syllabification. [This phrase made a great laugh when it was read.] This, that is rhyming, must have been found out very early,—

'Where are you, Adam ?' 'Here am I, Madam;'

but it can never have been habitually practised until after the Fall. The intrusion of tintinabulating terminations into the conversational intercourse of men and angels would have spoiled Paradise itself. Milton would not have them even in Paradise Lost, you remember. For my own part, I wish certain rhymes could be declared contraband of written or printed language. Nothing should be allowed to be hurled at the world or whirled with it, or furled upon it or curled over it; all eyes should be kept away from the skies, in spite of *as homini sublime dedit;* youth should be coupled with all the virtues except truth; earth should never be reminded of her birth; death should never be allowed to stop a mortal's breath, nor the bell to sound his knell, nor flowers from blossoming bowers to wave over his grave or show their bloom upon his tomb. We have rhyming dictionaries,—let us have one from which all rhymes are rigorously excluded. The sight of a poor creature grubbing for rhymes to fill up his sonnet, or to cram one of those voracious, rhyme-swallowing rigmaroles which some of our drudging poetical operatives have been exhausting themselves of late to satiate with jingles, makes my head ache and my stomach rebel. Work, work of some kind, is the business of men and women, not the making of jingles! No,—no,—no! I want to see the young people in our schools and academies and colleges, and the graduates of these institutions, lifted up out of the little Dismal Swamp of self-contemplating and self-indulging and self-commiserating emotionalism which is surfeiting the land with those literary sandwiches,—thin slices of tinkling sentimentality between two covers looking like hard-baked gilt-gingerbread. But what feces these young folks make up at my good advice! They get tipsy on their rhymes. Nothing intoxicates one like his—or her—own verses, and they hold on to their metre-ballad-mongering as the fellows that inhale nitrous oxide hold on to the gas-bag."

We laughed over this essay of the old Professor, though it hit us pretty hard. The best part of the joke is that the old man himself published a thin volume of poems when he was young, which there is good reason to think he is not very proud of, as they say he buys up all the copies he can find in the shops. No matter what they say, I can't help agreeing with him about this great flood of "poetry," as it calls itself, and looking at the rhyming mania much as he does.

How I do love real poetry! That is the reason I hate rhymes which have not a particle of it in them. The foolish scribblers that deal in them are like bad workmen in a carpenter's shop. They not only turn out bad jobs of work, but they spoil the tools for better workmen. There is hardly a pair of rhymes in the English language that is not so dulled and hacked and gapped by these 'prentice hands that a master of the craft hates to touch them, and yet he cannot very well do without them. I have not been besieged as the old Professor has been with such multitudes of would-be-poetical aspirants that he could not even read their manuscripts, but I have had a good many letters containing verses, and I have warned the writers of the delusion under which they were laboring.

You may like to know that I have just been translating some extracts from the Greek Anthology. I send you a few specimens of my work, with a Dedication to the Shade of Sappho. I hope you will find something of the Greek rhythm in my versions, and that I have caught a spark of inspiration from the impassioned Lesbian. I have found great delight in this work, at any rate, and am never so happy as when I read from my manuscript or repeat from memory the lines into which I have transferred the thought of the men and women of two thousand years ago, or given rhythmical expression to my own rapturous feelings with regard to them. I *must* read you my Dedication to the Shade of Sappho. I cannot help thinking that you will like it better than either of my two last, The Song of the Roses, or The Wail of the Weeds.

How I do miss you, dearest! I want you: I want you to listen to what I have written; I want you to hear all about my plans for the future; ***I want to look at you,*** and think how grand it must be to feel one's self to be such a noble and beautiful creature; I want to wander in the woods with you, to float on the lake, to share your life and talk over every day's doings with you. Alas! I feel that we have parted as two friends part at a port of embarkation: they embrace, they kiss each other's cheeks, they cover their faces and weep, they try to speak good-by to each other, they watch from the pier and from the deck; the two forms grow less and less, fainter and fainter in the distance, two white handkerchiefs flutter once and again, and yet once more, and the last visible link of the chain which binds them has parted. Dear, dear, dearest Euthymia, my eyes are running over with tears when I think that we may never, never meet again.

Don't you want some more items of village news? We are threatened with an influx of stylish people: "Buttons" to answer the door-bell, in place of the chambermaid; "butler," in place of the "hired man;" footman in top-boots and breeches, cockade on hat, arms folded à la Napoléon; tandems, "drags," dog-carts, and go-carts of all sorts. It is rather amusing to look at their ambitious displays, but it takes away the good old country flavor of the place.

I don't believe you mean to try to astonish us when you come back to spend your summers here. I suppose you must have a large house, and I am sure you will have a beautiful one. I suppose you will have some fine horses, and who wouldn't be glad to? But I do not believe you will try to make your old Arrowhead Village friends stare their eyes out of their heads with a display meant to outshine everybody else that comes here. You can have a yacht on the lake, if you like, but I hope you will pull a pair of oars in our old boat once in a while, with me to steer you. I know you will be just the same dear Euthymia you always were and always must be. How happy you must make such a man as Maurice Kirkwood! And how happy you ought to be with him!—a man who knows what is in books, and who has seen for himself what is in men. If he has not seen so much of women, where could he study all that is best in womanhood as he can in his own wife? Only one thing that dear Euthymia lacks. She is not quite pronounced enough in her views as to the rights and the wrongs of the sex. When I visit you, as you say I shall, I mean to indoctrinate Maurice with sound views on that subject I have written an essay for the Society, which I hope will go a good way towards answering all the objections to female suffrage. I mean to read it to your husband, if you will let me, as I know you will, and perhaps you would like to hear it,—only you know my thoughts on the subject pretty well already.

With all sorts of kind messages to your dear husband, and love to your precious self, I am ever your

LURIDA.

DR. BUTTS TO MRS. EUTHYMIA KIRKWOOD.

MY DEAR EUTHYMIA,—My pen refuses to call you by any other name. ***Sweet-souled*** you are, and your Latinized Greek name is the one which truly designates you. I cannot tell you how we have followed you, with what interest and delight through your travels, as you have told their story in your letters to your mother. She has let us have the privilege of reading them, and we have been with you in steamer, yacht, felucca, gondola, Nile-boat; in all sorts of places, from crowded capitals to "deserts where no men abide,"—everywhere keeping company with you in your natural and pleasant descriptions of your experiences. And now that you have returned to your home in the great city I must write you a few lines of welcome, if nothing more.

You will find Arrowhead Village a good deal changed since you left it. We are discovered by some of those over-rich people who make the little place upon which they swarm a kind of rural city. When this happens the consequences are striking,—some of them desirable and some far otherwise. The effect of well-built, well-furnished, well-kept houses and of handsome grounds always maintained in good order about them shows itself in a large circuit around the fashionable centre. Houses get on a new coat of paint, fences are kept in better order, little plots of flowers show themselves where only ragged weeds had rioted, the inhabitants present themselves in more comely attire and drive in handsomer vehicles with more carefully groomed horses. On the other hand, there is a natural jealousy on the part of the natives of the region suddenly become fashionable. They have seen the land they sold at farm prices by the acre coming to be valued by the foot, like the corner lots in a city. Their simple and humble modes of life look almost poverty-stricken in the glare of wealth and luxury which so outshines their plain way of living. It is true that many of them have found themselves richer than in former days, when the neighborhood lived on its own resources. They know how to avail themselves of their altered position, and soon learn to charge city prices for country products; but nothing can make people feel rich who see themselves surrounded by men whose yearly income is many times their own whole capital. I think it would be better if our rich men scattered themselves more than they do,—buying large country estates, building houses and stables which will make it easy to entertain their friends, and depending for society on chosen guests rather than on the mob of millionaires who come together for social rivalry. But I do not fret myself about it. Society will stratify itself according to the laws of social gravitation. It will take a generation or two more, perhaps, to arrange the strata by precipitation and settlement, but we can always depend on one principle to govern the arrangement of the layers. People interested in the same things will naturally come together. The youthful heirs of fortunes who keep splendid yachts have little to talk about with the oarsman who pulls about on the lake or the river. What does young Dives, who drives his four-in-hand

and keeps a stable full of horses, care about Lazarus, who feels rich in the possession of a horse-railroad ticket? You know how we live at our house, plainly, but with a certain degree of cultivated propriety. We make no pretensions to what is called "style." We are still in that social stratum where the article called "a napkin-ring" is recognized as admissible at the dinner-table. That fact sufficiently defines our modest pretensions. The napkin-ring is the boundary mark between certain classes. But one evening Mrs. Butts and I went out to a party given by the lady of a worthy family, where the napkin itself was a newly introduced luxury. The conversation of the hostess and her guests turned upon details of the kitchen and the laundry; upon the best mode of raising bread, whether with "emptins" (emptyings, yeast) or baking powder; about "bluing" and starching and crimping, and similar matters. Poor Mrs. Butts! She knew nothing more about such things than her hostess did about Shakespeare and the musical glasses. What was the use of trying to enforce social intercourse under such conditions? Incompatibility of temper has been considered ground for a divorce; incompatibility of interests is a sufficient warrant for social separation. The multimillionaires have so much that is common among themselves, and so little that they share with us of moderate means, that they will naturally form a specialized class, and in virtue of their palaces, their picture-galleries, their equipages, their yachts, their large hospitality, constitute a kind of exclusive aristocracy. Religion, which ought to be the great leveller, cannot reduce these elements to the same grade. You may read in the parable, "Friend, how earnest thou in hither not having a wedding garment?" The modern version would be, "How came you at Mrs. Billion's ball not having a dress on your back which came from Paris?"

The little church has got a new stained window, a saint who reminds me of Hamlet's uncle,—a thing "of shreds and patches," but rather pretty to look at, with an inscription under it which is supposed to be the name of the person in whose honour the window was placed in the church. Smith was a worthy man and a faithful churchwarden, and I hope posterity will be able to spell out his name on his monumental window; but that old English lettering would puzzle Mephistopheles himself, if he found himself before this memorial tribute, on the inside,—you know he goes to church sometimes, if you remember your Faust.

The rector has come out, in a quiet way, as an evolutionist. He has always been rather "broad" in his views, but cautious in their expression. You can tell the three branches of the mother-island church by the way they carry their heads. The low-church clergy look down, as if they felt themselves to be worms of the dust; the high-church priest drops his head on one side, after the pattern of the mediæval saints; the broad-church preacher looks forward and round about him, as if he felt himself the heir of creation. Our rector carries his head in the broad-church aspect, which I suppose is the least open to the charge of affectation,—in fact, is the natural and manly way of carrying it.

The Society has justified its name of Pansophian of late as never before. Lurida has stirred up our little community and its neighbors, so that we get essays on all sorts of subjects, poems and stories in large numbers. I know all about it, for she often consults me as to the merits of a particular contribution.

What is to be the fate of Lurida? I often think, with no little interest and some degree of anxiety, about her future. Her body is so frail and her mind so excessively and constantly active that I am afraid one or the other will give way. I do not suppose she thinks seriously of ever being married. She grows more and more zealous in behalf of her own sex, and sterner in her judgment of the other. She declares that she never would marry any man who was not an advocate of female suffrage, and as these gentlemen are not very common hereabouts the chance is against her capturing any one of the hostile sex.

What do you think? I happened, just as I was writing the last sentence, to look out of my window, and whom should I see but Lurida, with a young man in tow, listening very eagerly to her conversation, according to all appearance! I think he must be a friend of the rector, as I have seen a young man like this one in his company. Who knows?

Affectionately yours, etc.

DR. BUTTS TO MRS. BUTTS.

My BELOVED WIFE,—This letter will tell you more news than you would have thought could have been got together in this little village during the short time you have been staying away from it.

Lurida Vincent is engaged! He is a clergyman with a mathematical turn. The story is that he put a difficult problem into one of the mathematical journals, and that Lurida presented such a neat solution that the young man fell in love with her on the strength of it I don't think the story is literally true, nor do I believe that other report that he offered himself to her in the form of an equation chalked on the blackboard; but that it was an intellectual rather than a sentimental courtship I do not doubt. Lurida has given up the idea of becoming a professional lecturer,—so she tells me,—thinking that her future husband's parish will find her work enough to do. A certain amount of daily domestic drudgery and unexciting intercourse with simple-minded people will be the best thing in the world for that brain of hers, always simmering with some new project in its least fervid condition.

All our summer visitors have arrived. Euthymia—Mrs. Maurice Kirkwood—and her husband and little Maurice are here in their beautiful house looking out on the lake. They gave a grand party the other evening; You ought to have been there, but I suppose you could not very well have left your sister in the middle of your visit. All the grand folks were there, of course. Lurida and her young man—Gabriel is what she calls him—were naturally the objects of special attention. Paolo acted as major-domo, and looked as if he ought to be a major-general. Nothing could be pleasanter than the way in which Mr. and Mrs. Kirkwood received their plain country neighbors; that is, just as they did the others of more pretensions, as if they were really glad to see them, as I am sure they were. The old landlord and his wife had two arm-chairs to themselves, and I saw Miranda with the servants of the household looking in at the dancers and out at the little groups in the garden, and evidently enjoying it as much as her old employers. It was a most charming and successful party. We had two sensations in the course of the evening. One was pleasant and somewhat exciting, the other was thrilling and of strange and startling interest.

You remember how emaciated poor Maurice Kirkwood was left after his fever, in that first season when he was among us. He was out in a boat one day, when a ring slipped off his thin finger and sunk in a place where the water was rather shallow. "Jake"—you know Jake,—everybody knows Jake—was rowing him. He promised to come to the spot and fish up the ring if he could possibly find it. He was seen poking about with fish-hooks at the end of a pole, but nothing was ever heard from him about the ring. It was an antique intaglio stone in an Etruscan setting,—a wild goose flying over the Campagna. Mr. Kirkwood valued it highly, and regretted its loss very much.

While we were in the garden, who should appear at the gate but Jake, with a great basket, inquiring for Mr. Kirkwood. "Come," said Maurice to me, "let us see what our old friend the fisherman has brought us. What have you got there, Jake?"

"What I've got? Wall, I'll tel y' what I've got: I've got the biggest pickerel that's been ketched in this pond for these ten year. An' I've got somethin' else besides the pickerel. When I come to cut him open, what do you think I found in his insides but this here ring o' yourn,"—and he showed the one Maurice had lost so long before. There it was as good as new, after having tried Jonah's style of house-keeping for all that time. There are those who discredit Jake's story about finding the ring in the fish; anyhow, there was the ring and there was the pickerel. I need not say that Jake went off well paid for his pickerel and the precious contents of its stomach. Now comes the chief event of the evening. I went early by special invitation. Maurice took me into his library, and we sat down together.

"I have something of great importance," he said, "to say to you. I learned within a few days that my cousin Laura is staying with a friend in the next town to this. You know, doctor, that we have never met since the last, almost fatal, experience of my early years. I have determined to defy the strength of that deadly chain of associations connected with her presence, and I have begged her to come this evening with the friends with whom she is staying. Several letters passed between us, for it was hard to persuade her that there was no longer any risk in my meeting her. Her imagination was almost as deeply impressed as mine had been at those alarming interviews, and I had to explain to her fully that I had become quite indifferent to the disturbing impressions of former years. So, as the result of our correspondence, Laura is coming this evening, and I wish you to be present at our meeting. There is another reason why I wish you to be here. My little boy is not far from the age at which I received my terrifying, almost disorganizing shock. I mean to have little Maurice brought into the presence of Laura, who is said to be still a very handsome woman, and see if he betrays any hint of that peculiar sensitiveness which showed itself in my threatening seizure. It seemed to me not impossible that he might inherit some tendency of that nature, and I wanted you to be at hand if any sign of danger should declare itself. For myself I have no fear. Some radical change has taken place in my nervous system. I have been born again, as it were, in my susceptibilities, and am in certain respects a new man. But I must know how it is with my little Maurice."

Imagine with what interest I looked forward to this experiment; for experiment it was, and not without its sources of anxiety, as it seemed to me. The evening wore along; friends and neighbors came in, but no Laura as yet. At last I heard the sound of wheels, and a carriage stopped at the door. Two ladies and a gentleman got out, and soon entered the drawing-room.

"My cousin Laura!" whispered Maurice to me, and went forward to meet her. A very handsome woman, who might well have been in the thirties,—one of those women so thoroughly constituted that they cannot help being handsome at every period of life. I watched them both as they approached each other. Both looked pale at first, but Maurice soon recovered his usual color, and Laura's natural rich bloom came back by degrees. Their emotion at meeting was not to be wondered at, but there was no trace in it of the paralyzing influence on the great centres of life which had once acted upon its fated victim like the fabled head which turned the looker-on into a stone.

"Is the boy still awake?" said Maurice to Paolo, who, as they used to say of Pushee at the old Anchor Tavern, was everywhere at once on that gay and busy evening.

"What! Mahser Maurice asleep an' all this racket going on? I hear him crowing like young cockerel when he fus' smell daylight."

"Tell the nurse to bring him down quietly to the little room that leads out of the library."

The child was brought down in his night-clothes wide awake, wondering apparently at the noise he heard, which he seemed to think was for his special amusement.

"See if he will go to that lady," said his father. Both of us held our breath as Laura stretched her arms towards little Maurice.

The child looked for an instant searchingly, but fearlessly, at her glowing cheeks, her bright eyes, her welcoming smile, and met her embrace as she clasped him to her bosom as if he had known her all his days.

The mortal antipathy had died out of the soul and the blood of Maurice Kirkwood at that supreme moment when he found himself snatched from the grasp of death and cradled in the arms of Euthymia.

In closing the New Portfolio I remember that it began with a prefix which the reader may by this time have forgotten, namely, the ***First Opening.*** It was perhaps presumptuous to thus imply the probability of a second opening.

I am reminded from time to time by the correspondents who ask a certain small favor of me that as I can only expect to be with my surviving contemporaries a very little while longer, they would be much obliged if I would hurry up my answer before it is too late. They are right, these delicious unknown friends of mine, in reminding me of a fact which I cannot gainsay and might suffer to pass from my recollection. I thank them for recalling my attention to a truth which I shall be wiser, if not more hilarious, for remembering.

No, I had no right to say the ***First Opening.*** How do I know that I shall have a chance to open it again? How do I know that anybody will want it to be opened a second time? How do I know that I shall feel like opening it? It is safest neither to promise to open the New Portfolio once more, nor yet to pledge myself to keep it closed hereafter. There are many papers potentially existent in it, some of which might interest a reader here and there. The Records of the Pansophian Society contain a considerable number of essays, poems, stories, and hints capable of being expanded into presentable dimensions. In the mean time I will say with Prospero, addressing my old readers, and my new ones, if such I have,—

"If you be pleased, retire into my cell And there repose: a turn or two I'll walk, To still my beating mind."

When it has got quiet I may take up the New Portfolio again, and consider whether it is worth while to open it.

THE END.

The Codes Of Hammurabi And Moses
W. W. Davies

QTY

The discovery of the Hammurabi Code is one of the greatest achievements of archaeology, and is of paramount interest, not only to the student of the Bible, but also to all those interested in ancient history...

Religion   **ISBN:** *1-59462-338-4*   **Pages:132**
MSRP $12.95

The Theory of Moral Sentiments
Adam Smith

QTY

This work from 1749. contains original theories of conscience amd moral judgment and it is the foundation for systemof morals.

Philosophy   **ISBN:** *1-59462-777-0*   **Pages:536**
MSRP $19.95

Jessica's First Prayer
Hesba Stretton

QTY

In a screened and secluded corner of one of the many railway-bridges which span the streets of London there could be seen a few years ago, from five o'clock every morning until half past eight, a tidily set-out coffee-stall, consisting of a trestle and board, upon which stood two large tin cans, with a small fire of charcoal burning under each so as to keep the coffee boiling during the early hours of the morning when the work-people were thronging into the city on their way to their daily toil...

Childrens   **ISBN:** *1-59462-373-2*   **Pages:84**
MSRP $9.95

My Life and Work
Henry Ford

QTY

Henry Ford revolutionized the world with his implementation of mass production for the Model T automobile. Gain valuable business insight into his life and work with his own auto-biography... "We have only started on our development of our country we have not as yet, with all our talk of wonderful progress, done more than scratch the surface. The progress has been wonderful enough but..."

Biographies/   **ISBN:** *1-59462-198-5*   **Pages:300**
MSRP $21.95

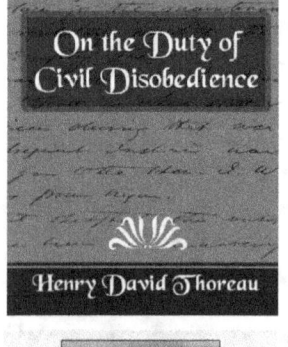

The Art of Cross-Examination
Francis Wellman

QTY

I presume it is the experience of every author, after his first book is published upon an important subject, to be almost overwhelmed with a wealth of ideas and illustrations which could readily have been included in his book, and which to his own mind, at least, seem to make a second edition inevitable. Such certainly was the case with me; and when the first edition had reached its sixth impression in five months, I rejoiced to learn that it seemed to my publishers that the book had met with a sufficiently favorable reception to justify a second and considerably enlarged edition. ..

Pages:412

Reference   **ISBN:** *1-59462-647-2*   *MSRP $19.95*

On the Duty of Civil Disobedience
Henry David Thoreau

QTY

Thoreau wrote his famous essay, On the Duty of Civil Disobedience, as a protest against an unjust but popular war and the immoral but popular institution of slave-owning. He did more than write—he declined to pay his taxes, and was hauled off to gaol in consequence. Who can say how much this refusal of his hastened the end of the war and of slavery ?

Law   **ISBN:** *1-59462-747-9*   **Pages:48**

MSRP $7.45

Dream Psychology Psychoanalysis for Beginners
Sigmund Freud

QTY

Sigmund Freud, born Sigismund Schlomo Freud (May 6, 1856 - September 23, 1939), was a Jewish-Austrian neurologist and psychiatrist who co-founded the psychoanalytic school of psychology. Freud is best known for his theories of the unconscious mind, especially involving the mechanism of repression; his redefinition of sexual desire as mobile and directed towards a wide variety of objects; and his therapeutic techniques, especially his understanding of transference in the therapeutic relationship and the presumed value of dreams as sources of insight into unconscious desires.

Pages:196

Psychology   **ISBN:** *1-59462-905-6*   *MSRP $15.45*

The Miracle of Right Thought
Orison Swett Marden

QTY

Believe with all of your heart that you will do what you were made to do. When the mind has once formed the habit of holding cheerful, happy, prosperous pictures, it will not be easy to form the opposite habit. It does not matter how improbable or how far away this realization may see, or how dark the prospects may be, if we visualize them as best we can, as vividly as possible, hold tenaciously to them and vigorously struggle to attain them, they will gradually become actualized, realized in the life. But a desire, a longing without endeavor, a yearning abandoned or held indifferently will vanish without realization.

Pages:360

Self Help   **ISBN:** *1-59462-644-8*   *MSRP $25.45*

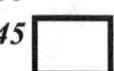

www.bookjungle.com *email: sales@bookjungle.com fax: 630-214-0564 mail: Book Jungle PO Box 2226 Champaign, IL 61825*

QTY

The Rosicrucian Cosmo-Conception Mystic Christianity by *Max Heindel*   ISBN: *1-59462-188-8*   **$38.95**
The Rosicrucian Cosmo-conception is not dogmatic, neither does it appeal to any other authority than the reason of the student. It is: not controversial, but is: sent forth in the, hope that it may help to clear...   *New Age/Religion Pages 646*

Abandonment To Divine Providence by *Jean-Pierre de Caussade*   ISBN: *1-59462-228-0*   **$25.95**
"The Rev. Jean Pierre de Caussade was one of the most remarkable spiritual writers of the Society of Jesus in France in the 18th Century. His death took place at Toulouse in 1751. His works have gone through many editions and have been republished...   *Inspirational/Religion Pages 400*

Mental Chemistry by *Charles Haanel*   ISBN: *1-59462-192-6*   **$23.95**
Mental Chemistry allows the change of material conditions by combining and appropriately utilizing the power of the mind. Much like applied chemistry creates something new and unique out of careful combinations of chemicals the mastery of mental chemistry...   *New Age Pages 354*

The Letters of Robert Browning and Elizabeth Barret Barrett 1845-1846 vol II   ISBN: *1-59462-193-4*   **$35.95**
by *Robert Browning* and *Elizabeth Barrett*   *Biographies Pages 596*

Gleanings In Genesis (volume I) by *Arthur W. Pink*   ISBN: *1-59462-130-6*   **$27.45**
Appropriately has Genesis been termed "the seed plot of the Bible" for in it we have, in germ form, almost all of the great doctrines which are afterwards fully developed in the books of Scripture which follow...   *Religion/Inspirational Pages 420*

The Master Key by *L. W. de Laurence*   ISBN: *1-59462-001-6*   **$30.95**
In no branch of human knowledge has there been a more lively increase of the spirit of research during the past few years than in the study of Psychology, Concentration and Mental Discipline. The requests for authentic lessons in Thought Control, Mental Discipline and...   *New Age/Business Pages 422*

The Lesser Key Of Solomon Goetia by *L. W. de Laurence*   ISBN: *1-59462-092-X*   **$9.95**
This translation of the first book of the "Lernegton" which is now for the first time made accessible to students of Talismanic Magic was done, after careful collation and edition, from numerous Ancient Manuscripts in Hebrew, Latin, and French...   *New Age/Occult Pages 92*

Rubaiyat Of Omar Khayyam by *Edward Fitzgerald*   ISBN:*1-59462-332-5*   **$13.95**
Edward Fitzgerald, whom the world has already learned, in spite of his own efforts to remain within the shadow of anonymity, to look upon as one of the rarest poets of the century, was born at Bredfield, in Suffolk, on the 31st of March, 1809. He was the third son of John Purcell...   *Music Pages 172*

Ancient Law by *Henry Maine*   ISBN: *1-59462-128-4*   **$29.95**
The chief object of the following pages is to indicate some of the earliest ideas of mankind, as they are reflected in Ancient Law, and to point out the relation of those ideas to modern thought.   *Religiom/History Pages 452*

Far-Away Stories by *William J. Locke*   ISBN: *1-59462-129-2*   **$19.45**
"Good wine needs no bush, but a collection of mixed vintages does. And this book is just such a collection. Some of the stories I do not want to remain buried for ever in the museum files of dead magazine-numbers an author's not unpardonable vanity..."   *Fiction Pages 272*

Life of David Crockett by *David Crockett*   ISBN: *1-59462-250-7*   **$27.45**
"Colonel David Crockett was one of the most remarkable men of the times in which he lived. Born in humble life, but gifted with a strong will, and indomitable courage, and unremitting perseverance...   *Biographies/New Age Pages 424*

Lip-Reading by *Edward Nitchie*   ISBN: *1-59462-206-X*   **$25.95**
Edward B. Nitchie, founder of the New York School for the Hard of Hearing, now the Nitchie School of Lip-Reading, Inc, wrote "LIP-READING Principles and Practice". The development and perfecting of this meritorious work on lip-reading was an undertaking...   *How-to Pages 400*

A Handbook of Suggestive Therapeutics, Applied Hypnotism, Psychic Science   ISBN: *1-59462-214-0*   **$24.95**
by *Henry Munro*   *Health/New Age/Health/Self-help Pages 376*

A Doll's House: and Two Other Plays by *Henrik Ibsen*   ISBN: *1-59462-112-8*   **$19.95**
Henrik Ibsen created this classic when in revolutionary 1848 Rome. Introducing some striking concepts in playwriting for the realist genre, this play has been studied the world over.   *Fiction/Classics/Plays 308*

The Light of Asia by *sir Edwin Arnold*   ISBN: *1-59462-204-3*   **$13.95**
In this poetic masterpiece, Edwin Arnold describes the life and teachings of Buddha. The man who was to become known as Buddha to the world was born as Prince Gautama of India but he rejected the worldly riches and abandoned the reigns of power when...   *Religion/History/Biographies Pages 170*

The Complete Works of Guy de Maupassant by *Guy de Maupassant*   ISBN: *1-59462-157-8*   **$16.95**
"For days and days, nights and nights, I had dreamed of that first kiss which was to consecrate our engagement, and I knew not on what spot I should put my lips..."   *Fiction/Classics Pages 240*

The Art of Cross-Examination by *Francis L. Wellman*   ISBN: *1-59462-309-0*   **$26.95**
Written by a renowned trial lawyer, Wellman imparts his experience and uses case studies to explain how to use psychology to extract desired information through questioning.   *How-to/Science/Reference Pages 408*

Answered or Unanswered? by *Louisa Vaughan*   ISBN: *1-59462-248-5*   **$10.95**
Miracles of Faith in China   *Religion Pages 112*

The Edinburgh Lectures on Mental Science (1909) by *Thomas*   ISBN: *1-59462-008-3*   **$11.95**
This book contains the substance of a course of lectures recently given by the writer in the Queen Street Hail, Edinburgh. Its purpose is to indicate the Natural Principles governing the relation between Mental Action and Material Conditions...   *New Age/Psychology Pages 148*

Ayesha by *H. Rider Haggard*   ISBN: *1-59462-301-5*   **$24.95**
Verily and indeed it is the unexpected that happens! Probably if there was one person upon the earth from whom the Editor of this, and of a certain previous history, did not expect to hear again...   *Classics Pages 380*

Ayala's Angel by *Anthony Trollope*   ISBN: *1-59462-352-X*   **$29.95**
The two girls were both pretty, but Lucy who was twenty-one who supposed to be simple and comparatively unattractive, whereas Ayala was credited, as her Bombwhat romantic name might show, with poetic charm and a taste for romance. Ayala when her father died was nineteen...   *Fiction Pages 484*

The American Commonwealth by *James Bryce*   ISBN: *1-59462-286-8*   **$34.45**
An interpretation of American democratic political theory. It examines political mechanics and society from the perspective of Scotsman James Bryce   *Politics Pages 572*

Stories of the Pilgrims by *Margaret P. Pumphrey*   ISBN: *1-59462-116-0*   **$17.95**
This book explores pilgrims religious oppression in England as well as their escape to Holland and eventual crossing to America on the Mayflower, and their early days in New England...   *History Pages 268*

QTY

The Fasting Cure by *Sinclair Upton*   ISBN: *1-59462-222-1* **$13.95**
In the Cosmopolitan Magazine for May, 1910, and in the Contemporary Review (London) for April, 1910, I published an article dealing with my experiences in fasting. I have written a great many magazine articles, but never one which attracted so much attention... New Age/Self Help/Health Pages 164

Hebrew Astrology by *Sepharial*   ISBN: *1-59462-308-2* **$13.45**
In these days of advanced thinking it is a matter of common observation that we have left many of the old landmarks behind and that we are now pressing forward to greater heights and to a wider horizon than that which represented the mind-content of our progenitors... Astrology Pages 144

Thought Vibration or The Law of Attraction in the Thought World   ISBN: *1-59462-127-6* **$12.95**

by *William Walker Atkinson*   Psychology/Religion Pages 144

Optimism by *Helen Keller*   ISBN: *1-59462-108-X* **$15.95**
Helen Keller was blind, deaf, and mute since 19 months old, yet famously learned how to overcome these handicaps, communicate with the world, and spread her lectures promoting optimism. An inspiring read for everyone... Biographies/Inspirational Pages 84

Sara Crewe by *Frances Burnett*   ISBN: *1-59462-360-0* **$9.45**
In the first place, Miss Minchin lived in London. Her home was a large, dull, tall one, in a large, dull square, where all the houses were alike, and all the sparrows were alike, and where all the door-knockers made the same heavy sound... Childrens/Classic Pages 88

The Autobiography of Benjamin Franklin by *Benjamin Franklin*   ISBN: *1-59462-135-7* **$24.95**
The Autobiography of Benjamin Franklin has probably been more extensively read than any other American historical work, and no other book of its kind has had such ups and downs of fortune. Franklin lived for many years in England, where he was agent... Biographies/History Pages 332

Name	
Email	
Telephone	
Address	
City, State ZIP	

☐ **Credit Card**   ☐ **Check / Money Order**

Credit Card Number	
Expiration Date	
Signature	

Please Mail to: Book Jungle
PO Box 2226
Champaign, IL 61825
or Fax to: 630-214-0564

ORDERING INFORMATION

web: *www.bookjungle.com*
email: *sales@bookjungle.com*
fax: *630-214-0564*
mail: *Book Jungle PO Box 2226 Champaign, IL 61825*
or PayPal *to sales@bookjungle.com*

Please contact us for bulk discounts

DIRECT-ORDER TERMS

**20% Discount if You Order
Two or More Books**
Free Domestic Shipping!
Accepted: Master Card, Visa,
Discover, American Express

www.ingramcontent.com/pod-product-compliance
Lightning Source LLC
Chambersburg PA
CBHW080904020726
47502CB00008B/2342